THE NECKLACE
AND
OTHER TALES

GUY DE MAUPASSANT

THE NECKLACE

AND

OTHER TALES

*Compiled and newly translated
by Joachim Neugroschel*

Introduction by Adam Gopnik

THE MODERN LIBRARY

NEW YORK

LIBRARY OF CONGRESS CATALOGING-IN-PUBLICATION DATA
Maupassant, Guy de, 1850–1893.
[Short stories. English. Selections]
The necklace and other tales / Guy de Maupassant; translated and compiled by
Joachim Neugroschel; introduction by Adam Gopnik.
    p.   cm.
ISBN 0-375-75717-1 (pbk.)
1. Maupassant, Guy de, 1850–1893—Translations into English.
I. Neugroschel, Joachim. II. Title.
PQ2349.A4 E5 2003
843'.8—dc21   2002032575

Modern Library website address: www.modernlibrary.com

2 4 6 8 9 7 5 3 1

Guy de Maupassant

Guy de Maupassant, the French naturalist writer generally considered a master of the short story, was born into a cultivated family of
prosperous means on August 5, 1850, at the Château de Miromesnil
near the town of Dieppe in Normandy. After a bitter and unhappy life
together, his parents separated when he was eleven years old. There-
after, Maupassant and his younger brother Hervé lived with their
mother in Étretat, a fishing village on the Channel coast that was a
newly fashionable resort for writers and artists. In 1863 he entered the
Institution Ecclésiastique in nearby Yvetot. Expelled from the school
in 1868 for writing sacrilegious verse, he completed his education at
the Lycée Corneille in Rouen. Upon passing the *baccalauréat* examination in 1869, Maupassant enrolled as a law student in Paris, but his
legal studies were interrupted by the outbreak of the Franco-Prussian
War, during which he served in the quartermaster corps. Afterward, a
reversal of family fortunes forced him to secure employment as a civil
servant, first with the Ministry of the Navy (1872–78) and later with
the Ministry of Public Education (1878–82). While working in Paris

during this period, Maupassant came under the influence of Gustave Flaubert, a childhood friend of his mother. "He's my disciple and I love him like a son," remarked the novelist, who encouraged Maupassant's literary ambitions and introduced him to a circle of writers that included Émile Zola, Ivan Turgenev, and Henry James.

The publication in 1880 of "Boule de Suif" ("Butterball") in *Les Soirées de Médan,* a collection of stories about the Franco-Prussian War compiled by Zola, brought Maupassant instant acclaim. "I consider 'Boule de Suif' a *masterpiece,*" exclaimed Flaubert. "Nothing more nor less than a masterpiece." *Des Vers,* a volume of Maupassant's poetry, appeared almost simultaneously, but it was his tale of the prostitute who acts with honor that captured public attention. Over the next decade Maupassant wrote some three hundred short stories portraying everyday life in France during the early years of the Belle Époque. His work often appeared in the newspapers *Le Gaulois* and *Gil Blas* and eventually filled fifteen collections: *La Maison Tellier* (1881), *Mademoiselle Fifi* (1882), *Contes de la bécasse* (1883), *Claire de lune* (1883), *Miss Harriet* (1884), *Les Sœurs Rondoli* (1884), *Yvette* (1884), *Contes du jour et de la nuit* (1885), *Monsieur Parent* (1885), *Toine* (1886), *La Petite Roque* (1886), *Le Horla* (1887), *Le Rosier de Madame Husson* (1888), *La Main gauche* (1889), and *L'Inutile Beauté* (1890). At the time, Henry James hailed Maupassant as "a lion in the path" of moralistic nineteenth-century critics because of the frankly erotic nature of his work, and Tolstoy deemed him a genius who "saw things in their essentials, and therefore involuntarily discovered truth." "[Maupassant] is the most uncompromising of all the French realists," observed Irish critic Sean O'Faolain. "There are no suggestive half-lights in Maupassant. We see the prostitute, the beastly peasant, the timid bourgeois, the civil servant—his favorite subjects—in an unpitying light."

Though best remembered for his short stories, Maupassant also wrote six novels. He enjoyed enormous popular success with *Une vie* (1883; translated as *A Woman's Life* in 1885), a tale of female disillusionment often compared to *Madame Bovary; Bel-Ami* (1885; translated into English in 1891), a biting satire involving a handsome young provincial who is determined to succeed in the corrupt Paris of the Third Republic; and *Pierre et Jean* (1888; translated as *The Two Brothers* in 1889), a psychological novel focusing on one man's tragic jealousy of his half-brother. Less well received were *Mont-Oriol* (1887; translated into English in 1891), a novel of manners chronicling the establishment of a spa in a small Auvergne town; and *Fort comme la mort* (1889; translated as *Strong as Death* in 1899), a story of unrequited autumnal love that explores the pain of aging. His final novel, *Notre cœur* (1890; translated as *The Human Heart* in 1890), considers the impossibility of love amid Parisian high society. In addition, Maupassant published three travel journals: *Au soleil* (1884; translated as *African Wanderings* in 1903); *Sur l'eau* (1888; translated as *Afloat* in 1889); and *La Vie errante* (1890; translated as *In Vagabondia* in 1903).

Maupassant's meteoric career lasted but ten years. Driven insane by the final stages of syphilis, a disease he had contracted as a young man, Maupassant attempted suicide on January 1, 1892, and was institutionalized at a clinic in Passy. Guy de Maupassant died on July 6, 1893, and was buried in the cemetery at Montparnasse. Three volumes of his short stories were issued posthumously: *Le Père Milon* (1899), *Le Colporteur* (1900), and *Les Dimanches d'un bourgeois de Paris* (1901). "[Maupassant gave the short story] a stature that it had never known before," reflected his biographer Francis Steegmuller. "Only with Chekhov (as has so often been said) has the short story reached comparable heights." "[Maupassant] is one of the dead-sure geniuses," concluded V. S. Pritchett. "Life itself seems to be writing his best stories, to have inked itself upon the page."

Contents

THE NECKLACE AND OTHER TALES

INTRODUCTION

Adam Gopnik

By now, Guy de Maupassant has become a high school classic, even in France, where it is possible to find, among the *bouquinistes,* secondhand copies of his stories dutifully diagrammed by young readers for their meanings (circle around the incident, arrow pointing to its attendant irony), as sentences are diagrammed in grammar books for verbs and objects. It may be odd that we give fourteen-year-olds the work of a writer whose great subject is the amorality of sexual appetite, yet we do, chiefly because he is both smart and simple-seeming, not small virtues for young readers, or old ones either.

This early exposure, though, can make Maupassant appear to be a writer of the snappy second rank, well below his master, Flaubert, or his contemporary Baudelaire, famous for his O. Henry endings and his bleak, acid picture of petit bourgeois French life. The common Anglo-American reader, or anyway, the reader who reads and runs, may recall the one with the surprise ending about the necklace and the one about the rowers and the girl, and that is, more or less, that. His contemporaries among the makers of modern French literature—

Flaubert, Baudelaire, Rimbaud, later on Proust—are writers we still approach with reverence, even a sense of the divine, as the Gods of the Early Modern. Maupassant seems more narrowly companionable, and we read him as grown-ups, if we do at all, for kicks.

Yet it is important to recall just how big a writer he once seemed in order to grasp how big a writer he might remain, particularly to Americans, for whom he should have something of the status of an Apostle, or Founding Father. Both Henry James and Hemingway, to name the two apparent bookends of our literature, were shaped by Maupassant's example—and any writer big enough to loom over both James's surplus economy of sentences and Hemingway's parsimonious one is a very big writer. For James, who wrote perhaps his finest critical essay on the French master (finest because there is something noble in a writer addressing a sensibility fundamentally discordant to his own while still recognizing his opposite's unique value). Maupassant was the high standing challenge, the realest of the realists. Where even Flaubert was still an aesthete and a shaper of sentences, Maupassant, for James, made the absolute realist demand: What would happen if you fearlessly wrote down what life is actually like? This involved truths about sex and greed, in particular, which were, to James, as upsetting as they were undeniable. (James, under the gravitational pull of the example but temperamentally unsuited to it, turned Maupassant's challenge inside out and took as his subject what would happen if you conscientiously wrote down what life was *not* actually like—if you took up the not-quite-realized, not-yet-actual world of dim motive that lay before the facts of life. Maupassant is present in James's later work as what his characters can only dream of becoming, guiltless and amoral actors.)

Forty years on, Maupassant became the first influence on Hemingway, too, who put two stories in this collection, "Boule de Suif" (here, called bravely "Butterball," in this fine and wonderfully idiomatic new translation) and "La Maison Tellier," first on his list of compulsory reading for a young writer, ahead even of *The Red and the Black* and *Madame Bovary,* and who once said that he had found himself when he trimmed up good to go nine rounds with Maupassant, and thought he had managed it. What Hemingway took from Maupassant was still another side of Maupassant's talent—not the challenge to be truthful but the courage to be brief. For Hemingway, Maupassant was the model of indirection and point and the amazing force of the no-comment narrator. (Beyond that, Hemingway's real gift was for the evocative and poetic and pastoral, none of which Maupassant is much good at, while he was too egocentric to be skilled at the close observation of social classes and manners, which is almost the whole of Maupassant.)

Through Hemingway's influence, this side of Maupassant's accomplishment passed on to become the pattern for the American short story. The still underappreciated John O'Hara depended largely on Maupassant's example, as did Stephen Crane, while Frank O'Connor drew on him so entirely that he calls one of his most Maupassant-like tales "A Story by Maupassant." An entire vein of the modern story—crisply told, underplaying implicitly tragic or farcical material and avoiding theatrical climaxes or obvious appeals to emotion, using a slightly God-like narrator, always barely visible but amused, like an Oriental deity, and usually with an ironic turn at the end that involves making a flat statement ("We don't always have something to celebrate" ["The Tellier House"]) newly alive with a secondary meaning—all of this is Maupassant's, and all of it is ours. This kind of influence, for range equaled only—to bring in another Modern Divine to whom Maupassant is not often enough compared—by Chekhov's, is brightened by, though it does not depend on, the additional superficial things that make Maupassant seem engagingly "French." His gleeful accounts of adulteries—as in this collection's "The Jewels," where the husband's grief over his dead wife is alleviated when he discovers that her pathetic costume jewelry were actually lavish gifts from her lovers—are ornamented with the style of a civilization.

———

Maupassant works small but feels big, and he writes about sex as a matter of fact. Maupassant always chooses the aesthete's tiny canvas:

his stories are often "sketches" in every sense. Yet he is never an exquisitist. Maupassant is to Zola as Degas is to Courbet: the man who made realism small and metropolitan, intense in focus and large in resonance. (Next to Maupassant, even Flaubert, with whom he studied so diligently, is a tapestry maker, weaving together a picture of an entire world.) The action of his typical story is at most an anecdote, rarely an entire "tale": a whore gives her favors to a Prussian officer, another group of whores go to see a first communion. (That is most of, if not the whole of, those two famous stories.) Maupassant's sketches share Degas's faith that the strange or sideways glance sees more in modernity than a straight-ahead gaze can, because it is in the nature of its subject to be in motion. This is true both in a literal sense—journeys of all kinds, coach and railroad and boat, fill these stories; his people, pinned in jobs and marriages, seek release through sheer movement— and symbolically—his bourgeois are restless in their social roles, too, always yearning for the next necklace or decoration or position or woman or even just for the next meal. In such an unsettled world, Maupassant knew, quick takes told more than long gazes.

This urban speed effects his prose style, too. Where in Flaubert we are slowly impressed with the style as style, with the sentences themselves, Maupassant, though never careless, is often conventional. His units are of behavior, not evocation. He can sum up a scene or the action of social classes in a phrase or paragraph, as in this from "Butterball" when a Prussian officer summons the contents of a coach out to be inspected:

> The two nuns were the first to obey, showing the docility of devout women accustomed to all forms of submission. Next the count and the countess stepped down, followed by the manufacturer and his wife, then Loiseau pushing his better and bigger half before him. Upon setting foot on the ground, he greeted the officer: "Bonjour, Monsieur," more out of prudence than politeness. The officer, insolent like any omnipotent man, eyed him without responding.

Where most of his contemporaries work by metaphor, as most writers do, Maupassant works by microcosms. We recall his circumstances more than his characters. Although the title figure in his novel *Bel Ami* remains a byword for a certain kind of sexual adventurer in Paris, he is not a personage in the sense that Madame Bovary is: he is an atom who significantly explodes in collisions with other atoms. Where Maupassant comes alive is in his ability to put types into relation with one another; he creates small, credible worlds that contain all of France. In "Butterball," again, we are never less than persuaded that the action is just the action—that the kindly dim whore with vague patriotic intimations could be pressured by her petty bourgeois traveling companions into sleeping with a Prussian officer. Nothing obvious is "at stake," as Hollywood people like to say; all that is at stake, in fact, is the convenience of the travelers. But all of France and its reactions to defeat are there, too; "Boule de Suif" is not just a masterpiece of the 1870 war, but of 1940, too. Even in smaller, meaner tales, like "The Model," which seem at first hardly more than literary grimaces, we are conscious that Maupassant makes what hardly at first seems to register as an event into a world-in-miniature: One of the central poetic relationships of the nineteenth century, that between the avant-garde artist and his model, is given a terrible twist of dependency, and the "twist" here is not an O. Henry-style surprise but instead has the ring of fatality: life is random and its turns are random, too. "How little it takes to doom you or save you," as Madame Loisel meditates at the end of "The Necklace." From a seeming inconsequence of incident, Maupassant again and again draws a momentous point about the randomness of fate.

As a constructor, too, Maupassant is extraordinary; his years of apprenticeship with Flaubert are most visible in the effortless technical perfection of his stories: he knows how to vary drama and dialogue better, perhaps, than any other storyteller. See, for instance, the long concluding section of "The Tellier House," where the whores' drinking song becomes a dramatic chorus against the action. Maupassant, in fact, is a genius at such counterpointed effects, which would not become part of the language of popular art until the advent of the movies.

Although his subjects often jarringly remind us of the subjects of his contemporaries among the Impressionists, we are always struck, too, by how unlike their picture of the world seems. "A Day in the Country," for instance, is a Renoir painting come to life, but what dark clouds intervene! It would be conventional to say that Maupassant sees what Renoir leaves out, but of course Renoir, a man of the world, knew perfectly well what the world was like, and what his boaters and drinkers and girls were up to, or down to, as anyone. (The pathos of his pictures lies exactly in his readiness to leave all that out for now; pictures step outside of time, and they allow us to have pleasures without consequences, too.)

With his gift for the intense, casual-seeming relationship of two or three people in a tale of greed or vanity, Maupassant, far more even than the more often cited Dickens, is the prose writer whose style most anticipates the language of film, and still gives the most to it. It would take fifty years, and Jean Renoir, rather than Auguste, to bring to visual life "A Day in the Country." Movies, as we often forget, are extremely ill-suited to the full-length novel—they're just too short; an adaptation of even a modest novel just goes on and *on*—and, because they are so easily and rapidly "visual," materializing in bare half-seconds battlefields and cityscapes that would take a writer pages, they do not do very well with the sensual or evocative, either. (Movies show, they don't evoke, and the show is over in a second.) But short, cruel black-and-white sketches of greed and desire are their ideal subjects, subjects that Maupassant mastered first. No writer has ever done more for the movies, or been better done in the movies, from Renoir to Max Ophuls to Stanley Kubrick (who adapted Stephen King's Maupassant-inspired novel, *The Shining*) than Maupassant. In fact, a formula for a good movie might be, simply, to take a Maupassant story and modernize it.

———

But Maupassant's stature finally depends not on his "influence" nor even on his picture of a moment in civilization. It rests on an original view of human nature. Maupassant can seem cold to us, even, at times, to take pleasure in cruelty. The sourness of his pictures of women in particular can sometimes recall less the impassive honesty of Degas than the nettled caricaturing of Lautrec. Chekhov, the good doctor, seems more humane—yet, on longer acquaintance, there is a residual optimistic mysticism in Chekhov that makes him impatient with his people's futilities. Maupassant's acceptance of the sensual basis of human conduct—not cynical so much as detached—is, by contrast, oddly cheering in its sense of permanence; appetite and disappointment, on and on forever. Maupassant is a humanist in the core, classical sense: nothing human is alien to him, even inhumanity. In Chekhov, there remains a vaguely Christian sense of aspiration, of sacrifice and the unattainable: we want and don't get because what we want is so remote and intangible as not to be gettable; for Maupassant, we want and don't get not because what we want can't be had but because there just is never enough of it to go around. His people are denied what they want not because of the injustice of their society or even because of their failures as people, but because of what used to be called "the cruelty of fate" and might now be called the randomness of existence.

This view of life doesn't offer much consolation, but it isn't without feeling. Trollope, a wise man once said, reminds us that sanity need not be philistine; Maupassant reminds us that humanism need not be soft-hearted. Again and again in his stories, the climax occurs when someone breaks down in tears, and the tears of Maupassant's people, though often comic, are never entirely ridiculous. In "The Tellier House," for instance, when the whores weep at their lost hopes and the befuddled priest imagines that grace has descended on his nasty little church, we are meant, for certain, to feel the absurdity of the whores' brief sentimental moment, and of the priest's sanctimonious misunderstanding. But Maupassant wants us to feel, too, that life has given them, as it gave him, and gives to all of us, more than enough to cry about.

———

ADAM GOPNIK is the author of *Paris to the Moon*.

Translator's Note

Joachim Neugroschel

In the nineteenth and twentieth centuries, the European and American short story developed within a new context: newspapers, magazines, and journals, which constituted the new mass media. Nowadays, American newspapers no longer provide their readers with fiction and poetry, while ethnic newspapers like the Yiddish *Forward* still run tales and serials—indeed, a number of Isaac Bashevis Singer's novels were actually serialized in that newspaper.

When short stories appeared in European newspapers, they offered an ambivalent presence—fiction vying with nonfiction. The Italian term *novella* means both "tale" and "news"—as does its French cognate *nouvelle*. Oddly enough, the use of the same word for a literary story and a news story provides a coy dialectic that blurs the line between fact and fiction—as does the French word *journal,* which means "newspaper" and "journal" as well as "diary" and "magazine."

On the other hand, France has always kept a rigid distinction between high culture and popular culture, so that the publication of tales and serials in factual *journaux* broke through a rigid barrier.

While Guy de Maupassant published in these new mass media, he nevertheless kept a sharp distance from their facticity or sensationalism. To avoid becoming "popular"—falling prey to the masses, that is—he developed an intricate style that combined terseness with complex syntax, precise rendering with sometimes harsh lyricism. His inspiration was Gustave Flaubert, whose Ciceronian sentences loom out against the lucidity of normal French style, a product of the French Enlightenment.

Please don't get me wrong. Flaubert and Maupassant certainly wanted to be as "real" as any newspaper item. Indeed, Flaubert's *Madame Bovary* derives from a newspaper item that he happened to read. But this quest for realism involves an endless struggle in which language forms a rampart against newsworthiness.

In rendering Maupassant into English, I've tried to offer a representative gamut of his themes, moods, and subjects, while employing his complex diction as the unifying element: a rich vocabulary, an elaborate syntax, an obscure rhythm and music. Since I have to decontextualize him from the world of journals and gazettes and provide only short stories, I feel that his language, delicately adumbrating the minds and manners of his characters and their situation, is a major clue to his genius.

THE NECKLACE
AND
OTHER TALES

THE NECKLACE

She was one of those pretty and charming girls who, as if through some blunder of fate, are born into a family of pen pushers. She had no dowry, no prospects, no possibility of becoming known, appreciated, loved, of finding a wealthy and distinguished husband. And so she settled for a petty clerk in the Ministry of Education.

Unable to adorn herself, she remained simple, but as miserable as if she'd come down in the world. For women have no caste or breed; their beauty, their grace, and their charm serve them in lieu of birth and family background. Their native finesse, their instinct for elegance, their versatile minds are their sole hierarchy, making shopgirls the equals of the grandest ladies.

She suffered endlessly, feeling that she was meant for all delicacies and all luxuries. She suffered from the poverty of her apartment, the dinginess of the walls, the shabbiness of the chairs, the ugliness of the fabrics. All these things, which wouldn't have even been noticed by any other woman of her station, tortured her and infuriated her. The sight of the Breton girl who did her humble housework aroused woeful regrets in her and desperate dreams. She fantasized about hushed antechambers with Oriental hangings, illuminated by high, bronze torchères, and with a pair of tall footmen wearing knee breeches and napping in spacious easy chairs because of the air made heavy by the heater. She fantasized about large drawing rooms lined with ancient silk, about fine furniture carrying priceless knickknacks, about small, fragrant, dainty parlors meant for five o'clock chats with the most intimate friends, well-known and sought-after men whose attention was envied and desired by all women.

Whenever she sat down for supper at the circular table covered with the same tablecloth for three days, she faced her husband, who, removing the lid from the tureen, ecstatically declared: "Ah! A good stew! I don't know of anything better!"

But she fantasized about elegant dinners, about shiny silverware, about tapestries filling the walls with ancient figures and exotic birds in the midst of a magic forest; she fantasized about exquisite courses served in wondrous vessels, about gallantries whispered and listened to with sphinxlike smiles, while the diners consumed the rosy flesh of a trout or the wings of a grouse.

She had no wardrobe, no jewels, nothing. And those things were all that she loved; she felt that they were what she'd been born for. She so dearly wanted to be liked, to be envied, to be seductive and in demand.

She had a rich friend, from convent-school days, whom she stopped visiting because she suffered so deeply upon coming home. And she'd weep for entire days, weep with chagrin, with regret, with despair, and with distress.

———

Now, one evening, her husband came home exuberantly, clutching a large envelope. "Look," he said, "here's something for you."

She ripped it open and pulled out a printed card bearing these words:

THE MINISTER OF EDUCATION AND MADAME GEORGES RAMPONNEAU
ASK MONSIEUR AND MADAME LOISEL FOR THE PLEASURE OF THEIR COMPANY
AT A SOIRÉE AT THE MINISTRY ON MONDAY, 18TH OF JANUARY.

Instead of being thrilled, as her spouse had hoped, she resentfully hurled the invitation on the table, muttering: "What do you want me to do with this?"

"But darling, I thought you'd be pleased. You never go out, and this is an occasion, a wonderful occasion! I went to endless trouble to get our names on the list. Everyone wants an invitation. They're greatly desired, and not too many clerks are invited. You'll see the entire official world there."

She glared at him, irritated, and snapped impatiently: "What do you expect me to wear?"

Her spouse hadn't considered that; he stammered: "Why, the gown you wear to the theater. It strikes me as very nice. . . ."

He held his tongue, stupefied, bewildered, upon seeing his wife crying. Two big tears rolled slowly from the corners of her eyes toward the corners of her mouth. He stuttered: "What's wrong? What's wrong?"

But with a violent effort, she repressed her pain, and, wiping her moist cheeks, she answered in a calm voice: "Nothing's wrong. Except that I've got nothing to wear and consequently I can't go to that ball. Give your card to some colleague whose wife's got a better wardrobe than I."

He was desolated. He went on: "Look, Mathilde. How much would it cost—a suitable gown that you could use on other occasions, something very simple?"

She mulled for several instants, making estimates in her head, trying to hit on a figure that she could ask for without drawing an immediate refusal and terrified exclamation from the frugal clerk.

At last, she hesitantly responded: "I'm not sure about an exact sum, but I think I could manage with four hundred francs."

He blanched slightly, for he had saved up that very amount to buy himself a rifle and go hunting that summer on the plain of Nanterre, with friends who'd be shooting larks on Sundays.

Nevertheless he said: "Fine. I'll give you four hundred francs. But try to have a beautiful gown."

———

The night of the ball was approaching, and Madame Loisel appeared sad, worried, anxious. Still, her gown was ready.

One evening, her husband said to her: "Listen, what's wrong? You've been acting funny for three days now."

And she replied: "I'm annoyed that I don't have any jewelry—not a single gem, nothing to put on. I'll look downright poverty-stricken. I'd almost rather not go to the ball."

He rejoined: "You'll wear real flowers. They're very chic this season. For ten francs you'll have two or three magnificent roses."

She wasn't convinced. "No. . . . There's nothing more humiliating than looking like a pauper in the middle of rich women."

But her husband exclaimed: "How silly you are. Go to your friend Madame Forestier and ask her to lend you some jewelry. The two of you are close enough for you to do that."

She uttered a cry of joy. "You're right! It didn't occur to me!"

The next day, she went to her friend and explained her distress. Madame Forestier went to a mirrored armoire, removed a large case, brought it over, opened it, and said to Madame Loisel: "Take your pick, my dear."

Madame Loisel looked first at some bracelets, then at a pearl necklace, then at a marvelously crafted Venetian cross made up of gold and precious stones. She tried the pieces on before the mirror, wavering, unsure whether to keep them or leave them. She kept asking: "Don't you have anything else?"

"Of course. Keep searching. I can't tell what you'll like."

All at once, in a black satin box, Madame Loisel unearthed a superb diamond necklace, and her heart began pounding with unrestrained desire. Her hands trembled when she picked up the necklace. She placed it on her throat, against her high-necked dress, and remained ecstatic in front of her reflection. Then, hesitant and fearful, she asked: "Can you lend me this, nothing but this?"

"Of course, by all means."

Madame Loisel flung her arms around her friend, hugged her passionately, then fled with her treasure.

———

The night of the ball arrived. Madame Loisel was a grand success. She was lovelier than any other woman, elegant, gracious, smiling, and wild with joy. All the men gazed at her, asked for her name, and tried to get introduced. All the cabinet attachés wanted to waltz with her. The minister noticed her.

She danced, intoxicated, swept away, heady with pleasure, thinking of nothing, in the triumph of her beauty, in the glory of her conquest, in something like a cloud of happiness made of all that homage, all that admiration, all that awoken yearning, all that complete victory that is so dear to a woman's heart.

She left around four in the morning. Since midnight her husband had been dozing in a small, deserted salon with three other men whose wives were having a wonderful time.

Monsieur Loisel, bringing the wraps for their exit, tossed them over her shoulders: they were the modest garments of ordinary life, their poverty clashing with the elegance of the ball gown. She sensed the discord and wanted to flee, to avoid being noticed by the other women, who were bundling up in expensive furs.

Loisel held her back: "Just wait. You'll catch cold out there. I'll hail a cab."

But she didn't listen, she hurried down the stairs. Out in the street, they couldn't find a cab; so they began searching, shouting at the drivers whom they saw riding by in the distance.

They walked down to the Seine, desperate, shivering. Finally, on a quay, they found one of those old, nocturnal broughams that you see in Paris only at night as if they were ashamed of their squalor by day. It brought them to their front door on Rue des Martyrs, and they sadly trudged up to their apartment. It was all over for her. And as for him, he knew he had to be at the Ministry by ten A.M.

Stripping off the wraps that had enveloped her shoulders, she stood in front of the mirror to view herself in her glory again. But suddenly she uttered a cry. The necklace was gone from her neck!

Her husband, already half undressed, asked her: "What's the matter?"

She turned toward him, panic-stricken: "I . . . I . . . I don't have Madame Forestier's necklace."

He rose in horror: "Huh? What do you mean?! That's impossible! . . ."

And they searched the folds of her gown, the folds of her coat, the pockets—everywhere. They did not find the necklace.

He asked her: "Are you sure you had it when we left the ball?"

"Yes, I touched it in the vestibule of the Ministry."

"Well, if you'd lost it in the street, we'd have heard it fall. It must be in the cab."

"Yes. Probably. Did you jot down the number?"

"No. What about you? Did you get it?"

"No."

Their eyes locked in terror. Finally Loisel put his clothes back on.

"I'm going to scour the entire distance that we walked—I'll see if I can find it."

And he left. Too feeble to go to bed, she remained in her gown, sprawling on a chair, her heart inert, her mind blank.

Her husband returned at around seven. He had found nothing.

He went to the police station, to the cab companies, to the newspapers, promising a reward—he went wherever a glimmer of hope beckoned.

She waited all day, still bewildered by that dreadful disaster.

Loisel came back in the evening, his face gaunt and pale; he had discovered nothing.

"You have to write your friend," he said, "that you broke the clasp of her necklace and that you're having it fixed. That'll buy us some time."

She wrote as he dictated.

———

By the end of a week, they had lost all hope.

And Loisel, who had aged five years, declared: "We have to see about replacing the necklace."

The next day they took the jewel case to the jeweler whose name was inside. He consulted his books.

"Madame, I'm not the one who sold this necklace, I only furnished the case."

So, both of them sick with chagrin and anguish, they traipsed from jeweler to jeweler, seeking a necklace that looked like the other one, consulting their memories.

In a boutique at the Palais-Royal, they found a diamond chaplet that struck them as entirely similar to the one they were searching for. The price was forty thousand francs. They could have it for thirty-six thousand.

They begged the jeweler to put it on reserve for three days. And he agreed to take it back for thirty-four thousand if the first necklace were found by the end of February.

Loisel had eighteen thousand francs that his father had left him. He would borrow the rest.

He borrowed, asking for a thousand francs from one person, five hundred from another, five louis here, three louis there. He signed promissory notes, accepted ruinous conditions, dealt with usurers, with all the races of moneylenders. He compromised his entire life, risked his signature without even knowing if he could honor it; and, terrified at the thought of future anguish, the black misery that would overwhelm him, the prospect of all the physical deprivations and all the mental tortures, he went to pick up the new necklace, placing thirty-six thousand francs on the merchant's counter.

When Madame Loisel returned the necklace to Madame Forestier, the latter said, with a slight show of annoyance: "You should have brought it back sooner, I might have needed it."

Madame Forestier did not open the case, which her friend had feared she would do. Had she detected the substitution, what would she have thought? What would she have said? Wouldn't she have taken Madame Loisel for a thief?

———

Madame Loisel now knew the horrible life of necessity. However, she did her part, thoroughly, heroically. The ghastly debt had to be repaid. She would repay it. They dismissed the maid; they moved to a garret.

She performed the gross household tasks, the odious kitchen chores. She washed the dishes, wearing down her rosy nails on greasy pots and on the bottoms of pans. She washed the dirty linen, the shirts and the dishcloths, and let them dry on a line. She lugged the garbage down to the street every morning and hauled up the water, stopping at every landing to catch her breath. And, dressed like a pauper, she went to the produce store, the grocer, the butcher, her basket on her arm, haggling, insulted, defending her miserable cash sou by sou.

Every month, they had to pay off some IOUs, renew others, gain time.

The husband worked evenings, putting a businessman's accounts in order, and spent many nights doing copies at five sous a page.

And this life dragged on for ten years.

At the end of ten years, they had repaid everything, everything, at the rates of loan sharks and with the accumulation of compound interest.

Madame Loisel looked old now. She had become the strong, and hard, and crude woman of poor households. Her hair ill kempt, her skirts awry, and her hands red, she spoke loudly and she washed the floors with big buckets of water. But sometimes, when her husband was at the office, she would sit down at the window and daydream about that long-ago ball, where she had been so beautiful and so celebrated.

What would have happened if she hadn't lost the necklace? Who knows? Who knows? How strange life is, how full of changes! How little it takes to doom you or save you!

———

Now one Sunday, as she was walking along the Champs-Élysées, trying to recover from her weekday chores, she suddenly noticed a woman strolling with a child. It was Madame Forestier, still young, still beautiful, still seductive.

Madame Loisel felt a surge of emotion. Should she speak to her? Yes, of course. And now that she had paid off her debt, she would tell Madame Forestier everything. Why not?

She walked over.

"Good day, Jeanne."

The other woman didn't recognize her, she was astonished at being addressed so familiarly by this housewife. She stammered: "But . . . Madame! . . . I don't know . . . You must be mistaken."

"No. I'm Mathilde Loisel."

Her friend uttered a cry: "Oh! . . . My poor Mathilde, how you've changed! . . ."

"Yes, I've had a hard life since I last saw you. And lots of misery. . . . And all because of you! . . ."

"Because of me? . . . What are you saying?"

"Do you recall that diamond necklace you lent me to attend the ball at the Ministry?"

"Yes. What about it?"

"Well, I lost it."

"What? But you returned it to me."

"I brought you a different one, identical with yours. And we've been paying it off for the past ten years. You realize it wasn't easy for us, we had nothing. . . . At last it's over, and I'm thoroughly glad of it."

Madame Forestier paused.

"You say you bought a diamond necklace to replace mine?"

"Yes. You didn't catch on, did you? They were fairly alike."

And she smiled with a proud and naïve joy.

Madame Forestier, deeply moved, took hold of Madame Loisel's hands.

"Oh, my poor Mathilde! My necklace was paste. It was worth at most five hundred francs! . . ."

Butterball

For several days in a row, the vestiges of the routed French army had been straggling across the city. These weren't troops so much as disbanded hordes. Their beards were long and filthy, their uniforms tattered, and they slogged on at a slack pace, not bearing any flags, not divided into regiments. They all looked overwhelmed, exhausted, incapable of thought or resolution, marching purely out of habit and collapsing with fatigue the instant they halted. Most of them had been mobilized, they were peaceful, tranquil men of independent means, bending under the weight of a rifle; little, alert militiamen, easily terrified and readily enthusiastic, prepared for both attack and flight. Then, in their midst, a few red breeches, the remnants of a division that had been thoroughly ground up in a major battle; somber artillerists aligned with these diverse foot soldiers, and, sometimes, the brilliant helmet of a sluggish dragoon who was arduously following the easier march of the infantrymen.

Legions of snipers with heroic appellations—Avengers of the Defeat, Citizens of the Tomb, Partakers of Death—passed by in turn, acting like bandits.

Their leaders, former cloth or grain merchants, soap or bacon mongers, temporary warriors, made officers thanks to their escutcheons or the length of their mustaches, covered with weapons, flannel, and braids, spoke in ringing tones, discussing campaign plans and claiming to be the sole support of a France in the throes of dying on their swaggering shoulders. But at times they feared their own soldiers—jailbirds, often daredevils, plunderers and debauchees.

The Prussians, rumor had it, were about to enter Rouen.

The French National Guard, which, for two months now, had been very prudently reconnoitering the nearby woods, sometimes gunning down its own sentries or preparing for combat the instant a small rabbit stirred in the underbrush, had gone home. Its weapons, its uniforms, all the death-dealing implements with which the National Guard had just recently haunted the boundaries of national highways within a radius of three leagues, had suddenly disappeared.

The last French soldiers had finally crossed the Seine to reach Pont-Audemer via Saint-Sever and Bourg-Achard; and bringing up the rear and flanked by two aides-de-camp, the despairing general trudged along, unable to try anything with those motley odds and ends and bewildered by the huge debacle of a nation accustomed to victory and disastrously beaten despite its legendary valor.

Next, a profound calm, a hushed and terrified foreboding came and hovered over the town. Many potbellied burghers, emasculated by years of wheeling and dealing, queasily awaited the conquerors, fearful that their roasting spits or their large kitchen knives might be considered weapons.

Life seemed to have halted, the stores were closed, the streets mute. Now and then an inhabitant, intimidated by the silence, glided along the walls.

The agony of waiting made them wish for the arrival of the enemy.

In the afternoon of the day following the departure of the French troops, a few uhlans, emerging from goodness knows where, galloped across the town. Then, a bit later, a dark mass plunged down Saint Catherine's Hill, while two other waves of invaders came pouring along the roads from Darnetal and Boisguillaume. The advance guards of all three forces reached Town Hall Square at precisely the same instant; and the German army kept lunging through the neighboring streets, spreading its battalions, with the cobblestones ringing under their hard, staccato tread.

Orders shouted by an unfamiliar, guttural voice echoed along the houses, which looked dead and deserted, while, from behind the closed shutters, eyes peered at these victorious men, who, by "right of war," had become the masters of the town, the commanders of the fate and the lives of the populace. The inhabitants, in their darkened rooms, suffered the kind of panic triggered by cataclysms, by tremendous and murderous upheavals of the earth, against which all wisdom and all strength are useless. For the same feeling recurs whenever the established order of things is upset, when security no longer exists, when everything that protected human or natural laws is at the mercy of irrational and ferocious brutality. The earthquake that crushes an entire population under tumbling houses; the overflowing river that sweeps drowned farmers together with carcasses of cows, with beams torn from roofs; or the glorious army that massacres people defending themselves and brings back the survivors as prisoners, looting by right of the Sword and thanking their God to the booming of cannon— these are all terrifying scourges that cripple any faith in eternal justice, any trust that we have been taught to place in divine protection and human reason.

Small detachments now knocked on each door, then vanished inside the houses. It was the occupation after the invasion. The conquered were now obliged to act gracious toward the conquerors.

After a while, a new calm settled in, once the initial terror had dissipated. Many families ate their meals with the Prussian officers. Some of the latter, being well bred, were polite enough to feel sorry for France and express their repugnance at participating in this war. The French were grateful for these sentiments; besides, sooner or later, they might need an officer's protection. If they humored him, he might keep down the number of men they would have to quarter. And why offend someone on whom you were totally dependent? Such behavior would be less courageous than foolhardy. And foolhardiness is no longer a foible of the burghers of Rouen as it was in the days of the heroic defenses that made their city so illustrious. And finally, drawing a supreme rationale from the tradition of French politesse, the citizens argued that it was quite legitimate for them to be courteous in their own homes, provided they did not act familiar with the foreign soldiers in public. Outdoors they ignored one another, but indoors they chatted freely, and the German stayed with them longer and longer each evening, warming himself at their fireplace.

The town itself gradually regained its normal appearance. The French still rarely ventured out, but the streets were teeming with Prussian soldiers. Furthermore, the officers of the Blue Hussars, arrogantly dragging their huge instruments of death over the sidewalks, did not appear to despise the simple citizens much more than the officers of the light infantry, who had been drinking in the same cafés the previous year.

Yet there was something in the air, something subtle and unfamiliar, an unendurable alien atmosphere, like a widespread odor, the odor of invasion. It filled the homes and the public squares, it changed the taste of food, it made people feel as if they were traveling very far away, among barbarous and dangerous tribes.

The victors demanded cash, lots of cash. The inhabitants kept forking it over; and they were rich enough to do so. But the more opulent a Norman businessman becomes, the more badly he suffers for any sacrifice of his money, any bit of his fortune that passes into someone else's hands.

Meanwhile, some five or six miles downstream, toward Croisset, Dieppedalle, or Biessart, mariners and fishermen often hauled in a corpse from the watery depth, a bloated, uniformed German who had been stabbed with a knife, or kicked to death, or shoved off a bridge, or whose head had been crushed by a rock. The river's mud buried these obscure reprisals, these both savage and legitimate retaliations, these anonymous deeds of heroism, these voiceless attacks, which were more perilous than battles in broad daylight and which brought no echoes of glory.

For hatred of the Foreigner will always hearten a few Intrepid souls who are ready to die for an Ideal.

Eventually, since the invaders, though subjecting the town to their iron discipline, inflicted none of the atrocities that they were rumored to have committed throughout their triumphal march, the citizens plucked up their courage, and the need for commerce resurged in the hearts of the merchants. A few of them, having major business interests in Le Havre, which was occupied by the French, wanted to try to reach that port by taking the overland route to Dieppe, where they would disembark.

Utilizing the influence offered by acquaintances among the German officers, these merchants obtained a departure pass from the commanding general.

And so, once a large four-horse coach was hired for the trip, with ten people reserving seats, they decided to start out on a Tuesday morning—at the crack of dawn to avoid drawing a crowd.

For some time now, the frost had been hardening the ground, and at around three o'clock that Monday, huge black clouds drifting in from the north brought snow, which fell steadily all evening and all night.

At four-thirty A.M., the travelers gathered in the courtyard of the Hôtel de Normandie, where they were supposed to board the coach.

Still half-asleep, they were shivering with cold under their wraps. It was so dark that they could barely discern one another, and the pileup of their heavy winter garments made all these bodies look like rotund priests in their long cassocks. However, two men did recognize each other, a third man came over, and they launched into a chat.

"I'm taking my wife," said one.

"So am I."

"Me, too."

The first one added: "We're not going to be returning to Rouen, and if the Prussians close in on Le Havre, we'll sail to England."

Being of the same temperament, they all had the same plans.

However, the horses still weren't hitched. Every so often, a small lantern carried by a stablehand emerged from one dark doorway and instantly vanished into another. Hooves of horses pounded the ground, muffled by the dung in the litter, and a male voice, talking to the animals and swearing, burst from the depths of the building. A faint jingling of bells announced that the harnesses were being handled; and this jingling soon became a loud and continuous jangle, following the cadence of the animal's movement, stopping at times, then resuming with a brusque jerk accompanied by the dull thuds of an iron horseshoe whacking the ground.

Suddenly the gate shut. All noise faded. The frozen passengers were silent; they remained rigid and immobile.

A curtain of white flakes kept endlessly sparkling as it descended toward the earth; it blurred all shapes, powdered all things with an icy froth; and in the vast, calm, wintry hush of the buried city, all that could be heard was the vague, elusive, indefinable rustle of falling snow—more a feeling than a sound, a mingling of airy atoms that seemed to fill all space and blanket the whole world.

The man reappeared, with his lantern, pulling a woeful and reluctant horse at the end of a rope. He placed the creature between the shafts, attached the traces, and spent a long time adjusting the harness, for he could use only one hand while holding the light in the other. Going for the second horse, he noticed all those inert travelers, who were already white with snow. And he said: "Why don't you get into the coach? You'll at least be sheltered."

This idea hadn't crossed their minds, no doubt, and they dashed over. The three husbands installed their wives at the far end of the interior, then climbed in after them. Next, the other dim and hazy figures took the remaining seats without exchanging a word.

The floor was covered with straw, and their feet sank into it. The ladies in back, having brought small copper foot warmers fueled by chemicals, lit their apparatuses and murmured softly for a while, enumerating the advantages, repeating things they had known for a long time.

At last, when the horses were hitched up—six instead of four because of the additional work caused by the weather—an exterior voice asked: "Has everyone gotten in?" And an interior voice replied: "Yes."

The coach crept off.

It lumbered slowly, slowly, very laboriously. The wheels sank into the snow; the entire vehicle groaned and creaked; the horses slipped, panted, steamed, and the driver's gigantic whip cracked nonstop, flitted every which way, twisting up and then uncoiling like a slender serpent, and suddenly lashing some hefty rump, which then tensed in a more vehement effort.

However, the day was brightening imperceptibly. The airy flakes, which one passenger, a purebred native of Rouen, had compared to a shower of cotton, stopped falling. A grimy light filtered through huge, dark, heavy clouds, and they, by contrast, intensified the dazzling whiteness of the countryside, which revealed now a row of high, frosted trees, now a cottage with a snowy cowl.

Inside the coach, the passengers exchanged curious stares in the dismal light of that dawn.

At the far end of the vehicle, in the best seats, Monsieur and Madame Loiseau [Bird], wholesale wine dealers on Rue Grand-Pont, were dozing opposite each other.

Formerly the clerk of a merchant who'd gone bankrupt, Loiseau had purchased the business and made a fortune. He sold very cheap and very bad wine to the small rural retailers and was known among his friends and acquaintances as a crafty rogue, a true Norman, full of cunning and joviality.

His reputation as a reprobate was so well established that one evening at the county seat, Monsieur Tournel, a local celebrity who wrote songs and stories, a man with a mordant and delicate wit, had proposed to the slightly drowsy ladies that they play cards—Loiseau would teach them the "tricks." The bon mot spread through all the drawing rooms in the county seat, then the city, and for an entire month, the jawbones throughout the province had a good laugh.

Loiseau was also famous for all kinds of pranks, for his good or bad jokes, and no one could mention his name without instantly adding, "He's priceless—that Loiseau!"

A scraggy manikin, he had a belly like a balloon, surmounted by a red face between salt-and-pepper whiskers.

His wife, big and stout, resolute and decisive, with a shrill voice, ran the business and did the books, while her husband kept the firm going with his joyful hustle and bustle.

Next to them in the coach sat Monsieur Carré-Lamadon, more dignified and part of a superior caste, a man of substance with a solid footing in the cotton trade, the owner of three cotton mills, an officer in the Legion of Honor, and a member of the county council. In the days of the Empire, he had remained the head of the benevolent opposition purely in order to obtain a higher price for rallying to the cause he had battled against with what he called "courteous weapons."

Madame Carré-Lamadon, much younger than her husband, remained the consolation of officers with good backgrounds who were garrisoned in Rouen. She now sat across from her husband, very tiny, very dainty, very pretty, snuggling in her furs and gazing with woebegone eyes at the lamentable interior of the coach.

Her neighbors, Count and Countess Hubert de Bréville, bore one of the oldest and noblest names in Normandy. With the artifices of his wardrobe, the count, an elderly and distinguished-looking aristocrat, tried to emphasize his natural resemblance to King Henry IV, who, according to a legend that was the glory of the family, had impregnated a lady in Bréville, whose husband had therefore been made a count and a governor of a province.

An associate of Monsieur Carré-Lamadon in the county council, Count Hubert represented the Orleanist Party in the department. The story of his marriage to a small shipowner's daughter in Nantes had always remained a mystery. But since the countess had high-and-mighty airs, entertained better than anyone else, and was even said to have been loved by a son of Louis Philippe's, she was fêted by the entire nobility, and her salon endured as the finest in the countryside, the only salon preserving old-world gallantry and exclusivity.

As for their fortune, which was fully invested in landed property, the Brévilles were said to have an income of nearly half a million pounds a year.

These six passengers occupied the far end of the coach, embodying the social class of independent means, serene and solid, upright and honorable people who have Religion and Principles.

By some bizarre coincidence, all the women were seated on the same side, whereby the countess's neighbors were two nuns, who kept telling long strings of beads while murmuring the Lord's Prayer and the Hail Mary. One nun was an old woman with a pockmarked face that looked as if it had received a broadside of grapeshot point-blank. The other nun, a very puny woman, had pretty but sickly features over a consumptive chest ravaged by the devouring faith that produces martyrs and illuminati.

Across from the nuns sat a man and a woman who drew everyone's attention.

The man, well known, was Cornudet the democrat—the terror of respectable people. For twenty years now, he had been dipping his red beard in the beer mugs of all the pro-democratic cafés. Together with his friends and cohorts, he had squandered a rather decent fortune left him by his father, a retired confectioner. Cornudet impatiently looked forward to the arrival of the Republic, eager to finally obtain the position he merited by dint of so many revolutionary expenditures. With the uprising of the fourth of September [1870], Cornudet, perhaps through some practical joke, had gotten it into his head that he had been appointed prefect. But upon his attempting to take office, the office boys, now the sole masters of the prefecture, had refused to acknowledge him, thereby forcing him to retreat. A good-natured type, however, obliging and inoffensive, he had devoted an incomparable ardor to organizing the defense of the town. He had had the citizens dig pits in the surrounding plains, layer the branches of all the young trees in the nearby forests, scatter booby traps on all the roads; and, at the approach of the enemy, Cornudet, satisfied with his preparations, had dashed back to the city. He now figured he'd be more useful in Le Havre, where new entrenchments would be necessary.

The woman, the kind known as being of easy virtue, was famous for her premature embonpoint, which had earned her the nickname of Butterball. Round and pudgy, as fat as lard, with bloated fingers squeezed in at the joints and looking like strings of short sausages, she had a taut, shiny skin and enormous breasts spilling out of her dress; still, her freshness was so delightful that she remained appetizing and popular. Her face was a red apple, a peony bud on the verge of blossoming; and at the top of her face, magnificent black eyes opened up, eyes shaded and deepened by large, thick lashes; beneath the eyes, there was a charming narrow mouth, moist for kisses, with a set of glossy, microscopic teeth.

Moreover, she was, people said, full of inestimable qualities.

The instant she was recognized, the respectable women started whispering, and the words "prostitute" and "disgrace" were muttered so loudly that she raised her head. She glared at her fellow passengers with such brazen defiance that they promptly lapsed into a deep silence, all of them lowering their eyes, except for Loiseau, who stared at her with an exhilarated air.

Soon, however, the conversation resumed among the three ladies, who had suddenly become fast friends, almost intimates, because of that woman's presence. The three ladies felt that, with their dignity as wives, they should form a united front against this shameless hussy; for legal love always looks down on its free colleague.

The three men, likewise brought together by a conservative instinct vis-à-vis Cornudet, started talking about money with a certain tone of disdain for the poor. Count Hubert told about the havoc inflicted on him by the Prussians, the losses resulting from cattle thefts and ruined harvests, and he spoke with the self-assurance of a lord, a millionaire ten times over, who would be inconvenienced for scarcely a year by those ravages. Monsieur Carré-Lamadon, badly hurt in the cotton industry, had, as he did on all occasions, put something by for a rainy day, taking the precaution of transferring six hundred thousand francs to England. As for Loiseau, he had managed to sell all the cheap wine in his cellar to the French military, so that the government owed him a formidable sum, which he planned to collect in Le Havre.

And the three men exchanged quick and friendly glances. While belonging to different social classes, they felt like brothers by dint of money, in the vast freemasonry of men who possess, who can jingle gold by slipping a hand into their trouser pockets.

The coach plodded along so slowly that by ten A.M. it had covered only ten miles. The men had gotten out three times to climb a hill on foot. The passengers started worrying, for they were scheduled to have lunch at Tôtes and now they despaired of arriving there by nightfall. Each passenger was trying to spot a roadside inn when the coach bogged down in a snowdrift, and it took them two hours to haul it out.

Their appetite grew, affecting their spirits, and not a single cheap tavern appeared, not a single wine shop; the approach of the Prussians and the passage of starving French troops had driven away all commerce.

The gentlemen hurried over to buy provisions at wayside farms, but they couldn't even dig up some bread, for the distrustful farmers hid their reserves, afraid of being looted by the soldiers, who, without a bite of food, were forcibly grabbing anything they chanced on.

Toward one in the afternoon, Loiseau announced that there was no doubt about it, he had an awful void in his stomach. Like him, the others had been suffering for a long time, and the violent hunger, growing all the while, had killed any conversation.

From time to time, somebody yawned; somebody else promptly imitated him; and each person in turn, according to breeding, character, and social position, opened his mouth noisily or modestly, his hand quickly covering the gaping and steaming hole.

Butterball kept leaning over as if searching for something under her petticoats. She would hesitate for an instant, peer at her neighbors, and then tranquilly sit erect again. The faces were pale and drawn. Loiseau declared that he'd pay a thousand francs for a knuckle of ham. His wife gestured as if to protest, then she calmed down. Hearing anything about wasted money caused her great discomfort, and she couldn't even understand jokes about that subject. "The fact is," said the count, "that I don't feel well. Why didn't I think of bringing provisions?" Each passenger was reproaching himself for the same oversight.

Cornudet, however, had a flask of rum; he offered it: he was coldly refused. Only Loiseau accepted a drop or two; and when he handed back the flask, he thanked Cornudet: "It's good all the same, it warms you up, and it staves off your hunger." The alcohol put him in a good mood, and, like the crew in the song about the little boat, he proposed that they eat the fattest of the travelers. This subtle allusion to Butterball shocked the well-bred passengers. They didn't respond; only Cornudet smiled. The two nuns had stopped mumbling their rosaries, and, burying their hands in their big sleeves, they remained motionless, obstinately lowering their eyes and, no doubt, offering up to heaven the anguish it was sending them.

Finally, at three P.M., when they were in the heart of an interminable plain, without a single village in sight, Butterball, sharply leaning down, reached under her seat and removed a basket, a large basket covered with a white napkin.

First she produced a small faïence plate, a fine silver mug, next a huge terrine in which two whole chickens were carved up and conserved in their aspic. And the travelers perceived more goodies wrapped up in the basket: pâtés, fruit, tidbits, provisions for a three-day trip, to avoid having to touch the fare dished up at inns. The necks of four bottles jutted out from among the packages of food. She took a chicken wing and started daintily eating it with one of those rolls that the Normans call Regencies.

All eyes were glued to Butterball. Then the aroma drifted about, making nostrils flare, creating abundant saliva in the mouths and a painful contraction of the jaws under the ears. The contempt that the ladies felt toward this hussy become ferocious, they practically longed to kill her or pitch her out into the snow—her, her mug, her basket, and her provisions.

But Loiseau's eyes devoured the chicken terrine. He said: "Fine, Madame took more precautions than we did. There are people who always manage to think of everything."

She looked up at him: "Would you care for something, Monsieur? It's hard fasting since this morning."

He bowed: "My goodness! Frankly, I won't refuse, I can't go on any longer. War is war—isn't that so, Madame?" And looking all around, he added: "At moments like this, it's so nice to find people who'll help you out." He had a newspaper, which he spread on his lap to avoid soiling his trousers; and with the point of a knife that he always kept in his pocket, he stabbed a jelly-glazed drumstick, shredded it with his teeth, then munched away with such blatant gusto that the coach was filled with a loud sigh of distress.

However, Butterball, in a gentle and humble voice, invited the nuns to share her snack. Both of them instantly accepted, and, without looking up, they began eating very quickly after stammering their thanks. Nor did Cornudet reject his neighbor's offers, and together with the nuns they formed a makeshift table by unfolding newspapers on their knees.

Mouths opened and closed incessantly, chewing, swallowing, ravenously wolfing down. Loiseau, in his corner, was hard at work, and he kept softly urging his wife to do the same. She resisted for a long time; but then, after a convulsion swept through her innards, she yielded. Her husband suavely asked his "charming companion" whether she'd allow him to offer Madame Loiseau a small morsel.

Handing him the terrine with an amiable smile, Butterball replied: "Why yes, help yourself, Monsieur."

An awkward situation arose when the first bottle of Bordeaux was uncorked: there was only one mug. Each person passed it along after wiping it. Cornudet alone, out of gallantry no doubt, put his lips to the spot that had been moistened by the female lips.

Surrounded by munchers and suffocating under the emanations from the food, the Count and Countess de Bréville, as well as Monsieur and Madame Carré-Lamadon, suffered the odious torture that has preserved the name of Tantalus. All at once, the manufacturer's young wife heaved a sigh that made all heads turn; she was as white as the snow outside the coach; her eyes shut, her forehead drooped: she had blacked out. Her terrified husband begged the others for help. They were all panic-stricken, but then the older nun, supporting the victim's head, slipped Butterball's mug between the woman's lips and made her swallow a few drops of wine. The pretty lady stirred, opened her eyes, smiled, and declared in a moribund voice that she now felt quite fine. However, to prevent any recurrence, the nun compelled her to drink a full mug of Bordeaux, adding: "She's hungry—that's all."

Butterball, blushing and embarrassed, looked at the four fasting travelers and stammered: "My goodness, if I dared to offer these gentle-men and these ladies . . ." She lapsed into silence, fearing their outrage.

Loiseau took the floor: "Well, by God! In such cases, we are all brothers and are bound to help each other. Come on, ladies, no cere-mony. My goodness! Why not accept?! Do we know if we'll even find a house to spend the night in? At the rate we're going, we won't reach Tôtes before noon tomorrow."

The others hesitated, no one daring to assume responsibility for saying yes. The count settled the matter. He turned toward the intimi-dated fat girl, and, assuming his grand, aristocratic air, he told her: "We gratefully accept, Madame."

The first step was the hardest. Once the Rubicon was crossed, they all tucked in royally. The basket was emptied. It also contained a pâté de foie gras, a lark pâté, a piece of smoked tongue, Crassane pears, a wedge of Pont-L'Évêque cheese, petits fours, and a jar of pickled gherkins and onions, for, like all women, Butterball loved pungent fla-vors.

Now, they couldn't very well eat the girl's provisions without speak-ing to her. So they chatted: first with reserve; then, since she conducted herself so nicely, they relaxed more and more. Madame de Bréville and Madame Carré-Lamadon, who had a lot of savoir faire, acted gra-cious and delicate. The countess in particular showed that friendly condescension of very high gentlewomen, whom no contact can soil, and she was charming. But the powerful Madame Loiseau, who had the soul of a martinet, remained grouchy, saying little and eating lots.

They talked about the war, of course. They told about atrocities committed by the Prussians and brave deeds performed by the French; and all these fleeing travelers paid homage to one another's courage. Soon they launched into personal stories; and with true agi-tation and with the heated speech sometimes used by girls to express their natural passions, Butterball described her departure from Rouen.

"At first I thought I could stay. My home was full of provisions, and

I preferred feeding a couple of soldiers to finding shelter goodness knows where. But when I saw those Prussians, I couldn't help it. They made my blood boil, and I was so ashamed that I cried all day. Oh, my! If I were a man! I watched them from my window—those big pigs with their pointed helmets—and my maid grabbed my arms to prevent me from dumping my furniture on their backs! Then they tried to lodge one of them in my home—I jumped at his throat. They're no harder to strangle than anyone else! And I would have polished him off, that Prussian, if I hadn't been pulled away by my hair. I had to go into hiding after that. Eventually, when I had an opportunity, I skipped town. And here I am."

Butterball was showered with congratulations. She grew in the esteem of her companions, who hadn't shown such guts. And Cornudet, listening to her, maintained the approving and benevolent smile of an apostle, the way a priest hears a devotee praise God, for democrats with flowing beards have a monopoly on patriotism just as men in cassocks have a monopoly on religion. In his turn, Cornudet spoke in a doctrinaire tone, with the bombast learned from the proclamations that were pasted on walls each day; and he finished with a bit of eloquence, giving a sound thrashing to that "low-down Napoleon III!"

But this promptly infuriated Butterball, for she was a Bonapartist. She grew redder than a beet and stuttered with indignation: "I'd like to have seen what you'd all have done in his place. That would have been a fine mess—oh yes! You're the ones who betrayed that man! We'd have no choice but to leave France if we were governed by scoundrels like you!"

Cornudet, impassive, maintained a disdainful and superior smirk, and they all sensed the coming of foul words; however, the count stepped in and, not without difficulty, calmed the exasperated girl by declaring authoritatively that all sincere opinions should be respected. However, the countess and the manufacturer's wife, both of them fostering the irrational hatred that genteel people level at the Republic, felt the instinctive tenderness that all women nurture for all swaggering and despotic governments; and so despite themselves, those two ladies were drawn to this highly dignified prostitute, whose convictions overlapped with theirs.

The basket was empty. The ten passengers had easily exhausted it, regretting only that it wasn't larger. The conversation drifted on for a while, cooling slightly once they were done eating.

Night was falling, the darkness gradually thickened, and the cold, more acute during a period of digestion, made Butterball shiver despite her fat. Madame de Bréville offered Butterball her heater, which had been refueled several times since that morning, and Butterball instantly accepted because her feet were frozen. Madame Carré-Lamadon and Madame Loiseau lent their heaters to the nuns.

The coachman had lit his lanterns. Their vivid glow brightened a cloud of vapor above the sweaty horse rumps and illuminated the snow, which seemed to unfurl on both sides of the road, under the moving reflections of the lights.

Nothing could be made out in the coach; but all at once, there was movement between Butterball and Cornudet; and Loiseau, scanning the darkness, thought he saw the thick-bearded man jump away as if he'd been dealt a strong and silent blow.

Tiny dots of fire emerged on the road ahead. It was Tôtes. The coach had been rolling for eleven hours, not counting the four half-hour stops for letting the horses catch their breath and gobble up some oats. Now the coach lurched into the small market town and drew up at the Commerce Hotel.

The door opened! A familiar noise made all the passengers tremble: it was the banging of a scabbard on the ground. A German voice instantly shouted something.

Even though the coach was immobile, the passengers stayed put—as if expecting to be massacred when descending. Then the driver appeared, clutching a lantern, which suddenly lit up the entire coach with its two rows of terrified faces, their mouths gaping and their eyes bulging in surprise and panic.

Next to the coachman, in full glare, stood a German officer, young and tall, immoderately blond and thin, squeezed into his uniform like a girl into her corset, and wearing, on one side of his head, his flat, glossy cap, which made him look like a page boy in a British hotel. His enormous mustache, with its long, straight hairs, tapering off undiscernibly and terminating on either side in a single blond thread so fine that its end disappeared, seemed to weigh on the corners of his mouth and, by pulling down his cheek, made his lips appear droopy.

Speaking bluntly in Alsatian French, he invited the travelers to come out: "Pleasse tescent, laities and tchentlemen?"

The two nuns were the first to obey, showing the docility of devout women accustomed to all forms of submission. Next the count and the countess stepped down, followed by the manufacturer and his wife, then Loiseau pushing his better and bigger half before him. Upon setting foot on the ground, he greeted the officer: "Bonjour, Monsieur," more out of prudence than politeness. The officer, insolent like any omnipotent man, eyed him without responding.

Butterball and Cornudet, though closest to the door, were the last to descend; grave and haughty, they faced the enemy. The fat girl tried to control herself and stay calm; the democrat kept twisting his long, reddish beard with a tragic and slightly quivering hand. They were eager to uphold their dignity, realizing that in such encounters each individual to some degree represents his country. Both were revolted by the servility of their companions: Butterball attempted to act more arrogant than the respectable women she was traveling with, while Cornudet, feeling he ought to set an example, maintained his full attitude of resistance—a mission he had begun by helping to break up the roads.

They entered the vast kitchen of the inn, where the German, after checking the departure pass signed by the commanding general and listing each traveler's name, description, and profession, studied all these people for a long time, comparing them with the written data.

Then he abruptly exclaimed: "Very goot!" and vanished.

Everyone heaved a sigh of relief. They were still hungry; supper was ordered. It would be ready in half an hour; and, while two serving girls seemed to be preparing it, the travelers went to their rooms. These rooms all lined a long corridor that was closed off by a glazed door bearing the numeral 100, the sign of a toilet.

Finally, they were about to sit down at the table when the innkeeper himself appeared. He was a former horse-dealer, a burly asthmatic, who kept wheezing and hawking with a raspy larynx. His father had encumbered him with the name of Follenvie [Wild Desire].

He asked: "Mademoiselle Élizabeth Rousset?"

Butterball shuddered, she turned around.

"That's me."

"Mademoiselle, the Prussian officer wants to talk to you right away."

"Me?"

"Yes, if you're Mademoiselle Élizabeth Rousset."

Butterball was flustered, she mulled for a second, then declared flat out: "Let him, I'm not going."

The others stirred all around her; everyone debated, everyone tried to pinpoint the reason for that order. The count came over.

"You're wrong not to go, Madame, your refusal can entail serious difficulties, not only for you but also for all your fellow travelers. One should never resist anyone who has the upper hand. I'm certain your compliance won't expose you to any danger; it probably involves some neglected formality."

Everyone sided with him; they begged her, they coaxed her, they preached to her, and they eventually convinced her; for they all feared the complications that might result from her defiance. At last she said: "I'm only doing it for your sakes, believe me!"

The countess took her hand: "And we're grateful to you."

Butterball left. Rather than sitting down at the table, they waited for her to return. Each person was upset at not having been asked instead of that violent and irascible girl, and they mentally rehearsed platitudes just in case they were summoned in turn.

Ten minutes later, however, she reappeared with a crimson face, gasping, choking, fuming. She kept stammering: "Oh, that bastard! That bastard!"

They all crowded around her, trying to learn what had happened; but she held her tongue; and since the count persisted, she replied with great dignity: "No, it doesn't concern you, I can't say anything."

They sat down to a deep soup tureen from which the smell of cabbage wafted up. Despite the unpleasant incident, the supper was cheerful. The cider was good, the Loiseaus and the nuns imbibed it for economy's sake. The others asked for wine; Cornudet requested beer. He had his special way of opening the bottle, pouring a nice head, and inspecting the liquid by tilting the glass between the lamp and his eyes in order to appreciate the color. When he drank, his large beard, turning the same hue as his favorite beverage, seemed to shiver with tenderness; and he squinted so as to keep sight of his mug; he acted as though he were carrying out the one function he'd been born for. It was as if his mind were establishing a rapport, virtually an affinity, between the two great passions that ruled his life: pale ale and the Revolution; and he certainly couldn't savor one without musing about the other.

Monsieur and Madame Follenvie dined at the far end of the table. The innkeeper, rattling like an exhausted locomotive, was too congested to talk while eating; but his wife talked a blue streak. She recounted all her impressions of the arrival of the Prussians, what they did, what they said; she execrated them, first because they were costing her money and second because she had two sons in the army. Flattered to be chatting with a lady of quality, she focused on the countess.

Then she lowered her voice to say delicate things, while her husband interrupted every so often: "You really ought to hold your tongue, Madame Follenvie." But she paid no heed, she babbled on.

"Yes, Madame, those people do nothing but eat potatoes and pork, and then pork and potatoes. And you mustn't think they're clean. Not on your life. Why, they relieve themselves everywhere, if you'll pardon my frankness. And if you saw them drilling for hours and days on end . . . They're all out in the fields. And forward march and backward march, and turn this way and turn that way. If they at least did a little farming or repaired the roads in their own country! But oh no, Madame! Those soldiers aren't useful for anybody! So the poor population has to feed them so that all they do is learn how to massacre! I'm only an old, uneducated woman, that's true. But when I see them trampling from dawn till dusk, ruining their constitutions, I say to myself: 'If there are people who discover so many useful things, why do others have to go to so much trouble to wreck things?! Honestly, isn't it an abomination to kill people, whether they're Prussians or else Englishmen, or Poles, or Frenchmen?' If you get back at somebody for doing you dirt, that's bad, because you'll get punished. But when they gun down our boys like game, that's fine and dandy, because they give medals to the soldier who's killed the most. No, I tell you, I'll never understand that!"

Cornudet spoke up: "War is barbaric when you attack a peaceful neighbor, but it's a sacred duty when you defend your country."

The old woman lowered her head.

"Yeah, when you're defending yourself, that's different. But shouldn't we kill all the kings who're fighting wars for their own pleasure?"

Cornudet's eyes flamed.

"Bravo, Citizeness," he said.

Monsieur Carré-Lamadon was lost in thought. Despite his fanatical support of illustrious captains, this peasant woman's common sense reminded him of the prosperity that could be generated in a country by so many idle and therefore destructive hands, so many unproductive forces, if they could be deployed in the huge industrial projects that would take centuries to carry out.

But Loiseau, leaving his chair, went to have a whispered exchange with the innkeeper. The burly man laughed, coughed, spit; his enormous belly quavered joyfully at his neighbor's jokes, and he purchased six small casks of Bordeaux to be delivered in spring, once the Prussians were gone.

Barely had the worn-out travelers finished supper, when they turned in.

Loiseau, however, who'd been observing things, put his wife to bed, then glued now his ear, now his eye to the keyhole, trying to expose what he termed "the secrets of the corridor."

Roughly an hour later, he heard a rustling, took a quick peek, and spotted Butterball, who looked even pudgier in a blue cashmere dressing gown lined with white lace. She was clutching a candlestick and heading for the toilet at the far end of the corridor. But a door opened on the side, and when she returned several minutes later, Cornudet, in his suspenders, followed her. They spoke in whispers, then they paused. Butterball seemed to be energetically defending the entrance to her room. Unfortunately, Loiseau couldn't make out anything, but eventually, when they raised their voices, he managed to catch a few words. Cornudet was spirited and insistent. He said: "C'mon, you're being silly! What's the difference?"

Apparently indignant, she retorted: "No, my dear! There are times when those things aren't done. And besides, it would be shameful here."

He didn't catch her drift, no doubt, and he asked her why. She blew up and spoke louder.

"Why? You don't understand why? When there are Prussians in the same house, maybe in the next room?"

He held his tongue. This patriotic modesty in a hooker, who absolutely refused to be caressed with the enemy nearby, must have awoken the sense of dignity faltering in Cornudet's heart; for, after merely kissing her, he crept back to his door.

Loiseau, now greatly aroused, abandoned the keyhole, capered across the room, put on his head scarf, and pulled back the sheet covering the bony carcass of his spouse, whom he awoke with a kiss, murmuring: "Do you love me, darling?"

Then the entire house fell silent. But soon, some undetermined quarter that could have been the basement or the attic emitted a powerful, regular, monotonous snoring, a prolonged and muffled noise, quavering like a pressure-fed boiler. Monsieur Follenvie was asleep.

Having agreed to get going at eight A.M., the passengers assembled in the kitchen. However, the coach, with its snow-covered top, was waiting solitary in the middle of the courtyard, with no horses and no driver. They searched the stables, the haylofts, the coach house, but to no avail. The men then decided to scour the area and they set out. They wound up in the town square, with the church at one end, and, on both sides, squat cottages, where they sighted Prussian soldiers.

The first Prussian they saw was peeling potatoes. The second one, farther on, was cleaning the barbershop. Another soldier, bearded up to his eyes, was hugging a wailing baby and dandling it on his lap, trying to calm it down. And the buxom peasant women, whose men were "away at war," used signs to instruct their obedient conquerors as to which chores they should perform: split wood, boil soup, grind coffee. One Prussian was even doing the laundry for his hostess, a helpless nanny.

The astonished count questioned the beadle, who was emerging from the rectory. The old church official responded: "Oh! These guys ain't nasty. They ain't even Prussians, I hear. They come from farther away—I ain't sure where. And each one left a wife and kids at home. The war ain't much fun for them, believe me! I'm sure their families are crying for their men just like our near and dear, and lousy times are coming for them and also for us. The locals ain't too miserable for now because the Prussians don't do no harm and they work like these were their own homes. Look, Monsieur, poor people gotta help each other. . . . It's the biggies who wage war."

Cornudet, indignant about the *entente cordiale* established between conquerors and conquered, withdrew, preferring to shut himself up at the inn. Loiseau had a ready quip: "They're repopulating!" Monsieur Carré-Lamadon had a serious retort: "They're atoning."

Meanwhile the coachman was nowhere to be found. But at last they discovered him in the village café, sharing a friendly table with the officer's orderly. The count addressed the coachman: "Weren't you told to hitch up the horses by eight A.M.?"

"Oh, well, yes. But then I was given a counterorder."

"Namely?"

"To not hitch up at all."

"Who gave you that counterorder?"

"Damn it! The Prussian commander."

"Why?"

"How would I know? Go and ask him. If I'm ordered not to hitch up, then I don't hitch up. And that's that!"

"Did he tell you so himself?"

"No, Monsieur. The innkeeper passed it on."

"When?"

"Last night, just as I was about to turn in."

The three men were extremely worried as they returned to the inn.

They asked for Monsieur Follenvie, but the maid replied that on account of his asthma monsieur never got up before ten. He even had a strict standing order that he wasn't to be awakened any earlier except in case of fire.

They tried to see the officer, but that was absolutely impossible even though he was lodging at the inn. Monsieur Follenvie alone was authorized to speak to him about civil matters. So they waited. The women went back up to their rooms, busying themselves with trifles.

Cornudet settled down by the high kitchen hearth, where a huge fire was blazing. He had them bring over one of the small café tables plus a bottle of beer, and he took out his pipe, which, in democratic circles, enjoyed a status almost like his, as though by serving Cornudet the pipe were serving the fatherland. It was a superb meerschaum, admirably seasoned and as black as its owner's teeth, but curved, glossy, and aromatic, feeling intimate in his hand and adding a final touch to his physiognomy. And he remained motionless, staring either at the flame in the hearth or at the head on his mug; and with each swallow, he would contentedly run his long, thin fingers through his long, greasy hair while sucking his foam-fringed mustache.

Loiseau, under the pretext of stretching his legs, went off to peddle wine among the retailers of the area. The count and the manufacturer began talking politics. They predicted the future of France. The count believed in the Orleans dynasty; the manufacturer in an unknown savior, a hero who would reveal himself when all seemed hopeless: a Du Guesclin, a Joan of Arc perhaps? Or another Napoleon I? Ah! If only the imperial prince were not so young? Cornudet, listening to them, smiled like someone privy to the secrets of destiny. The aroma of his pipe filled the kitchen.

At the stroke of ten, the innkeeper showed up. They showered him with questions; but all he could do was repeat two or three times without a variant: "The officer told me as follows: 'Monsieur Follenvie, you will refuse to prepare the coach of those travelers tomorrow. I don't want them to leave without my express order. You understand? That's all.'"

Now the passengers wanted to see the officer. The count sent him his card, to which Monsieur Carré-Lamadon added his name and all his distinctions. The Prussian sent word that he would receive these two men after having his lunch—that is, around one P.M.

The ladies reappeared, and everyone managed to get something down despite their anxiety. Butterball seemed ill and deeply troubled.

They were just finishing their coffee when the orderly came looking for those gentlemen.

Loiseau joined the first two. When they tried to take along Cornudet to make their case more urgent, he proudly declared that he intended never to have anything to do with the Germans, and he returned to his fireplace and ordered another bottle of beer.

The three men went upstairs and were ushered into the inn's finest room, where the officer received them, stretched out on an easy chair, propping his feet on the mantelpiece, smoking a long porcelain pipe, and swathed in a flamboyant dressing gown, pilfered, no doubt, from a home abandoned by some bourgeois with deplorable taste. The officer didn't rise, he didn't greet the visitors, he didn't look at them. He was an exemplar of the loutish behavior that comes naturally to a military victor.

After several moments, he finally said: "Vat do you vant?"

The count took the floor: "We wish to leave, Monsieur."

"No."

"May I dare to ask you for the cause of this refusal?"

"Becoss I don't vant it."

"May I respectfully point out, Monsieur, that your commander in chief has granted us a permit to go to Dieppe. And I don't believe that we have done anything to deserve your severe measures."

"I don't vant it. . . . And dat is dat. . . . You may go back downstairs."

After bowing, all three visitors retreated.

The afternoon was wretched. No one could fathom that German caprice, and they were all prey to the most singular thoughts. They lingered in the kitchen, debating interminably and imagining unlikely things. Perhaps the Prussians meant to hold them as hostages—but to what end? Or imprison them and take them away? Or rather demand a huge ransom? This prospect left them panic-stricken. The wealthiest of the travelers were the most terrified, already seeing themselves constrained to pour sackloads of gold into the hands of that insolent soldier in order to redeem their lives. They racked their brains, trying to hit on reasonable lies, to conceal their wealth, to pass themselves off as paupers, desperate paupers. Loiseau removed his watch chain and stashed it in his pocket. The thickening night increased their fears. The lamp was lit, and since dinner was two hours away, Madame Loiseau suggested that they play a round of Trente-et-un. It would be a distraction. Her idea was accepted. Cornudet himself, after courteously putting out his pipe, joined in.

The count shuffled the cards—and dealt them. Butterball got thirty-one immediately; and soon their interest in the game eased the fear that was haunting them. Cornudet noticed that Monsieur and Madame Loiseau had teamed up to cheat.

As the company was going in to dinner, Monsieur Follenvie reappeared; and in his mucous voice he stated: "The Prussian officer wishes to know whether Mademoiselle Élizabeth Rousset may have changed her mind after all."

Butterball remained standing, very pale. Then, suddenly turning crimson, she got so choked up with anger that she couldn't speak. Finally she exploded: "Tell that pig, that rat, that brute of a Prussian that I'll never want it. Do you hear me? Never, never, never!"

The burly innkeeper left. Butterball was then surrounded, interrogated, and beseeched by everyone to reveal the mystery of her visit. At first she resisted; but soon she was swept away by her exasperation.

"What he wants? . . . What he wants? . . . He wants to sleep with me!" she cried.

Her indignation was so intense that no one was shocked by that word. Cornudet broke his mug by slamming it down on the table. There was an uproar of reprobation against that ignoble soldier, a blast of outrage, a united front of resistance as if each of them had been asked to join in the sacrifice demanded of Butterball. The disgusted count declared that those people were behaving like ancient barbarians. The women, above all, showered her with energetic and affectionate commiseration. The nuns, who showed up only at meals, lowered their heads and said nothing.

Nevertheless, the travelers managed to dine once their initial wrath had petered out; but they barely spoke, they were mulling.

The ladies retired early; and the men, while smoking, organized a game of Écarté, to which they invited Monsieur Follenvie, hoping to question him tactfully about what means they could employ to overcome the officer's resistance. But Monsieur Follenvie, never listening, never answering, focused only on his cards; and he kept reiterating ceaselessly: "The game, gentlemen, the game." He was so thoroughly absorbed that he forgot to spit, thereby emitting occasional organ tones from his chest. His wheezing lungs ran the entire gamut of asthma, from grave, deep notes to the sharp, gargly squawks of young cockerels struggling to crow.

He refused to go upstairs even when his wife, who was keeling over with fatigue, came looking for him. She then left all alone, for she was a "morning person," always rising with the sun, while her husband was a "night owl," always ready to stay up all night with friends. He called out to her: "Put my eggnog in front of the fire," and he rejoined his game. When they saw that nothing was to be gleaned from him, they declared that it was time to turn in, and they each went to bed.

The next day, they rose at the crack of dawn, feeling a blurry hope, a greater desire to move on, and terrified at the thought of spending another day in this horrible little dump.

Alas! The horses remained in the stable, the coachman was still invisible. To while away the time, the travelers hung around the coach.

Lunch was quite dismal; and the others felt something like coolness toward Butterball, for, after a night of sleeping on their problem, they had slightly modified their judgments. They almost resented the prostitute for not having secretly visited the Prussian and thereby giving her companions a nice surprise upon their awakening. What could be simpler? Besides, who would have known? She could have kept up appearances by notifying the officer that she felt sorry for her companions in their distress. It was so unimportant for her!

But nobody voiced those thoughts as yet.

That afternoon, when they were bored to tears, the count suggested that they take a stroll on the outskirts of the village. They each carefully bundled up, and the small group left, except for Cornudet, who preferred staying near the fire, and the nuns, who spent their days at church or with the priest.

The cold, sharpening from day to day, cruelly nipped at ears and noses; feet hurt so badly that each step was torture. And when the countryside unrolled before them, it looked so dreadfully lugubrious under the boundless white that the strollers promptly turned back, with their souls frozen, their hearts saddened.

The four women strode in front, the three men followed at a short distance.

Loiseau, who grasped the situation, suddenly asked whether that "slut" was going to keep them much longer in a place like this. The count, ever chivalrous, said that such a painful sacrifice could not be demanded of a woman, and that she would have to make it of her own accord. Monsieur Carré-Lamadon remarked that if, given the situation, the French counterattacked the Prussians by way of Dieppe, the sole point of encounter would be Tôtes. This reflection made the two other men queasy.

"What if we continue on foot?" said Loiseau.

The count shrugged. "Do you really think so in this snow? With our wives? And besides, we'd be instantly pursued, they'd catch us within ten minutes and haul us back as prisoners, at the mercy of the soldiers."

It was true; they fell silent.

The women were talking about clothes; but a certain restraint seemed to drive them apart.

All at once, at the end of the street, the officer heaved into view. Tall and wasp-waisted in his uniform, he was silhouetted against the snow that closed off the horizon, and he was marching with his knees far apart, in that special movement of military men trying to avoid soiling their meticulously waxed boots.

He bowed when passing near the women and he disdainfully eyed the men, who, for their part, were sufficiently dignified not to bare their heads, even though Loiseau seemed about to do so.

Butterball blushed up to her ears; and the three wives felt profoundly humiliated at being discovered by this soldier in the company of this prostitute whom he had treated so cavalierly.

They then talked about him, about his appearance, his face. Madame Carré-Lamadon, who had met lots of officers and was quite the connoisseur, judged this one as not bad at all; she even regretted that he wasn't French because he'd make a very handsome hussar, whom all the women were sure to fall madly in love with.

———

Once the travelers were back at the inn, they wondered what next. Harsh words were exchanged about trivial things. The silent dinner was brief, and everyone then turned in, hoping to kill time by sleeping.

The next morning they descended with weary faces and exasperated hearts. The women hardly spoke to Butterball.

A church bell rang. It was for a baptism. The fat girl had a child who was being raised by farmers in Yvetot. She saw it at most once a year and never gave it a second thought. But, thinking about the baby that was going to be christened, she felt a sudden and violent tenderness for her own child and she absolutely insisted on attending the local ceremony.

When she was gone, the others exchanged glances, then shoved their chairs together, for they felt it was high time they hit on something. Loiseau had an inspiration: he figured that they should urge the officer to keep only Butterball and let the others leave.

Monsieur Follenvie once again took on the job of go-between, but then he promptly came back down. The German, who was familiar with human nature, had shown him the door. He said he would hold on to the entire group so long as his desire remained unsatisfied.

Now Madame Loiseau's riffraff temperament exploded.

"I'm not planning to die of old age here. Since that tramp makes her living by doing that with all men, I don't think she's got the right to act so picky. What's the difference, I ask you. Why, in Rouen, she took any man she found, even coachmen! Yes, Madame, the prefect's coachman. I know it for a fact, I do—he buys his wine from us. And today, when she could help us out of a jam, she gets stuck-up—that slut! . . . I personally find that he's behaving very nicely—that officer. He may've been deprived for a long time now, and he'd have preferred us three. But no, he's satisfied with a girl for all seasons. He respects married women. Just think: he's the master here. All he had to say was, 'I want,' and he could violate us with the help of his soldiers."

The other two women shivered. Pretty Madame Carré-Lamadon's eyes were shining, and she was a bit pale, as if already feeling violated by the officer.

The men, having debated off to the side, came over. Loiseau, furious, wanted to tie up "that miserable slut" hand and foot and deliver her to the enemy. However, the count, descended from three generations of ambassadors and endowed with a diplomat's look, favored a more sensitive approach.

"We must talk her into it," he said.

So they plotted.

The women huddled together, the voices were lowered, and the discussion became general, with everyone speaking his mind. It was all quite respectable, though. The ladies especially found discreet expressions, subtle and charming locutions to make the most indelicate points. The rules of suitable diction were observed so carefully that no outsider would have caught the slightest drift. But since the thin patina of propriety marking every sophisticated woman is quite flimsy, they basked in their smutty adventure, exulted wantonly in it, feeling that they were in their element while pursuing their amorous designs with the sensuality of a gluttonous cook preparing someone else's supper.

The whole business ultimately struck them as so funny that it restored their good mood. The count recited jokes that, albeit slightly risqué, were so well told as to bring smiles to all faces. Loiseau, in his turn, produced some bawdier yarns that no one took offense at. And his wife's brutally voiced challenge dominated all minds:

"Seeing as it's the slut's livelihood, why should she be inclined to reject him more than someone else?"

Indeed, genteel Madame Carré-Lamadon even seemed to imagine

that had she been in Butterball's place, she'd have been less inclined to turn down the Prussian.

They spent a long time preparing the blockade as if they were beleaguering a fortress. They agreed on the role each person would play, the arguments he would advance, the maneuvers he should perform. They drew up the plans of attacks, the ruses to employ, and the sneak assaults that would force this living citadel to receive the enemy in her stronghold.

Cornudet, however, remained aloof, a complete stranger to this whole venture.

They were all so deeply preoccupied that no one heard Butterball return. The count then uttered a soft "shh," which made all eyes look up. She was here. Everyone quickly hushed, and at first they were too embarrassed to speak to her.

However, the countess, more accustomed than the rest to the duplicities of high society, inquired: "Was it fun—that baptism?"

The fat girl, still deeply moved by the ceremony, provided a blow-by-blow description of the faces, the demeanors, and the very appearance of the church. She added: "It's so good to pray occasionally."

Still, until lunchtime, the ladies contented themselves with being amiable to her in order to make her more trusting and more compliant to their advice.

But once they were seated, the groundwork began. First they had a vague conversation about devotion. Ancient examples were cited: Judith and Holofernes, then, gratuitously, Lucretia with Sextus, Cleopatra bedding down with all the enemy generals and thereby reducing them to slavish servitude. Next came a freakish story concocted in the imaginations of these ignorant millionaires: supposedly the women of Rome had gone to Capua and lulled Hannibal to fall asleep in their arms and, along with him, his lieutenants and the phalanxes of his mercenaries. They listed all the women who had stopped conquerors in their tracks by turning their own bodies into battlefields, into utensils of domination, into weapons, women who, with their heroic caresses, had defeated hideous or hated creatures, sacrificing their own chastity to vengeance and devotion. They even spoke in veiled terms about a certain British gentlewoman who had let herself be inoculated with a dreadful contagious disease in order to transmit it to Napoleon, who, at the moment of the fateful rendezvous, had been miraculously saved by a sudden indisposition.

And all these tales were told in a subdued and seemly manner, with occasional bursts of contrived enthusiasm aimed at provoking emulation.

Ultimately one might have believed that a woman's only role in this world consisted of perpetual sacrifice of her person and constant submission to the whims of undisciplined soldieries.

The two nuns, lost in deep thought, seemed to hear nothing. Butterball never spoke.

They let her reflect throughout the afternoon. But, instead of addressing her as "madame," which they had done until now, they simply called her "mademoiselle," though nobody really knew why. It was as if they wanted to bring her down by one notch in the esteem she had achieved, and to make her feel her shameful situation.

As soup was being served, Monsieur Follenvie reappeared and stated the same message as yesterday: "The Prussian officer wishes to know whether Mademoiselle Élizabeth Rousset may have changed her mind after all."

Butterball retorted curtly: "No, Monsieur."

At dinner, however, the coalition weakened. Loiseau uttered three unfortunate remarks. The travelers were cudgeling their brains, trying to unearth more examples but finding none, when the countess, unpremeditatedly perhaps, and feeling a murky need to pay tribute to Religion, questioned the older nun about the great deeds in the lives of saints. Now, many of them had done things that would be crimes in our eyes; but the Church fully absolves those atrocities if they are perpetrated for the glory of God or for the benefit of one's neighbor.

It was a powerful argument; the countess made the most of it. And so, through one of those tacit understandings, through one of those veiled connivances at which all wearers of ecclesiastic garb excel, or merely because of a felicitous stupidity, an auspicious absence of intelligence, the old nun provided the conspiracy with a formidable support. The others had viewed her as timid; she proved to be bold, long-winded, violent. She wasn't even bothered by the trials and errors of casuistry; her doctrine seemed ironclad; her faith never faltered; her conscience had no scruples. She judged Abraham's sacrifice of his son Isaac to be quite natural, for she would have killed her father and mother without further ado if she had received an order from on high; and nothing, in her opinion, could displease the Lord if the intention was praiseworthy. The countess, profiting from the sacred authority of her unexpected confederate, incited her to come out with an edifying paraphrase of that moral axiom, "The end justifies the means."

The countess asked the nun: "So, Sister, you believe that God accepts any and all means and forgives the misdeed if the motive is pure?"

"Who could doubt it, Madame? An action that is blameworthy in and of itself often becomes meritorious because of the thought that inspires it."

And so on they went, illuminating God's wishes, foreseeing His decisions, and trying to arouse His interest in things that were really none of His concern.

This entire discussion was guarded, adroit, discreet. Yet each and every word of the holy sister in the coif struck a breach in the courtesan's indignant resistance. Then the conversation took a slightly different course: the woman with the hanging rosary talked about the houses of her order, her mother superior, herself, and her darling companion, dear Sister Saint-Nicéphore. They had been called to the hospitals in Le Havre to care for hundreds of soldiers afflicted with smallpox. She described those miserable victims, depicted their illness in detail. And while the two nuns were being detained at the whims of that Prussian, a huge number of French lives that these sisters might have saved would be lost! This was her specialty: tending soldiers; she had been in Crimea, in Italy, in Austria, and, when evoking her campaigns, she suddenly revealed herself as being one of those fife-and-drum nuns who seem destined to follow army camps, gathering the wounded in the wake of battles, and, better than any commander, squelching old and undisciplined troopers with a single word—a true rat-a-tat sister, whose ravaged face, pitted with countless pockmarks, presented the very image of the devastations of war.

Her depictions were so vivid that no one spoke after her.

When the meal was over, they hurried up to their rooms and didn't come back down until fairly late the next morning.

Lunch was quiet. The seeds sown the previous evening were given time to sprout and bear fruit.

That afternoon, the countess suggested that they go for a walk. The count, as had been agreed, took Butterball's arm and lagged behind the others. He spoke to her in that familiar, paternal, and slightly disdainful tone that staid men employ when dealing with prostitutes. Calling her "my dear child," he talked down to her from the very acme of his social position, his undisputed respectability. He immediately cut to the chase.

"So you would rather make us stay here, vulnerable like you yourself to all the violence that would follow a setback of the Prussian troops—you prefer that to bestowing one of those favors that you have so often lavished in your life?"

Butterball didn't respond.

He tried gentleness, he tried reasoning, he tried appealing to her emotions. Throughout that time, he managed to remain "Monsieur le Comte," while playing the ladies' man when necessary, paying her compliments and generally acting congenial. He glorified the service she would render them, he spoke about their gratitude. Then, all at once, using the familiar form, he cheerfully said: "And you know, my dear, he might boast about enjoying a pretty girl of whom he couldn't find many in his country."

Butterball didn't respond, she caught up with the other strollers. Upon returning to the inn, she immediately went up to her room and did not reappear. The travelers were extremely worried. What was she going to do? How awkward if she kept resisting!

Dinnertime came; they waited for her in vain. Then, entering the room, Monsieur Follenvie announced that Mademoiselle Rousset was indisposed and that they could start the meal without her. They all pricked up their ears.

The count approached the innkeeper and whispered: "Everything all right?"

"Yes."

For propriety's sake, the count said nothing to his companions, but he did signal them with a slight nod. Instantly a great sigh emerged from all chests, and all faces beamed with delight. Loiseau cried: "Praise the Lord! The champagne's on me if we can find any in this establishment."

And Madame Loiseau was horrified when the innkeeper actually returned with four bottles. The group suddenly became chatty and noisy; hearts were filled with ribald gaiety. The count seemed to notice that Madame Carré-Lamadon was charming, while the manufacturer kept complimenting the countess. The conversation was lively, frolicsome, and full of wit.

Out of the blue, Loiseau, with an anxious face and raised arms, yelled: "Silence!" Everybody hushed, they were surprised and almost terrified. Loiseau then pricked up his ear, motioning the others to shush, peered up at the ceiling, listened again, and resumed in his normal voice: "You needn't worry, everything's going smoothly."

At first they didn't catch on, but then a grin swept across their faces.

A quarter hour later, Loiseau repeated his farce, which he kept reprising throughout the evening; and he pretended to address someone on the next floor, giving advice, double entendres, drawn from his traveling-salesman mind. At times he lapsed into a sad mood and sighed, "Poor thing!" Or else he furiously muttered between his teeth, "You Prussian rat, damn you!" Occasionally, when least expected, he kept reiterating in a rousing voice, "Enough! Enough!" And, as if talking to himself, he added, "So long as we get to see her again! I hope he doesn't kill her—that creep!"

Although in deplorable taste, these jokes were amusing and they wounded no feelings, for indignation, like anything else, depends on its milieu, and the atmosphere that had gradually developed around these people was charged with lewd thoughts. At dessert, the ladies themselves dropped witty and discreet hints. All eyes glistened; the company had drunk a lot. The count, who maintained his exalted appearance of gravity even when deviating from accepted standards of conduct, drew a comparison, greatly relished, with icebound polar vessels and the joy of their crews when the southern route reopens at winter's end.

And there was no stopping Loiseau, who got to his feet, clutching a flute of champagne: "I drink to our deliverance!" Everyone stood up; they saluted him. The two nuns, urged on by the ladies, agreed to wet their lips in this bubbly wine, which they had never tasted. They declared that it resembled a sparkling lemonade, but had a more subtle flavor.

Loiseau summed up the overall feeling: "Too bad there's no piano, otherwise we could dance a quadrille."

Cornudet hadn't uttered a single word, hadn't made a single move: he appeared to be totally absorbed in very grave thoughts, and at times he fiercely yanked his large beard as if wanting to lengthen it farther. Finally, toward midnight, when they were about to disperse, Loiseau, lurching toward Cornudet, suddenly tapped him on the belly and mumbled: "You're no fun tonight. Don't you have anything to say, Citizen?"

Cornudet brusquely raised his head, and, scowling at the company with his shiny and dreadful eyes, he snapped: "I tell all of you that you've done something infamous!" He rose, got to the door, repeated the word "infamous," and disappeared.

At first, this left a pall on the revelers. Loiseau, knocked for a loop, was stupefied; but he regained his composure, and, then suddenly laughing his head off, he exclaimed: "Sour grapes, pal, sour grapes." Since no one caught his drift, he described the "secrets of the corridor." This triggered a new blast of merriment. The ladies guffawed like crazy. The count and Monsieur Carré-Lamadon laughed till they cried. They couldn't believe it.

"What? You're sure? He wanted . . . ?"

"I tell you I saw him."

"And she turned him down. . . ."

"Because the Prussian was in the next room."

"Impossible."

"I swear."

The count was choking with mirth. The manufacturer was splitting a gut. Loiseau went on: "So you see why he didn't enjoy the evening—not at all."

And the three men kept going, half-sick, breathless, gasping.

At this point, the party broke up. When Monsieur and Madame Loiseau were turning in, the wife, who was as prickly as nettle, remarked that "the little Carré-Lamadon bitch" had been forcing her laughter all evening: "You know! When a woman desires a man in uniform, he can be French or Prussian—my goodness, it's all the same to her. Good Lord, that's such a pity!"

And all through the night, the darkness of the corridor bristled with shivers, faint, breathlike, barely audible noises, the grazing of bare feet, imperceptible creaks. It was obvious that nobody went to sleep until very late, for thin strips of light shimmered on the thresholds for a long time. Champagne has that effect; it supposedly interferes with sleep.

The next day brought dazzling snow in a clear winter sun. The coach, ready at last, stood waiting at the door, while an army of white pigeons, with thick plumage and with rosy eyes and black pupils, strutted earnestly among the legs of the six horses, pecking for nourishment in the steaming turds that lay scattered about.

The coachman, bundled up in his sheepskin, was smoking a pipe on the box, while the exhilarated travelers were all quickly packing food for the rest of the trip.

They were waiting only for Butterball. She appeared.

She seemed a bit troubled, shameful; and she shuffled timidly toward her companions, who uniformly turned their backs as if they hadn't noticed her. With great dignity, the count took his wife's arm and led her away from that impure contact.

The fat girl halted, dumbfounded; then, marshaling all her courage, she greeted the manufacturer's wife, humbly murmuring: "Good morning, Madame." The wife barely offered an insolent nod while glowering with outraged virtue. Everyone looked very busy and they gave her a wide berth as if she were bringing an infection in her petticoats. Then they dashed over to the coach, which she reached alone, the last passenger, silently taking the seat she had occupied during the first part of the trip.

They pretended not to see her, not to know her; but Madame Loiseau, indignantly glowering at her from far away, murmured sotto voce to her husband: "It's lucky I'm not sitting next to her."

The heavy coach lumbered off, and the journey resumed.

At first, no one spoke. Butterball didn't dare raise her eyes. She felt both enraged toward all her neighbors and humiliated for yielding, for being sullied by the kisses of that Prussian, into whose arms they had hypocritically thrown her.

But the countess, turning toward Madame Carré-Lamadon, soon broke that distressing hush.

"I believe you know Madame Etrelles?"

"Yes, she's a friend of mine."

"What a charming woman!"

"Delightful! A truly remarkable person—very educated to boot, and artistic to her very fingertips. She sings divinely and she draws to perfection."

The manufacturer was chatting with the count, and amid the clattering of the windows, a word stuck out here and there: "Dividend—due date—premium—mature."

Loiseau, having swiped the inn's ancient pack of cards, which were greasy with five years of friction on grimy tables, launched into a game of Bezique with his wife.

The nuns, taking the long rosaries dangling from their belts, jointly crossed themselves, and suddenly their lips began moving vividly, faster and faster, their vague, murmured prayers scampering along as if running a race; and from time to time, the nuns kissed a medal, crossed themselves again, then recommenced their rapid and continuous mumbling.

Cornudet sat inert, lost in thought.

After three hours of rolling along, Loiseau gathered his cards. "I'm hungry," he said.

His wife reached for a package, untied it, and pulled out a chunk of cold veal. She cut it neatly into thin, firm slices, and the two of them dove in.

"Why don't we do the same," said the countess. They agreed, and she unwrapped the snacks prepared for the two couples. In one of those long receptacles with a porcelain hare on the cover to indicate the contents, there was a hare pâté, its succulent cold, brown flesh crisscrossed by white streaks of bacon fat and mixed with other finely chopped meats. A lovely slab of Gruyère was ensconced in a sheet of newsprint, revealing the words "News in Brief" on its oily exterior.

The two nuns unreeled a round of sausage, which smelled of garlic; and Cornudet plunged both hands into the vast pockets of his sackcloth overcoat, retrieving four hard-boiled eggs from one pocket and a crusty heel of bread from the other. He removed the shells, tossed them into the straw at his feet, and bit into the eggs, littering his huge beard with bright yellow particles that twinkled like stars.

That morning, Butterball had hurried out of bed, too bewildered to focus on anything; and now, exasperated and choking with rage, she watched all these people eating placidly. At first, convulsed with tumultuous anger, she opened her mouth to give them a tongue-lashing, inundate them in a flood of insults that were on the tip of her tongue. But she was so strangled by her indignation that she couldn't speak.

No one glanced at her, thought about her. She felt she was drowning in the scorn of those respectable scoundrels, who had first sacrificed her, then rejected her like something unclean and useless. She recalled her huge basket filled with goodies that they had gobbled up, two chickens in glossy aspic, her pâtés, her pears, her four bottles of Bordeaux; and with her anger suddenly abating, like a rope that snaps when it's stretched too tight, she felt ready to burst into tears. She made a terrible effort at self-control, bracing herself and choking back her sobs like a child; but the tears welled up, shining on the edges of her eyelids, and soon two big drops, leaving her eyes, rolled slowly down her cheeks. Like water oozing from a rock, more rapid tears followed, landing rhythmically on the swelling curve of her bosom. She remained erect, her eyes gaping, her face pale and rigid, and she hoped that no one would see her.

But the countess did notice her and signaled her husband. He shrugged as if saying, "What do you want? It's not my fault."

Madame Loiseau, chuckling in mute triumph, murmured: "She's weeping because she's ashamed of herself."

The two nuns had resumed their prayers after coiling up their left-over sausage in some paper.

Then, digesting his eggs, Cornudet stretched out his long legs under the opposite seat, leaned back, smiled like a man who has just thought up some fun, and began whistling "The Marseillaise."

All faces darkened. The popular song certainly didn't sit well with his fellow travelers. They grew nervous, irritated, and seemed about to howl like dogs hearing an organ-grinder.

He noticed their state of mind but he didn't stop. At times he even hummed the lyrics:

> Oh, sacred love of our Country,
> Lead us, support our vengeful arms,
> Ah, Liberty, sweet Liberty,
> Come, fight with your defenders, fight.

The coach was rolling faster since the snow was harder; and all the way to Dieppe, during the long, bleak hours, across the bumps in the road, through the thickening night, then in the profound darkness of the vehicle, Cornudet, with ferocious obstinacy, continued his vindictive and monotonous whistling, compelling his weary and exasperated listeners to follow the anthem from start to finish, recalling each word and applying it to each appropriate note.

And Butterball was still crying; and now and then, a sob that had gotten the better of her slipped out between two verses and melted into the darkness.

THE TELLIER HOUSE

They headed there every evening, toward eleven o'clock, casually, as if going to their regular café.

There were six or seven men, always the same ones, not roisterers but solid citizens, businessmen, young men about town; and they sipped their Chartreuse while teasing the girls or else conversing earnestly with Madame, whom they all treated with respect.

By midnight most of them had gone home to bed; a few of the young men remained.

The house was cozy—very small, painted yellow on the outside, located at a street corner behind Saint Stephen's Church; and from the windows of the house, you could see the basin full of ships being un-loaded, the big salt marsh known as "the Reservoir," and, in the back-ground, the Slope of the Virgin with its old, utterly gray chapel.

Madame, who came of good peasant stock in the Eure department, had accepted this profession as readily as if she'd become a milliner or a linen draper. While the bias against prostitution may be intense and inveterate in towns, no such stigma exists in the Norman countryside.

The farmer says, "It's a good occupation." And he sends his daughter off to manage a harem of girls just as he would send her off to be headmistress of a finishing school.

Moreover, this house had been left to Madame by its owner, an old uncle. Monsieur and Madame Tellier, who had once kept an inn in Yvetot, had immediately liquidated their business, judging that the establishment in Fécamp would be more profitable. And so one fine morning, they arrived and started running the enterprise, which had been jeopardized by the lack of a proprietor.

The Telliers were decent folk, who instantly won the hearts of their employees and their neighbors.

Two years later, Monsieur died of a stroke. With his new profession keeping him in indolence and inertia, he had grown very fat, so that he'd been felled by his good health.

As a widow, Madame was desired in vain by all the habitués of the establishment; but she was said to be absolutely celibate, and even her charges had never managed to unearth anything to the contrary.

She was tall, fleshy, prepossessing. Her complexion, now pallid in the dim light because the shutters were always closed, glistened as if under an oil varnish. A slender fringe of stray curls, false and crisp, ensconced her forehead, giving her a youthful look that clashed with the ripeness of her shapely figure. Invariably cheerful, with a candid face, she had a good sense of humor, though with a touch of reserve that her new pursuits had not yet managed to overcome. She was always a bit shocked by crude language; and whenever an ill-bred fellow used the proper name for her establishment, she felt angry and repulsed. In short, she had a delicate sensibility, and while treating her girls as friends, she was quick to reiterate that they "were not of the same mold."

Sometimes during the week, she rented a carriage and rode off with a section of her flock; and they romped about on the grassy banks of the creek that flows through the valley of Valmont. They were like schoolgirls on the loose, running wild races, playing childhood games,

with the sheer joy of recluses intoxicated by the fresh air. They pic-
nicked on cold cuts, washing them down with cider, and they returned
at nightfall, sweetly moved and deliciously exhausted; and inside the
carriage, they hugged and kissed Madame like a wonderful mother, in-
dulgent and obliging.

The house had two entrances. On the corner, a kind of low dive
opened in the evening, catering to workers and sailors. Two of the
women assigned to the main commerce of the place were specifically
geared to the needs of this faction of the clientele. With the help of
the waiter, Frédéric, who was short, blond, beardless, and as strong as
an ox, these two women served mugs of wine and bottles of beer on
the wobbly marble tables, where, sitting on the laps of the drinkers
and coiling their arms around their necks, they urged them to keep
buying.

The three other ladies (there were only five in all) formed a sort
of aristocracy that was reserved for the upstairs visitors, provided,
however, that these women weren't needed down below and that the
upstairs was empty.

The Jupiter Salon, where the local burghers got together, was covered with blue wallpaper and embellished by a large picture showing
Leda stretched out under a swan. You reached this area through a winding staircase that was accessed from the street by a narrow, humble-
looking door; above it, behind a lattice, a small lantern burned all night,
similar to the ones still lit in certain towns, at the feet of Madonnas
embedded in wall niches.

The building, old and humid, had a vaguely musty aroma. At times,
a puff of cologne wafted through the corridors; or else, the shouts of
the rabble sitting at tables on the ground floor burst through a half-
open door, shaking the entire house like a clap of thunder and leaving
nervous and disgusted expressions on the faces of the upstairs gentlemen.

Although Madame, on friendly and familiar terms with her customers, never left the Salon, she was interested in the rumors they

brought to her from the town. Her grave discourse was a distraction from the incoherent chitchat of the three girls; it provided a restful lull in the smutty banter of the potbellied individuals who spent each evening indulging in that respectable and third-rate debauchery of drinking a glass of liqueur in the company of prostitutes.

The three upstairs ladies were named Fernande, Raphaële, and Rosa the Bitch.

Given the small size of the personnel, they tried to make each girl an exemplar, a female prototype, so that any consumer could find more or less the embodiment of his ideal.

Fernande represented "the beautiful blonde": very large, almost obese, flaccid, a hoyden, whose freckles refused to vanish, and whose hair, close-trimmed, towlike, limpid, virtually colorless, similar to hackled hemp, covered her head inadequately.

Raphaële, from Marseilles, a waterfront hooker, played the indispensable role of "la belle Juive," skinny, with high cheekbones plastered with rouge. Her black hair, greased with beef marrow, formed kiss curls on her temples. Her eyes would have been beautiful if the right one hadn't been marred by a white speck. Her aquiline nose stuck out over a powerful jaw, with two new teeth in the upper row contrasting unpleasantly with the lower teeth, which, in aging, had taken on a dark hue like old wood.

Rosa the Bitch, a small ball of flesh, all belly, with minuscule legs, sang from morning to evening, her raspy voice squawking ditties that were either scurrilous or sentimental. She told interminable and insignificant shaggy-dog stories, stopped talking only to eat and stopped eating only to talk, and was always on the move, as agile as a squirrel despite her corpulence and her puny feet. And her laugh, a cascade of shrieks, burst out incessantly, here, there, in bedroom, attic, or tavern, wherever, and for no particular reason.

The two main-floor girls were Louise, dubbed Wench, and Flora, nicknamed Seesaw because of her slight limp; Wench was always costumed as "Liberty" with a tricolor sash, and Seesaw as a fancy señorita with copper sequins that bobbed up and down in her ginger hair at each teetering step. The two girls resembled kitchen maids all gussied up for a Mardi Gras. They were like any lower-class girls, neither uglier nor lovelier, authentic tavern maids, and they were labeled the Two Pumps throughout the port.

An edgy but seldom ruffled peace endured among these five girls thanks to Madame's conciliatory wisdom and her inexhaustible cheeriness.

The establishment, the only one of its kind in the small town, was frequented assiduously. Madame had managed to provide a genteel atmosphere; she was so friendly, so accommodating to everyone; and she was so well known for her good heart that she was surrounded by a certain esteem. The regular customers went out of their way to oblige her and they exulted whenever she was more genial to them than normal. And if they happened to meet on daytime business, they would say, "See you tonight in the usual place," the way you say, "At the café, right? After dinner."

In short, the Tellier house was a handy gathering point, and customers hardly ever skipped the nightly rendezvous.

Now one evening in late May, the first client to arrive, Monsieur Poulin, a lumber dealer and former mayor, found the door locked. The small lantern behind its lattice was not burning; nor did any sound emerge from inside the house, which seemed dead. Monsieur Poulin knocked, tapping at first, then pounding; no one responded. He toddled back up the street, and, upon reaching the marketplace, he bumped into Monsieur Duvert, the shipowner, who was likewise heading toward the establishment. They went there together, but with no greater success. All at once, a racket burst out very close by; rounding the corner, they saw a gang of French and British sailors punching the closed shutters of the tavern.

The two solid citizens promptly fled to avoid getting involved; but they were stopped by a soft "Psst!" It was Monsieur Tournevau, the fish curer, who had recognized and hailed them. They apprised him of the situation, which perturbed him all the more since he, a closely scrutinized husband and father, came by only on Saturdays: *"securitatis causa,"* he would say, alluding to the periodic medical-police inspection, which his friend, Dr. Borde, had told him to observe. This just happened to be Monsieur Tournevau's evening, and now he was going to be deprived for a whole week.

The three men made a wide detour to the docks; en route they encountered young Monsieur Philippe, the banker's son and a regular, and Monsieur Pimpesse, the tax collector. Walking along Rue des Juifs, the group went back to the establishment for a last-ditch effort. But the exasperated sailors were besieging the house, yelling and hurling stones; the five upstairs clients therefore retreated as fast as their legs could carry them, and they began wandering the streets.

Now they ran into Monsieur Dupuis, the insurance agent, then Monsieur Vasse, the judge at the commercial court; and a long stroll ensued, leading first to the jetty. They sat down in a row on the granite parapet and watched the foaming waves. In the darkness, the froth on the crests produced a luminous whiteness, which faded almost upon appearing; and the monotonous thudding of the sea smashing against the rocks reverberated through the night, all along the cliff.

When the gloomy strollers had remained there for some time, Monsieur Tournevau declared: "This isn't much fun."

"It sure isn't," Monsieur Pimpesse replied. And they all trudged off.

After taking Sous-le-Bois, the road that dominates the coast, they returned across the plank bridge over the Reservoir, passed close to the railroad tracks, and wound up back in the marketplace, where an argument suddenly broke out between the tax collector, Monsieur Pimpesse, and the fish salter, Monsieur Tournevau, the bone of contention being an edible mushroom that one man claimed he had found in the vicinity.

Boredom had so soured their tempers that they might have come to blows if the others hadn't interfered. Monsieur Pimpesse furiously stomped away; and instantly a fresh altercation exploded between

Monsieur Poulin, the ex-mayor, and Monsieur Dupuis, the insurance agent, about the tax collector's salary and the perks he could create for himself. Insults were raining down on both sides when a tempest of formidable shouts erupted, and the gaggle of sailors, worn out from uselessly waiting outside a locked house, came surging into the square. They were striding in pairs, arm in arm, forming a long procession and hollering violently. The group of solid citizens hid out in a doorway, and the bellowing horde disappeared in the direction of the abbey. For a long time, the mayhem could be heard dying down like a fading storm; and silence was restored.

Monsieur Poulin and Monsieur Dupuis, enraged at each other, went their separate ways without saying good night.

The remaining four set off again, instinctively heading for the Tellier establishment. It was still locked, mute, impenetrable. A tranquil and obstinate drunkard was softly tapping on the shutters of the tavern, pausing to mumble Frédéric the waiter's name. Since there was no response, the drunkard decided to sit down on the doorstep and wait it out.

The burghers were about to disperse when the tumultuous gang of seamen loomed up at the end of the street. The French sailors were bawling "The Marseillaise," and the English sailors, "Rule Britannia." There was a general lurching toward the walls, then the torrent of hooligans resumed its rush toward the docks, where a battle flared up between the mariners of both nations. The fight left one Brit with a broken arm and one Frenchman with a split nose.

The drunkard, who had stayed at the door, was blubbering now like a boozer or a frustrated child.

The burghers finally scattered.

Little by little, calm was restored to the troubled town. Here and there, shrieks arose for an instant, then waned in the distance.

Only one man was still roaming: Monsieur Tournevau, the fish salter, despondent at having to hold out till next Saturday; and he was hoping for some kind of fluke, uncomprehending, exasperated that the police allowed the closing of a public utility that they supervised and controlled.

He returned there, skulking along the walls, seeking an explanation; and then he spotted a note glued to the door. He swiftly lit a wax vesta and read these words scrawled in large, uneven letters: "Closed for first communion."

He walked away, realizing that all was said and done.

The drunkard was dozing by now, stretched out full-length across the inhospitable doorway.

And the next day, every regular, each in turn, devised an excuse to pass by the house, holding a sheaf of papers under his arm to make a bold front. And with a furtive glance, they all read the mysterious announcement: "Closed for first communion."

—

You see, Madame had a brother who had established himself as a carpenter in their native hamlet, Virville, in Eure. While still an innkeeper in Yvetot, she had held her brother's daughter over the baptismal fonts and had named her Constance, Constance Rivet, since Madame herself was a Rivet through her father. The carpenter, who knew that his sister was well heeled, never lost sight of her even though they seldom got together, busy as they both were in their respective occupations and also living far apart. But since the little girl was going on twelve and scheduled to have her first communion that year, he seized the opportunity for a meeting by writing to his sister that he was counting on her for the ceremony. Their old parents were dead, she couldn't say no to the little girl; she agreed. Her brother, whose name was Joseph, hoped that, by showering his sister with attention, he might prod her to draw up a will in his daughter's favor since Madame had no offspring of her own.

His sister's profession didn't ruffle his scruples at all, and besides, no one in the region had the slightest clue. When speaking about her, they merely said, "Madame Tellier is a householder in Fécamp," which implied that she was a woman of independent means. Virville was at least twenty leagues from Fécamp; and an overland trip of twenty leagues is more arduous for a rustic than an ocean voyage for a cultivated sophisticate. The inhabitants of Virville had never gotten any farther than Rouen; and nothing tempted the inhabitants of Fécamp to visit a tiny village of five hundred homes, lost in the middle of a plain in a different department. As a result, no one there had the slightest inkling of Madame's line of work.

However, with the communion approaching, Madame found herself in a big predicament. She had no assistant and she didn't care to leave her house unsupervised for even a day. All the rivalries between the upstairs ladies and the downstairs ladies were bound to erupt; moreover, Frédéric was sure to get drunk, and when he was drunk, he would knock people down for no earthly reason. In the end, Madame decided to take everyone along, except for the waiter, whom she gave the day off.

Her brother, when consulted, didn't object, and he agreed to put up the entire company for one night. So, on Saturday morning, the eight A.M. express train carried Madame and her companions off in a second-class car.

Until reaching Beuzeville, they remained alone, jabbering like magpies. But at that station, a couple climbed in. The man was an old peasant in a blue blouse with a pleated collar and wide sleeves narrow at the wrists and decorated with small white embroidery; his head was covered with an old-fashioned high hat, its brownish nap looking shaggy, as if brushed against the grain. His one hand clutched an immense green umbrella, while his other hand grasped a huge basket, from which the heads of three terrified ducks poked out. The woman, rigid in her rustic getup, had the face of a hen with a nose that was pointed like a beak. She settled across from her husband and stayed utterly immobile, alarmed at finding herself in such excellent society.

And indeed, the compartment offered a dazzling array of splashy colors. Madame, all blue, in blue silk from head to foot, and over the silk a faux French cashmere, red, blinding, flashing. Fernande was gasping in a plaid frock, the bodice of which, so tightly laced by her companions, shoved up her droopy breasts in a constantly heaving double dome, which seemed jiggly under the tartan.

Raphaële, in a plumed bonnet that looked like a nestful of birds, wore a lilac frock spangled with gold—something Oriental that suited her Jewish physiognomy. Rosa the Bitch, in a pink skirt with wide flounces, looked like an overweight child or an obese dwarf; and the Two Pumps appeared to have cut their bizarre togs out of old window curtains, those old floral curtains dating back to the Restoration.

The instant they had company, the ladies donned grave miens and started talking about exalted things in order to make a good impression. However, in Bolbec, a gentleman with blond whiskers, sporting a few rings and a gold watch chain, entered and stowed packages wrapped in oilcloth onto the overhead rack. There was something facetious and good-natured about the newcomer. He bowed, smiled, and asked, free and easy: "Are you ladies switching to a new garrison?" His question left the group confused and embarrassed.

Madame finally regained her bearing, and, to vindicate the honor of the corps, she snapped: "You might try being polite!"

He apologized: "Forgive me. I meant to say 'convent.'"

Madame, too flustered to retort or perhaps deeming the correction sufficient, nodded with dignity and pursed her lips.

The gentleman, sitting between Rosa the Bitch and the old peasant, began winking at the three ducks, whose heads loomed out of the basket; then, upon feeling he had a captive audience, the gentleman began tickling those creatures under their beaks, delivering quips to make the travelers laugh: "We've weft our wittle po-ond! Quack! Quack! Quack! To roast on a wittle spit! Quack! Quack! Quack!"

The unfortunate birds twisted their necks to avoid his caresses and made horrible efforts to escape their wicker prison. Suddenly, all three ducks in unison uttered a lamentable shriek of despair: "Quack! Quack! Quack! Quack!" And the women exploded with laughter. They bent over, they jostled one another to get a good view; they were passionately interested in the ducks; and the gentleman outdid his usual battery of grace, wit, and heckling.

Rosa joined the fun: leaning across the gentleman's legs, she kissed the noses of the three animals. Each woman now wanted to kiss them in turn; and the gentleman sat the ladies on his lap, bouncing them up and down, pinching them; all at once, he was using the familiar form of address with them.

The peasant couple, even more terrified than their fowls, rolled their eyes like lunatics, not daring to stir; and no smile, no twitch crossed their old, wrinkled faces.

Next, the gentleman, a traveling salesman, jokingly offered those ladies shoulder straps, and, hauling down one of his packages, he opened it up. It was all a ruse, the package contained garters.

They were in blue silk, in pink silk, in crimson silk, in violet silk, in mauve silk, in flaming red silk, with metal clasps in the shapes of two gilded cupids embracing. The girls uttered shrieks of joy, and examined the samples, as naturally earnest as any woman inspecting an item of clothing. They consulted each other with glances or whispers, responding in the same way, and Madame longingly fondled a pair of orange garters that were wider and more imposing than the rest: the proper garters for a lady in charge.

The gentleman waited, forging a plan: "C'mon, my little pussycats," he said, "ya gotta try 'em on."

Those words unleashed a storm of exclamations; and the girls squeezed their petticoats between their legs as if fearing rape. Meanwhile, he calmly bided his time. Thereupon he declared: "If you don't want to, I'll wrap them up again." Then he taunted them: "I'll give a pair of her own choosing to any lady who tries them on." But, sitting very dignified, very upright, they refused. The Two Pumps, however, seemed so miserable that he repeated his offer. Flora Seesaw, above all, tortured with desire, was visibly faltering. He goaded her: "Go ahead, my girl, a bit of courage. Look, the lilac pair, it'll go nicely with your gown."

That settled it, and, tugging up her dress, she exposed a robust milkmaid-leg in a gross, ill-fitting stocking. The gentleman, stooping down, fastened the garter first under the knee, then over it; and he gently tickled her, forcing her to squeal and writhe. When he was done, he handed her the lilac pair and asked: "Who's next?"

They all chorused: "Me! Me!"

He began with Rosa the Bitch, who uncovered a roundish, shapeless thing with no ankle, a real "sausage leg," as Raphaële put it. Fernande was complimented by the traveling salesman, who was enraptured by her powerful columns. The scrawny shanks of "la belle Juive" were less successful. Louise the Wench, joking around, covered the gentleman with her skirt, and Madame was obliged to intervene and put a stop to that indecorous farce. At last, Madame herself thrust out her leg, a gorgeous Norman leg, fleshy and muscular; and the surprised and delighted salesman gallantly doffed his hat to salute this masterful calf like a true French cavalier.

The peasant couple, stark and stiff in their bewilderment, kept glancing askance from the corners of their eyes; and they so absolutely resembled chickens that the man with the blond whiskers crowed "cock-a-doodle-doo" right under their noses. Which unleashed a new hurricane of merriment.

The oldsters climbed out at Motteville, with their basket, their ducks, and their umbrella; and the woman could be heard telling her husband as they slogged away: "They're prostitutes going to that satanic Paris."

As for the amusing peddler, he got off in Rouen after behaving so grossly that Madame felt obliged to put him sharply in his place. She added as a moral: "That'll teach us to talk to just any man coming down the pike!"

They changed trains at Oissel, and, at a later stop, they found Monsieur Joseph Rivet waiting for them with a large farm cart stuffed with chairs and drawn by a white horse.

The carpenter politely embraced all these ladies and helped them into his vehicle. Three ladies sat on chairs in the back; Raphaële, Madame, and her brother sat on chairs in the front; while Rosa, having no chair of her own, settled for better or worse on tall Fernande's lap; then the cart lumbered off. From the very outset, however, the old nag's jerky trot shook the vehicle so wildly that the chairs started dancing about, hurling the passengers aloft, to the right, to the left, with puppetlike movements, terrified faces, and horrified shrieks that were abruptly cut short by a more violent quake. The women clung to the sides of the cart; their hats fell on their backs, over their noses, or toward their shoulders. And the white horse kept plodding along, its head lunging forward, and its tail rigid, a small, hairless rattail that whisked its buttocks every so often. Joseph Rivet, bracing one foot against the shaft, bending the other leg underneath himself, and keeping his elbows very high, clutched the reins while his throat released a sort of clucking that, by making the nag prick its ears, accelerated its speed.

The verdant country unrolled on both sides of the road. Here and there, a huge, wavy, yellow expanse of blossoming colza fields gave off a healthy and powerful fragrance, a sweet, pervasive smell that the breeze wafted very far away. In the rye, which already stood tall, cornflowers poked up their small azure heads, which the women wanted to pick; but Monsieur Rivet refused to stop. Every so often, an entire area was so thoroughly invaded by poppies that it looked bloodstained. And in the midst of those flower-colored plains, the cart, which in itself seemed to be carrying a bouquet of even more flamboyant colors, trundled along behind the trotting white horse and disappeared beyond the huge trees of a farm, reappearing at the edge of the foliage, pitching once more across the green and yellow crops speckled with red or blue as it conducted that dazzling cartload of women into the sunny distance.

One o'clock was striking when they drew up at the carpenter's door.

They were exhausted and pale with hunger, having eaten nothing since their departure. Madame Rivet hurried over and helped them step down one by one, giving them a peck the instant their feet touched the ground; and she tirelessly kissed her sister-in-law, hoping to win her over. They ate in the workshop, from which the benches had been cleared in preparation for tomorrow's dinner.

A good omelette, followed by a grilled-chitterlings sausage, washed down by a good tart cider, restored the general merriment. Rivet had picked up a glass in order to join the carousing, while his spouse cooked, served, brought the dishes, took them away, murmuring into each diner's ear: "Have you had enough?" Piles of boards leaning against the walls and heaps of shavings swept into the corners emitted the fragrance of planed wood, an aroma of carpentry, that resinous smell that seeps down to the very depths of the lungs.

They asked to see the little girl, but she was at church and not expected back until evening.

So the group went for a stroll.

The village was tiny and crossed by a highway. Some dozen houses lining that single road were inhabited by the local merchants, the butcher, the grocer, the carpenter, the café owner, the cobbler, and the baker. The church, at the end of what was vaguely a street, was surrounded by a narrow graveyard and fully shaded by four immense lindens growing at the entrance. The church itself was built of chipped flints, in no particular style, and topped with a slate-roofed belfry. Beyond the church, the open countryside unrolled anew, broken here and there by clusters of trees that shrouded the farms.

Rivet, out of courtesy and although in his working clothes, had taken his sister's arm and was escorting her with majestic dignity. His wife, astounded by Raphaële's gold-spangled frock, had interjected herself between her and Fernande. Behind them, chubby Rosa trotted along with Louise the Wench and Flora Seesaw, who was so frazzled that she hobbled worse than ever.

The townsfolk gathered at the doors, the children left off playing, a slightly raised curtain revealed a head in a calico cap; a purblind crone with a crutch crossed herself as if watching a religious procession.

And everyone kept watching and watching all these beautiful city ladies, who had come from so far away to attend the first communion of Joseph Rivet's little girl. In his reflected glory, the carpenter's prestige rose enormously.

Passing the church, the ladies heard the singing of children: a hymn sent heavenward by small, shrill voices; but Madame wouldn't let the group step inside lest they disturb those little cherubs.

After a detour through the countryside and an itemization of the principal farms, the yield of their soil, and the productivity of their cattle, Joseph Rivet walked his flock of women back and installed them in his home.

Since the house was quite small, they were put up two in a room.

Rivet, this one time, would bunk out on the shavings in his workshop; his wife would share her bed with her sister-in-law, and Fernande and Raphaële would sleep together in the next room. Louise and Flora would make do with a mattress on the kitchen floor; while Rosa had a small black cabinet to herself above the staircase, next to a cramped loft, where the communicant would spend the night.

When the little girl came home, she was showered with kisses; all the women wanted to caress her, with that need to show effusive tenderness, that routine of professional cajolery, which had moved them all to kiss the ducks on the train. Each visitor sat the little girl on her lap, played with her fine blond hair, squeezed her with outbursts of intense and spontaneous affection. The well-behaved child endured everything patiently and wistfully, as if shielded by the absolution she had just received.

After a day that had been arduous for everyone, they all quickly retired after dinner. The tiny village was enveloped in that endless, almost religious silence of the fields, a tranquil, pervasive silence that reaches the stars. The girls, accustomed to the tumultuous evenings at the public house, felt deeply affected by the mute repose of the slumbering countryside. They had gooseflesh, shivering not with cold but with the solitude of anxious and troubled hearts.

The instant they were paired off in their beds, they coiled their arms around one another as if protecting themselves from invasion by the earth's calm and profound sleep. However, Rosa the Bitch, alone in her black cabinet and unaccustomed to sleeping with empty arms, was seized with a hazy and cheerless emotion. She kept tossing and turning, unable to doze off, when all at once, from behind the wooden partition at her head, she heard feeble sobs, like those of a weeping child. A frightened Rosa called out softly, and a faint, broken voice responded. It was the little girl, who, usually sleeping in her mother's room, was scared in her cramped loft.

Rosa, delighted, got up and went to see the child very quietly, to avoid waking anyone up. She brought her to her very warm bed, pressed her against her bosom, kissed her, cuddled her, wrapped her up in the most exaggerated tenderness; then, having likewise calmed down, Rosa drifted off. And until daybreak, the communicant slept with her head on the prostitute's naked breast.

At five A.M., the small church bell, ringing the *Angelus* full force, woke up these ladies, who normally slept all morning—the sole remedy for their nightly fatigue. The villagers were already up. The local women bustled from door to door, buoyantly chatting and cautiously bringing either short muslin dresses starched as stiffly as cardboard or tremendous tapers with gold-fringed silk bows around the middle and with dents in the wax to indicate where to hold them. The sun, already high, was radiant in a sheer blue sky, which retained a slightly pinkish tint on the horizon, like a faint trace of dawn. Families of poultry roamed about in front of their houses; and here and there, a black rooster with a shiny neck raised its crimson-crested head, flapped its wings, and crowed its brassy cock-a-doodle-doo into the wind, provoking echoes from other roosters.

Carts were rolling in from neighboring communities, discharging their passengers at the thresholds: tall Norman women in dark dresses, with shawls crossed on their bosoms and clasped together by antique silver brooches. The men had slipped blue smocks over new frock coats or over old-fashioned green cloth suits, their two tails dangling underneath.

When the horses were in the stables, the entire highway was lined with two rows of rustic jalopies—carts, cabriolets, tilburies, charabancs—vehicles of all shapes and ages, tilted on their noses or else squatting on the ground with their shafts aloft.

The carpenter's home was as busy as a beehive. The ladies, in petticoats and loose jackets, and with their short, straggly hair scattered on their backs and looking worn and faded from too much dyeing, were busy dressing the girl.

She stood motionless on the table where Madame Tellier directed the movements of her fluttering battalion. They washed the girl's face, combed her, did her hair, dressed her, and with the aid of a whole multitude of pins, they adjusted the pleats in her frock, they took in the baggy waist, and they arranged her overall elegance. Once they were done, they had the long-suffering girl sit down and they told her not to budge; then the agitated troop of women rushed off to adorn themselves in turn.

The small church bell started pealing again. Its frail chiming wafted across the sky like an overly feeble voice, quickly melting into the blue immensity.

The communicants emerged from the doorways and headed toward the village hall, which contained the two schools and the mayor's office; the hall was located at one end of the hamlet, while the "house of God" occupied the other end.

The parents, in their Sunday best, with awkward faces and the clumsy movements of people unceasingly bent over their work, were following their kids. The little girls disappeared in clouds of snowy tulle resembling whipped cream, while the little men, like tavern waiters in embryo, their hair pomaded, walked astraddle to avoid soiling their black trousers.

It was a proud day for a family when a large number of relatives came from far away and surrounded the child: so the carpenter's triumph was complete. The Tellier legion, its employer at the head, followed Constance; and with the father giving his sister his arm, the mother walking next to Raphaële, Fernande next to Rosa, and the Two Pumps together, the troop strutted majestically like a general staff in regimentals.

The impact on the village was staggering.

At school, the girls fell in under the cornet of the nun, the boys under the hat of the schoolmaster, a handsome man who cut a fine figure; and they all set out, tackling a hymn.

The boys, heading the procession, strode in double file between the two rows of unhorsed vehicles, the girls followed in the same formation; and since all the villagers had respectfully given the city ladies precedence, they walked directly behind the girls, extending the double line of the procession, three ladies on the left, three on the right, their dresses as dazzling as the pièce de résistance of a fireworks display.

Their entrance into the church boggled all minds. The locals pushed and shoved and jostled to see the visitors. And pious women spoke almost aloud, stupefied by the spectacle of these ladies, who were bedizened more sumptuously than the cantors in their chasubles. The mayor offered them his pew, the first pew to the right by the chancel, and Madame Tellier settled there with her sister-in-law, Fernande, and Raphaële. Rosa the Bitch and the Two Pumps occupied the second pew together with the carpenter.

The chancel was full of genuflecting children, girls on one side, boys on the other, and the long tapers they were holding looked like spears pointing every which way.

In front of the lectern, three basses stood, chanting at the top of their lungs. They prolonged the sonorous Latin syllables infinitely, eternalizing each "Amen" with an indefinite "a-a," bolstered by the serpent with its interminable and monotonous note bellowed by its vast gullet. A child's shrill voice would respond, and from time to time, a priest, sitting in a stall and wearing a square biretta, would get up, mumble something, and sit down again, while the three choristers sang away, gaping at the huge plainsong book, which lay open before them on the outspread pinions of a wooden eagle on a swivel.

Then a hush ensued. Everyone knelt down in unison, and the celebrant emerged, ancient, hoary, venerable, bending over the chalice, which he bore in his left hand. The two servers in red robes led the way, and he was followed by a throng of heavy-booted cantors, who lined up on either side of the chancel.

A small chime tinkled amid the vast stillness. The Divine Service was starting. The priest shuffled about in front of the golden tabernacle, genuflecting several times, while his broken voice, quavering with old age, droned out the preliminary prayers. No sooner was he done than all the choristers and the serpent exploded in one fell swoop, and some of the male congregants joined in with less robust and more humble voices, as befits ordinary worshipers.

Suddenly, the *Kyrie eleison* spurted heavenward, driven by all lungs and all hearts. Rattled by the vocal explosion, specks of dust and bits of worm-eaten wood actually tumbled from the ancient vaulted ceiling. The sun, beating down on the roof slates, was turning the tiny church into a furnace; and a billow of emotion, an anxious waiting, the approach of the ineffable mystery constricted the children's hearts and tightened their mothers' throats.

After sitting for a while, the priest trudged back to the altar, and, his bare head covered with silver hair, his hands quivering, he prepared for the supernatural act.

Turning toward the worshipers and stretching out his arms, he said: "*Orate, fratres.* Pray, my brethren." They all prayed. The old priest very quietly stammered the supreme and mysterious words; the little bell tinkled several times in quick succession; the prostrate assembly called to God; the children were swooning with inordinate anxiety.

It was at this point that Rosa, her forehead in her hands, suddenly remembered her mother, her village church, her own first communion. She felt as if she'd been carried back to that day, when she'd been so small, so deeply lost in her white dress, and she started whimpering. She wept softly at first: the tears oozed slowly from her eyelids; then, with her memories surging in, her emotions grew more ardent; and, her throat swelling, her bosom heaving, she started sobbing. Pulling out her handkerchief, she wiped her eyes, dabbed at her nose and her lips to keep from blubbering. But it was useless; a rattling sound emerged from her throat, and two deep, heartrending sighs responded; because her two mournful neighbors, Louise and Flora, overwhelmed by the same distant memories, were also moaning and shedding a deluge of tears.

What with tears being contagious, Madame, in turn, soon felt moisture in her eyelids, and, glancing at her sister-in-law, she saw that the entire pew was likewise weeping.

The priest was transforming bread and wine into God's flesh and blood. Their minds blank, the children were thrown to the floor by a kind of devout alarm; and, here and there, a wife, a mother, or a sister was soaking her checkered calico handkerchief, while forcefully pressing her left hand on her thumping heart, gripped by the enigmatic sympathy of agonizing emotions and also astonished at the sight of those kneeling beauties shuddering and hiccuping.

Like the spark that sends fire across an entire ripe crop, the tears shed by Rosa and her companions promptly infected the entire congregation. Men, women, oldsters, young guys in new blouses—soon they were all sobbing, and a superhuman entity appeared to be hovering over their heads, a spreading soul, the wondrous breath of an invisible and all-powerful being.

Next, the chancel emitted a thud; the nun, rapping on her missal, was signaling for the communion to start; and the children, shivering with a divine fever, approached the Lord's table.

An entire line of communicants knelt down. The old priest, clutching the gilt-silver ciborium, trudged along, offering them, between thumb and forefinger, the sacred host, the body of Christ, the redemption of the world. With their eyes shut, they opened their lips spasmatically, their pale faces grimacing nervously; and the long, white cloth under their chins rippled like flowing water.

Suddenly, a kind of madness swept through the church, the clamor of a delirious throng, a tempest of sobs and stifled cries. It passed like the gusts bending the trees in a forest; and the priest remained standing, immobile, clasping a wafer, paralyzed with emotion, whispering to himself: "It is God, God is among us, manifesting His presence, descending upon His kneeling people in response to my voice." And, at a loss for words, he stammered frenzied prayers, the prayers of a soul raging toward heaven.

He completed the communion with a faith so rapturous that his legs buckled underneath him; and when he himself had drunk the blood of his Lord, he collapsed in an act of tumultuous thanksgiving.

Behind him, the congregation was gradually calming down. The choristers, in all the dignity of their white surplices, recommenced their chanting, though in less certain and still tearful voices; and the serpent likewise sounded husky, as if it too had been crying.

Raising his arms, the priest gestured for silence, and, plodding between the two rows of ecstatically blissful communicants, he reached the chancel screen.

The assembly settled down amidst a clatter of chairs, and they all blew their noses boisterously. But upon sighting the priest, they fell silent, and he began murmuring very softly in a rasping and hesitant voice.

"My dear brethren, my dear sisters, my children, I thank you from the bottom of my heart: you have just given me the greatest joy of my life. I felt God descending on us in response to my prayers. He came, He was here, present, filling your souls, making your eyes overflow. I am the oldest priest in the diocese, and today I am also the happiest. A miracle has occurred among us, a true, a grand, a sublime miracle. While Jesus Christ penetrated the bodies of these little children for the first time, the Holy Ghost, the Celestial Dove, the breath of God descended upon you, seized hold of you, overpowered you, bending you like reeds in the wind."

Then, turning toward the two pews where the carpenter's guests were sitting, the priest went on in a clearer voice.

"Thank you, above all, my dear sisters, who have come from so far away, and whose presence among us, whose visible faith, whose profound piety have been a salutary example for all of us. You are the very edification of my parish, your deep feelings have warmed our hearts. But for you, this day might not have been so truly divine. Sometimes it takes a single chosen sheep to impel the Lord to descend to the flock."

His voice was failing. He added: "May you enjoy the Lord's grace. Amen." And he headed back to the altar so as to conclude the service.

Now the worshipers were in a hurry to leave. Even the children were agitated, worn out by such a lengthy emotional tension. Besides, they were hungry, and the parents, not waiting for the final Gospel, gradually dispersed in order to finish preparing the banquet.

A noisy swarm was mobbing the entrance, a hubbub of shrill voices speaking in a Norman singsong. The congregants formed two lines, and when the children appeared, each family swooped down on theirs.

Constance was grabbed, surrounded, hugged and kissed by the entire female household. Rosa in particular wouldn't weary of embracing her. Finally, she took one of the little girl's hands, Madame Tellier grasped the other hand; Raphaële and Fernande held the long train of the communicant's muslin skirt to keep it from dragging in the dust; Louise and Flora brought up the rear together with Madame Rivet; and the child, still bewildered, thoroughly penetrated by the God she carried inside herself, began walking in the midst of that guard of honor.

The feast was served in the workshop, on long planks resting on trestles.

The door, open to the street, brought in all the joy of the village. Everyone was tucking in. Through each window, merrymakers could be seen eating in their Sunday best, and tipsy cries resounded from the homes. The men, in shirtsleeves, were guzzling overflowing glasses of straight cider, and in the midst of each meal, you could see two children—two girls here, two boys there—dining with their respective families.

Sometimes, in the heavy noon heat, a charabanc, pulled by an old, hopping nag, would teeter through the countryside, and the driver, in his smock, would glance enviously at all that fanfare.

At the carpenter's shop, the hilarity was slightly restrained, still a bit affected, as it was, by the emotions of the morning. Rivet alone was unfazed and he kept boozing like mad. Madame Tellier kept checking the time nonstop, because, in order to avoid losing two workdays, they would have to catch the three-fifty-five train, which would deposit them at Fécamp toward evening.

The carpenter did his best to distract her and keep his guests until the next day; but Madame refused to be diverted: when it came to business, she never fooled around.

After coffee, she promptly ordered her charges to get ready as fast as possible. Then, turning to her brother, she said: "Listen, go and hitch up quickly"; and she herself went to make the final preparations.

When she came back down, her sister-in-law was waiting to talk to her about the little girl; a long conversation took place, but nothing was resolved. The mother finagled, pretending to be deeply moved; but Madame Tellier, with the child on her lap, refused to be pinned down and only made hazy promises: the girl would be taken care of, they had time, and they'd be getting together again anyway.

Meanwhile, the vehicle didn't show up, and the women didn't come down. But Madame did hear them guffawing, scuffling, yelling, clapping. Then, while her sister-in-law went over to the stable to see about the wagon, Madame finally headed upstairs.

Rivet, dead drunk and half unclad, was trying, though in vain, to rape Rosa, who was helpless with laughter. The Two Pumps were pulling him back by his arms, attempting to calm him down: they were shocked by this scene after the morning's ceremony. However, Raphaële and Fernande were goading the drunkard on, convulsed, as they were, with mirth and holding their sides; and they squealed and shrieked at each of his useless efforts. The furious man, red-faced, utterly disheveled, violently struggling to shake off the two clinging women, yanked Rosa's skirt with all his might, while stammering: "Slut, you don' wanna?!" However, Madame indignantly rushed over, grabbed his shoulders, and shoved him out of the room so ferociously that he crashed into the wall.

A minute later, they heard him in the courtyard, he was pumping water over his head. And by the time he reappeared with his cart, he was fully calmed down.

They started out as on the previous day, and the small white horse trotted off in its brisk and bouncy gait.

Under the blazing sun, the joy that had been stifled during the meal now exploded. This time, the girls were delighted by the jolts of the old jalopy, they even pushed one another's chairs, bursting into laughter at every moment, titillated by the thought of Rivet's fruitless attack.

A dazzling, almost blinding light hovered over the fields; and on the highway, the cartwheels twirled up two grooves of dust, which kept whirling behind the vehicle for a long time.

All at once, Fernande, who loved music, begged to sing; and Rosa brazenly launched into "The Fat Priest of Meudon." But Madame instantly shushed her, finding that ditty unsuitable on this of all days. She added: "Sing us something by Béranger." So Rosa, after wavering for a few seconds, made her choice and she warbled "Granny" with her worn-out vocal cords:

> At her birthday my granny said,
> After sipping a bit of pure wine
> And shaking her head:
> "How many lovers I've called mine!

> Oh, how I do miss
> My fleshy arms,
> My shapely legs,
> And my bygone charms!"

And the chorus of prostitutes, led by Madame herself, joined in the refrain:

> Oh, how I do miss
> My fleshy arms,
> My shapely legs,
> And my bygone charms!

"Why, that's fabulous!" Rivet declared, inflamed by the cadence; and Rosa instantly warbled on:

> "What, Granny, you weren't pure?" I said.
> "No! I learned at fifteen the delight,
> Of using my charms alone in bed,
> For I would never sleep at night."

They all bawled the refrain in unison; and Rivet tapped his foot on the shaft, beating out the time with the reins on the back of the old nag, which, as if likewise caught up in the rhythm, broke into a tempestuous gallop, causing the women to pile up on one another at the bottom of the vehicle.

The women got up, laughing frantically. And they continued the song at the top of their lungs, blaring it across the countryside, under the burning sky, amidst the ripening crops, to the raging trot of the little horse, which, at each repetition of the refrain, virtually bolted for a hundred yards, to the great joy of the travelers.

Here and there, a stonecutter straightened up and, through his wire mask, watched the furious and hollering cart swept away in the dust.

When the travelers climbed out at the railroad station, the carpenter became mushy: "Too bad you're leavin', we could've had a lotta fun."

Madame replied sensibly: "There's a time and a place for everything. You can't have fun every day!"

Rivet then had a bright idea. "Listen," he said, "I'll come and see you in Fécamp next month." And he leered at Rosa with his shifty, glowing eyes.

"C'mon," Madame concluded, "you've got to behave. You can visit if you like, but don't do anything stupid."

He didn't respond; and since they heard the whistling of the train, he immediately started hugging and kissing everyone. When it was Rosa's turn, he tried desperately to get at her mouth, but, laughing from behind closed lips, she kept eluding his efforts by swiftly turning her head. He held her in his arms but failed to reach his goal, hampered as he was by the long whip that he was clutching and hopelessly flailing behind the girl's back.

"All aboard for Rouen!" the conductor shouted.

The women got in.

A flimsy whistle was instantly echoed in the powerful hissing of the locomotive, which spewed out its first puff of steam while the wheels began grinding slowly and with a blatant strain.

Rivet, leaving the station, hurried over to the barrier for one last glimpse of Rosa; and when the railroad car with that load of human merchandise lurched past him, he started cracking his whip and hopping and bawling with all his strength:

> Oh, how I do miss
> My fleshy arms,
> My shapely legs,
> And my bygone charms!

Then he saw a white handkerchief waving as it faded into the distance.

—

The women slept all the way, with the peaceful sleep of a clear conscience; and when they arrived home, refreshed and well rested for their nightly task, Madame couldn't help asserting: "It doesn't matter, I was already getting homesick."

They had a quick supper; then, donning their battle gear, they waited for their regular clients; and the burning lantern, the small Madonna lantern, let passersby know that the flock had returned to the fold.

And the news spread in the twinkling of an eye—no one knew how, no one knew by whom. Monsieur Philippe, the banker's son, was even gracious enough to send an express letter to Monsieur Tournevau, a prisoner in his family.

The fish salter usually had several cousins to dinner every Sunday, and they were just sipping their coffee when a man presented himself at the door, grasping a letter. Monsieur Tournevau, deeply agitated, ripped open the envelope and blanched; all it contained were the following words in pencil: "Cod cargo traced; boat in harbor; good deal for you. Come quickly."

He rummaged in his pockets, gave the messenger twenty centimes, and suddenly reddening up to his ears, he said: "I have to go." And he handed the laconic and mysterious letter to his wife. He rang; then, when the maid appeared, he snapped: "My overcoat, quick, quick, and my hat!" Scarcely was he outdoors when he started running while whistling a tune, and he was so impatient that the road seemed twice as long as usual.

The Tellier establishment was in a festive mood. On the ground floor, the shouting and yelling of the waterfront denizens produced a deafening hurly-burly. Louise and Flora didn't know whom to respond to first; they drank with one man, drank with another, deserving more than ever their sobriquet, the Two Pumps. They were bellowed at from everywhere at once; the work was already more than they could handle; a laborious night lay ahead.

The upstairs coterie was complete by nine o'clock. Monsieur Vasse, the judge at the commercial court and Madame's eager but platonic suitor, was whispering with her in a corner; and they were both smiling as if on the verge of an agreement. Monsieur Poulin, the ex-mayor, had Rosa straddling his lap and, nose to nose, running her short hands through his white whiskers. Her yellow silk skirt was hiked up, exposing a bit of bare thigh that clashed with his black trousers, while her red stockings were kept in place by blue garters, a present from the traveling salesman.

Tall Fernande, stretched out on the sofa, had both feet propped on the belly of Monsieur Pimpesse, the tax collector, and her upper body on the vest of the young Monsieur Philippe: her right arm was coiled around his neck, and her left hand was clutching a cigarette.

Raphaële seemed to be parleying with Monsieur Dupuis, the insurance agent, and she terminated the negotiation with these words: "Yes, darling, tonight, I want to." Then, with a swift and solo waltz across the salon, she cried: "Tonight, anything anyone likes."

The door flew open, and Monsieur Tournevau appeared. He was welcomed with enthusiastic shouts: "Hurray for Tournevau!" And Raphaële, who was still swiveling, threw herself on his chest. He grabbed her and hugged her wildly, and, without a word, he lifted her up like a feather, marched across the salon, reached the opposite door, and, with his live burden, he vanished in the staircase leading to the higher rooms—accompanied by loud applause.

Rosa, trying to inspire the ex-mayor by showering him with kisses, tugging on both his whiskers at once to keep his head erect, urged him to follow the salter's example: "C'mon, do the same." The man then stood up, and, adjusting his vest, he followed the girl while fumbling in his pocket, where his money lay dormant.

Fernande and Madame remained alone with the four men, and Monsieur Philippe exclaimed: "The champagne's on me. Madame Tellier, send for three bottles." Next, Fernande, embracing him, murmured into his ear: "Why don't you play us something to dance to, huh?" He stood up, and, settling at the ancient spinet that was languishing in the corner, he forced out a waltz, a rasping, maudlin waltz, from the wheezing belly of that contraption. The tall girl squeezed the tax collector, Madame abandoned herself to Monsieur Vasse's arms; and the two couples twirled about, exchanging kisses. Monsieur Vasse, who had once danced at society shindigs, was so graceful that Madame gazed at him with captivated eyes, the eyes that respond yes, a "yes" more discreet and more delicious than any spoken word!

Frédéric brought in the champagne. The first cork popped, and Monsieur Philippe launched into the opening bars of a quadrille.

The four dancers strutted through it with a fashionable demeanor, grand and dignified, with elegant manners and with bows and curtsies.

After which, they started drinking. Now Monsieur Tournevau reappeared, content, relieved, and radiant. He cried out: "I don't know what's going on with Raphaële, but she's perfect tonight." Then, when he was handed a flute, he tossed it off, murmuring: "Damn it! Nothing like bubbly deluxe!"

Monsieur Philippe promptly tackled a lively polka, and Monsieur Tournevau let loose with "la belle Juive," lifting her up, without letting her feet touch the floor. Monsieur Pimpesse and Monsieur Vasse lunged in with fresh verve. From time to time, one of the couples halted by the mantelpiece to gulp down a flute of champagne; and the dancers seemed ready to go on forever when Rosa, holding a candlestick, opened the door a crack. Her hair was undone, she was wearing slippers and a nightgown, and she was utterly ebullient and utterly flushed. "I wanna dance!" she exclaimed.

Raphaële asked her: "What about your old guy?"

Rosa guffawed: "Him? He's already asleep. He usually dozes off right away." She grabbed Monsieur Dupuis, who'd been idle on the divan, and the polka recommenced.

Unfortunately, the bottles were empty. "The next one's on me!" Monsieur Tournevau declared. "And the one after that's on me!" Monsieur

Vasse announced. "And I'll take care of the one after that!" Monsieur Dupuis concluded. Everyone clapped.

Things were shaping up, the evening was turning into a real ball. Now and then, Louise and Flora even came dashing in from below and did a quick waltz while their ground-floor customers grew impatient; then the two girls ran back to their tavern, much to their regret.

At midnight, the group was still dancing. Occasionally, a girl would disappear, and when somebody wanted her as a partner, it suddenly hit them that one of the men was likewise missing.

"Where are you coming from?" Monsieur Philippe asked friskily just as Monsieur Pimpesse was returning with Fernande.

"We watched Monsieur Poulin dozing," the tax collector replied. His quip brought down the house; and each person in turn went up to watch Monsieur Poulin dozing with one or another of the young ladies, who were inconceivably obliging that night. Madame turned a blind eye to all these goings-on; and, sitting in corners, she had long tête-à-têtes with Monsieur Vasse as if to supply the finishing touch to an arrangement that they had already agreed on.

Finally, at one A.M., the two married men, Monsieur Tournevau and Monsieur Pimpesse, proclaimed that they were retiring and they wished to settle their accounts. They were charged only for the champagne, and six francs a bottle at that instead of the usual ten francs. And when they expressed their astonishment at that generosity, a beaming Madame replied: "We don't always have something to celebrate."

On the Water

Last summer, I rented a small country cottage on the Seine, a few miles from Paris, and I would spend every night there. After several days, I made the acquaintance of a neighbor, a man in his thirties, who was the strangest character I have ever known. He was a veteran boatman, indeed a ferocious boatman, always near the water, always on the water, always in the water. He must have been born in a boat, and he is sure to die during a final boat ride.

One evening, as we were strolling along the Seine, I asked him to tell me a few anecdotes from his nautical life. My neighbor immediately livened up, was transfigured, waxed eloquent, almost poetic. He had a great passion in his heart, an all-consuming and irresistible passion: the river.

———

Ah! (he said). I've got countless memories of this river, which you see flowing there, next to us! You street-dwellers don't know what a river is. But just listen to a fisherman pronounce that word. For him it is something profound, mysterious, unknown, the land of mirages and phantasmagorias, where, at night, you see things that don't exist, where you hear noises you've never heard before, where you tremble without knowing why, like when you cross a graveyard. And indeed, the river is the most sinister of graveyards, the kind that has no graves.

For a fisherman, the land is limited, while, on a dark, moonless night, the river is infinite. A mariner doesn't feel the same way about the sea. The sea is often harsh and wicked, that's true; but it shouts, it howls, it's loyal—the open sea—while the river is silent and perfidious. It never roars, it always flows noiselessly; and this eternal motion of the flowing water is more terrifying for me than the towering waves of the ocean.

Dreamers claim that the sea hides in its bosom huge bluish countries, where drowned corpses roll among enormous fish, in the midst of weird forests and crystal grottoes. The river has nothing but black chasms, where the dead decay in the mire. Yet the river is beautiful when it shines in the rising sun and gently ripples to and fro between banks covered with murmuring reeds.

When writing about the ocean, Victor Hugo said:

> Oh, waves, what lugubrious tales you know!
> Deep waves, feared by kneeling mothers,
> You, who tell your tales to the rising tide.
> And you tell them with those desperate voices
> That you have when you come to us in the evening.

Well, I believe that those stories whispered by the slender reeds in their faint, sweet voices must be even eerier than the grim tragedies recounted by the howling waves.

But since you've asked me for some of my memories, I'm going to tell you about a singular adventure that I had a dozen years ago.

I was living, as I still do, in old Mother Lafon's home, and one of my best friends, Louis Bernet, who by now has given up boating, given up its pomps and havoc in order to become a state counselor, had settled in the village of C——, a couple of miles downstream. We dined together every night, alternating between his place and mine.

One evening, when I was rowing home all alone and quite worn out, barely managing to handle my boat, a twelve-footer that I always used at night, I halted for a few seconds to catch my breath near that reedy tongue over there, some two hundred yards before the railroad bridge. The night was magnificent; the moon was shining, the river was glowing, the air was calm and soft. That tranquillity was tempting; I figured it would do me good to smoke a pipe in that place. The thought was father to the deed: I grabbed my anchor and dropped it into the river.

The boat, drifting with the current, glided to the end of the anchor chain, then halted; I sat down aft on my sheepskin as comfortably as possible. I heard nothing, nothing: though now and then, I believed I caught the almost imperceptible lapping of the water against the shore, and I noticed higher clumps of reeds that took on surprising shapes and, at times, appeared to be moving.

The river was perfectly serene but I felt deeply affected by the extraordinary stillness around me. All the animals, frogs and toads, those nocturnal crooners of the swamps, were hushed. Suddenly, to my right, against me, a frog croaked. I shuddered; it fell silent again; I heard nothing more, and so I resolved to smoke a little by way of distraction. However, although I'm an inveterate pipe smoker, I couldn't manage; after a puff or two, I grew sick and I stopped. I began humming; but the sound of my voice was distressing; so I stretched out on the bottom of my boat and I gazed up at the sky. For a while, I remained tranquil; but soon, I was bothered by the vague swaying of the craft. I felt as if it were floating gigantic distances, yawing from bank to bank; next, it was as if an invisible force or some entity were slowly drawing it to the bottom, then raising it, only to let it sink again. I was tossed about as if in the thick of a tempest; I heard noises around me; I jumped up: the water was shimmering, everything was calm.

I realized that my nerves were a bit shaken and I decided to start moving again. I pulled on my chain; the boat stirred; then I felt some resistance. I yanked harder, the anchor wouldn't budge: it had snagged on to something in the depths, and I couldn't unhook it. I tried and tried, but it was useless. Then, hoping to change the position of the anchor, I grabbed my oars and made the boat turn around and point upstream. It didn't work, the anchor wouldn't budge. In a rage, I yanked and yanked the chain. Nothing stirred. Discouraged, I sat down and began mulling over my situation. I couldn't possibly hope to break or detach the chain, for not only was it huge, but it was also riveted to a fore-part chunk of wood that was thicker than my arm; however, since the weather was gorgeous, I figured some fisherman was bound to show up very soon and come to my rescue. My plight had calmed my nerves; I sat down and I could finally smoke my pipe. I had a bottle of rum aboard, and after draining two or three glasses, I laughed at my situation. The night was very hot, so that if push came to shove, I could easily sleep outdoors.

All at once, something bumped into the side of my boat. I was startled, and an icy sweat covered me from head to toe. That tap must have been caused by a piece of wood swept there by the current, but it was enough to unsettle me, and again I felt overwhelmed by a bad case of nerves. I seized the chain, and my body stiffened in a desperate effort. The anchor held fast. I sat down again, exhausted.

Meanwhile, the river was gradually blanketed by a very dense, white fog that hovered on the surface of the water, so that when I stood up, I could no longer see the river, or my feet, or my boat; all I could make out were the tips of the reeds and, farther away, the very pale, moonlit meadow, with dark, sky-high patches that were actually clusters of black Italian poplars. I was virtually buried up to my waist in a sheet of bizarre white cotton, and my mind conjured up wild fantasies. I imagined that somebody was trying to climb into my boat—which I could no longer discern—and that the river, concealed by that opaque fog, must be teeming with strange creatures that were circling around me. I felt horribly uncomfortable, my temples were throbbing, my heart was pounding intensely enough to suffocate me; and, losing all control, I thought of jumping into the river and swimming to safety. But then that very notion made me shudder in dread. I saw myself lost, fumbling about in the thick mist, floundering amid unavoidable reeds and plants, rattling with fear, not seeing the bank, not finding my boat; and I felt as if I'd be pulled by my feet to the very bottom of the black water.

Indeed, I would have to struggle against the current for at least five hundred yards before reaching a spot free of plants and rushes, where I could get a solid foothold; nine chances out of ten, I'd be unable to find my way in this fog and I would drown, good swimmer though I was.

I tried to reason with myself. I tried to will myself not to be afraid; but there was something in my mind besides my will, and that something was scared. I asked myself what I had to fear; my brave self poked fun at my cowardly self, and never have I grasped that conflict as sharply as on that night, that opposition between the two beings in our soul: the being that wills and the being that resists, each prevailing in turn.

My idiotic and inexplicable alarm kept growing more and more into terror. I remained inert, with open eyes and tense ears, waiting. For what? I didn't know, but it must have been something horrendous. I do believe that if, as often happens, a fish had decided to leap out of the water, it wouldn't have taken much for me to collapse in a dead faint.

Nevertheless, making a violent effort, I finally managed to more or less regain my senses, which I had been losing. I again picked up my bottle and guzzled some rum.

Then I had an idea and I started shouting at the top of my lungs, successively facing the four points of the compass. When my throat was absolutely paralyzed, I listened. A dog was howling, very far away.

I drank some more and then stretched out full length on the bottom of the boat. I remained like that, sleepless, with eyes open, for perhaps an hour, perhaps two, beleaguered by nightmares. I didn't dare stand up and yet I desperately wanted to; I kept putting it off from minute to minute. I told myself: "C'mon, stand up!"—but I was afraid to stir. Eventually I drew myself up with infinite caution, as if my life hinged on the slightest noise that I made, and I peered over the side of the boat.

I was flabbergasted by the most wondrous, the most astonishing spectacle that anyone could ever see. It was one of those phantasmagorias of fairyland, one of those visions described by travelers who return from far away and whom we listen to in disbelief.

The fog, which had been floating on the water for two hours, had gradually shifted a little and gathered on the shores. Leaving the river utterly free, it had formed an unbroken mound six or seven yards high, on either bank, and these mounds were shining in the moonlight, as dazzling as snow. They were so superbly blinding that nothing was visible except for that fiery river flowing between those two white mountains; and up above, over my head, a full, huge, broad moon illuminated a bluish and milky sky.

All the creatures of the water had awakened; the frogs were croaking furiously, while, from moment to moment, now from the right, now from the left, I heard that brief, mournful, monotonous note thrown at the stars by the ringing voices of the toads. It was odd, I was no longer afraid; I was in the midst of a landscape so extraordinary that I wouldn't have been surprised to encounter the most phenomenal things.

I can't tell how long that phantasm lasted, for I finally dozed off. By the time I reopened my eyes, the moon was gone and the sky was cloudy. The water lapped lugubriously, the wind blew, the air was cold, the darkness was profound.

I polished off the last of the rum; then, shivering, I listened to the rustling of the reeds and the eerie swishing of the river. I tried to see, but I couldn't make out my boat or even my hands when I held them up in front of me.

Bit by bit, however, the blackness grew less dense. Suddenly I thought I sensed a shadow gliding very close to me; I shouted, a voice responded: it was a fisherman. I called out to him, he rowed over, and I explained my predicament. He brought his boat alongside mine, and we both pulled on my anchor chain. The anchor wouldn't move. Dawn was coming, somber, gray, rainy, icy, one of those days that bring you sadness and misery. I sighted another boat, we hailed it. The boatman tried to help us; then, little by little, the anchor yielded. It rose, but slowly, slowly, and charged with a huge weight. We finally saw a black bulk and we hauled it aboard my boat.

It was the corpse of an old crone with a huge rock tied to her neck.

MADEMOISELLE FIFI

The Prussian commandant, Count von Farlsberg, a major, was almost done reading his mail in the depths of a big easy chair upholstered in tapestry; his booted feet were propped on the elegant marble of the fireplace, where, during the three months that he'd been occupying the Château d'Uville, his spurs had been digging two deep gashes, a bit deeper every day.

A cup of coffee was steaming on an inlaid pedestal table, which was stained by liqueurs, burned by cigars, notched by the penknife of the conquering officer, who, sometimes, pausing in the midst of sharpening a pencil, would scrawl figures or drawings on the graceful marble, whatever struck his capricious fancy.

Having read his mail and skimmed the German newspapers that his orderly had just brought him, he stood up; and, after tossing three or four huge chunks of green wood into the fire (for these gentlemen were gradually denuding the park in order to keep warm), he stepped over to the window.

A torrential rain was pouring down, a Norman rain that seemed to be hurled by some furious hand, a slanting rain, as thick as a curtain, virtually forming a wall with oblique stripes, a lashing, splattering, inundating rain, a typical rain of the Rouen area, that chamber pot of France.

The officer gazed and gazed at the sodden lawns and, farther away, at the swollen, overflowing Andelle River; his fingers were drumming a Rhenish waltz on the pane when a sudden noise made him whirl around: it was his second-in-command, Baron von Kelweingstein, whose rank was the equivalent of captain.

The major was a giant, with broad shoulders and a long, fan-shaped beard covering his chest like a sheet; his entire solemn person was the very image of a military peacock, a peacock spreading his tail all the way to his chin. His eyes were blue, cold, and gentle, one cheek was scarred from a saber cut he had received in Prussia's war with Austria; and he was said to be an honorable man as well as an honorable officer.

The captain, a short man with a ruddy face and a big, tightly belted paunch, had a fiery crew cut, which, in certain lights, made his face and his head look as if they had been rubbed with phosphorous. He had once lost two front teeth during a night of debauchery—though he couldn't remember how—and the gap made him splutter his garbled speech, which was not always understood. The top of his head was bald—a monkish tonsure with a short fringe of gilded, shiny, curly hair around that hoop of naked skin.

The commandant shook the captain's hand, and he tossed down his coffee (his sixth cup that morning) while listening to his subordinate's report on the incidents that had occurred; then both men walked over to the window, declaring that things didn't look so cheery. The major, a quiet sort, with a wife at home, was highly adaptable; but the captain baron, an obstinate Lothario, a denizen of low dives, a frantic skirt-chaser, was champing at the bit after three months of forced chastity in this godforsaken post.

Someone scratched on the door, and the commandant shouted:

"Come in!" A man, one of their military automatons, appeared in the open doorway, his mere presence indicating that lunch was served.

In the dining room, they found the three lower-ranking officers: a lieutenant, Otto von Grossling; plus two second lieutenants, Fritz Scheunaubourg and Marquis Wilhem von Eyrik, a blond manikin, proud and brutal with other men, harsh to the vanquished and as violent as a firearm.

Since his arrival in France, his buddies called him exclusively Mademoiselle Fifi. This nickname was inspired by his dainty figure, by his slender waist, which looked corseted, by his pale face with its scant wisp of a mustache, and also by his habit of expressing his sovereign disdain for things and people by constantly using the French locution "Fi, fi donc" [Fie, for shame], which he pronounced with a slight hiss.

—

The dining room of the Château d'Uville was a long, majestic hall, whose ancient crystal mirrors, now riddled with bullet holes, and whose high Flemish tapestries, now slashed to sometimes dangling ribbons, revealed what Mademoiselle Fifi did with himself during his idle moments.

On the walls, there were portraits of three family members—an armored knight, a cardinal, and a magistrate—who were now smoking long porcelain pipes inserted into the canvases, while, in her tarnished frame, a noblewoman with a cinched bust arrogantly sported an enormous charcoal mustache.

The officers lunched almost silently in that mutilated hall, which was gloomier because of the rain and mournful because of its look of defeat; whereby the old oaken parquet had become as grimy as a tavern floor.

Finishing their meal, and then smoking and drinking, they began, as on any other day, to talk about their boredom. Bottles of cognac and liqueur passed from hand to hand; and each of these men sat back in his chair, sipping and sipping, without removing from the corner of his mouth the long, curving stem that was terminated by the china bowl, daubed in all the colors of the rainbow as though to seduce a Hottentot.

Once a glass was empty, they refilled it with a gesture of resigned apathy. Mademoiselle Fifi, however, broke his glass every time, and a soldier instantly replaced it.

Engulfed in a fog of acrid smoke, they seemed to be absorbed in a sorrowful and intoxicated slumber, in that dreary state of drunkenness that afflicts people who have nothing to do.

Suddenly, however, the baron sat up. His body shook with rebellion: he cursed: "Damn it all! This can't go on! We have to come up with something."

Lieutenant Otto and Second Lieutenant Fritz, two Germans eminently endowed with grave and heavy German faces, responded in unison: "What, sir?"

He reflected for a couple of seconds, then resumed: "What? Well, we have to throw a party, if the commandant allows us to."

The major removed his pipe. "A party, Captain?"

The baron drew nearer: "I'll take care of everything, sir. I'll send Le Devoir [Duty] to Rouen to bring back some women. I know where to find them. We'll prepare a supper here; nothing is lacking anyway, and at least we'll have a great time."

Count von Farlsberg shrugged with a smile: "You're crazy, my friend."

However, all the officers had risen, they crowded around their superior and begged him: "Let the captain do it, Commandant, this place is so dismal."

In the end, the major yielded: "Fine." And the baron promptly summoned Le Devoir. The latter was an old petty officer, who had never been seen cracking a smile, but who fanatically executed any and every order he was given by the higher ranks.

Standing there, his face impassive, he received his instructions from the baron; then he left. Five minutes later, a huge army wagon, covered with a miller's dome-shaped canvas and pulled by four galloping horses, lurched off into the torrential rain.

The officers instantly seemed to awake with a quiver; their languishing bodies straightened, their faces brightened, and they started to chat.

Although the deluge kept raging as furiously as ever, the major asserted that it was less dark out, and Lieutenant Otto announced with conviction that the sky was about to clear up. Mademoiselle Fifi herself seemed unable to sit still. She got up, she sat down. Her hard, clear eyes looked around for something to break. Suddenly, focusing on the lady with a mustache, the small young blond drew his revolver.

"You're not gonna see this," he said; and without leaving his chair, he took aim. Two successive bullets gouged out the two eyes in the portrait.

Then he exclaimed: "Let's make a mine!" And instantly all conversations broke off as if some new and powerful interest had taken hold of everyone.

The mine was his invention, his method of destruction, his favorite amusement.

When fleeing his château, the legitimate owner, Count Fernand d'Amoys d'Uville, hadn't had time to carry off or conceal anything except for some silverware that he stashed inside a wall. Prior to his precipitous escape, he had enjoyed great wealth and a magnificent lifestyle, so that his grand salon, which opened into the dining hall, resembled a museum gallery.

The walls were hung with expensive paintings, drawings, and watercolors, while the furnishings, the étagères, and the vitrines displayed a thousand knickknacks: a bizarre and precious throng that filled the vast dwelling with large vases, statuettes, Dresden porcelain figures, grotesque Chinese creatures, ancient ivories, and Venetian glassware.

Few of those bibelots had survived. Not that they were pillaged: Count von Farlsberg wouldn't have stood for it; but from time to time,

Mademoiselle Fifi made a "mine"; and on that day, all the officers had five minutes' worth of real fun.

The little marquis went to the salon to find what he needed. He brought back a dainty Chinese teapot decorated with rosaceae and he filled it with cannon powder; next, he delicately inserted a long piece of tinder through the snout, ignited it, and quickly transferred that infernal machine to the adjoining room.

Then he swiftly returned and closed the door. The Germans all stood there, waiting, and smiling with childlike curiosity; and as soon as the explosion shook the château, they dashed over as one man.

Mademoiselle Fifi, the first to enter, deliriously applauded a terracotta Venus, whose head had finally been blown off; and each soldier picked up some porcelain fragments, surprised by their weird, jagged shapes, examining the new damage, contesting some ravages as products of an earlier explosion. And with a fatherly air, the major scanned the vast salon, which had been wrecked by that Neronian mayhem and was strewn with the debris of art objects. The major was the first to leave as he beamed: "A nice job this time."

Meanwhile, the smoke, whirling into the dining room and mingling with the tobacco fumes, was so dense that the men couldn't breathe. The commandant opened the window, and all the officers, checking in for a last snifter of cognac, gathered there.

The humid air came rushing into the room, conveying the smell of inundation and a kind of spray that speckled all beards. The officers gazed at the gigantic, rain-battered trees; at the broad, misty valley under low, dark clouds; and at the faraway church spire towering like a gray point in the clobbering downpour.

The church bell hadn't rung since the arrival of the Prussians. And that, incidentally, was the only local resistance that the invaders had encountered: the resistance of the belfry. The priest hadn't objected to receiving and feeding Prussian soldiers; a few times, he had even agreed to share a beer or a Bordeaux with the enemy commandant, who often used him as a benevolent intermediary. But it was futile asking him for even a single clang of his bell; he would rather have been shot. It was his own way of protesting the invasion—a peaceful protest, a silent protest, the only kind, he said, that suited a priest, a mild and not bloodthirsty man. And everyone within a radius of ten leagues praised the staunchness, the heroism shown by Father Chantavoine, who dared to affirm the public grief, to proclaim it through the obstinate hush of his church.

The entire village, inspired by his resistance, was ready to support its pastor come what may, to brave everything, for the villagers regarded that tacit protestation as a safeguard of their national honor. In line with that, they felt they deserved more of their country than Belfort and Strasbourg, that they were setting an equally sublime example, that the name of their hamlet would become immortal. Aside from that, they refused their Prussian conquerors nothing.

The commandant and his officers laughed at that inoffensive courage; and since the whole countryside proved obliging and cooperative, the invaders gladly tolerated that mute heroism.

Little Marquis Wilhem was the only one who wanted to force the priest to ring the bell. He was furious about his superior's politic acquiescence to the priest; and no day passed without his begging the commandant to ring "ding dong" just once, just one brief, single time, just for a wee bit of fun. And he would cajole the commandant like a cat, wheedle like a woman, mealy-mouth him like an obsessed mistress. But the commandant dug in his heels; and Mademoiselle Fifi consoled himself by making a "mine" in the Château d'Uville.

For several minutes, the five men clustered at the window, inhaling the muggy air. Finally, Lieutenant Fritz guffawed: "Doze ladies von't haf nice veader for deir drife."

That being said, they dispersed, each man attending to his own duties, while the captain had a lot of preparations to make for the dinner.

At nightfall, when they met again, they laughed upon seeing one another well scrubbed, well groomed as on inspection days—perfumed, pomaded, and very fresh. The commandant's hair seemed less gray than in the morning, and the captain was clean-shaven except for his mustache, which formed a fiery trail under his nose.

Despite the rain, they left the window open; and every so often, one of the men would go over and listen. At six-ten, the baron signaled that he had caught a distant rolling. They all dashed up; and soon, the huge vehicle arrived with its four galloping horses steaming, panting, and mud-splattered up to their backs.

And five women stepped down to the perron, five beautiful prostitutes carefully selected by the captain's friend, to whom Le Devoir had brought a card from his superior.

The women didn't play hard to get, they were sure to be well paid; for they'd gotten to know the Prussians in these three months of drawing them out and resigning themselves to men and to facts. "It's part of the job," they had told one another en route, responding, no doubt, to some secret prickle in a vestige of conscience.

The company instantly entered the dining room. Illuminated in its pitiful dilapidation, the room looked even more lugubrious; and, with the table groaning under its goodies, its rich china, and the silverware that had been found in the wall, it resembled a tavern where bandits dined after a pillage. As if dealing with familiar objects, the radiant captain took hold of the women, assessing them, kissing them, sniffing them, evaluating them as pleasure-givers. And since each of the three young men wanted to appropriate a girl, the captain authoritatively opposed them, reserving for himself the right to couple them off fairly, according to each man's rank, so as not to disturb the hierarchy.

And so, to avoid any challenge, any argument, any suspicion of partiality, he lined the women up in size place and, addressing the tallest, asked in a forceful voice: "Your name?"

With a touch of menace, she retorted: "Pamela."

The captain proclaimed: "Number one, called Pamela, is awarded to the commandant."

Having kissed Blondine, the next tallest, as a sign of his ownership, he earmarked fat Amanda to Lieutenant Otto, Eva the Tomato to Second Lieutenant Fritz, and Rachel, the shortest of them all, to the youngest officer, the frail Marquis Wilhem von Eyrik; Rachel, a very young brunette with inky-black eyes, was a Jew whose snub nose constituted the exception proving the rule that assigns hooked noses to her entire race.

All the girls, incidentally, were pretty and fleshy and, being devoid of distinctive features, were more or less similar in appearance and expression because of their daily sexual routine and the uniform life in brothels.

The three young men wanted to take their women upstairs right off the bat, on the pretext of offering them soap and brushes for cleaning up. But the captain wisely stopped them, asserting that the women were clean enough for dinner, and that the men who went upstairs would, upon coming back down, prefer to change partners, thereby disturbing the other couples. His experience won out. All they did for now was kiss a lot—kisses of expectation.

Suddenly, Rachel started choking and coughing until tears came to her eyes while smoke emerged from her nostrils. The marquis, purporting to kiss her, had blown a spurt of tobacco smoke into her mouth. She didn't lose her temper, she didn't say a word, but she glared at her possessor with an anger lurking in the very depths of her black eyes.

They settled round the table. The commandant actually seemed enchanted; he sat Pamela on his right, Blondine at his left, and, unfolding his napkin, he declared: "You've had a charming idea, Captain."

Lieutenants Otto and Fritz, as polite as if entertaining socialites, intimidated their women slightly; but Baron von Kelweingstein, giving free rein to his vices, beamed and made smutty remarks, virtually on fire with his crown of red hair. He mouthed sweet nothings in Rhenish French; and his tavern compliments, expectorated through the gap in his teeth, reached the girls in a salvo of saliva.

In any case, the girls understood nothing; and their intelligence seemed to awaken only when he spewed out obscene words and crude expressions mangled by his accent. The girls would all then shriek with laughter and collapse on their neighbors, repeating the phrases that the baron wantonly garbled in order to make the girls talk dirty. They disgorged as much ribaldry as he wished since they got drunk with the first bottles of wine; and, again becoming themselves, opening up to their usual habits, they kissed mustaches to the right and left, pinched arms, shouted furiously, drank out of all the glasses, and warbled French ditties plus snatches of German songs that they had picked up in their daily association with the enemy.

Soon the men themselves, intoxicated by that display of female flesh under their noses and under their hands, went berserk, yelling, smashing dishes, while behind them, the soldiers kept waiting on them matter-of-factly.

The commandant alone maintained his self-control.

Mademoiselle Fifi had put Rachel on his lap, and, pretending to grow excited, he wildly kissed the ebony curls on her neck, sniffing the tiny space between her frock and her skin and inhaling the sweet warmth of her body and all the pleasant smell of her person—or else he savagely pinched her through her dress, forcing out her shrieks, raging ferociously, tormented by his need to plunder. Often, while holding her tight, clinging as if to fuse with her, he kept his mouth on the Jewess's fresh lips, kissing her on and on until she was unable to breathe. Then suddenly, he bit her so hard that a trail of blood trickled down to the young woman's chin and rolled into her bodice.

Once again, she gazed at him, face to face, and, washing the injury, she muttered: "You're gonna pay for this."

He guffawed harshly. "I'll pay," he said.

It was time for dessert; they poured champagne. The commandant stood up, and, in the same tone he would have used to toast the health of Germany's Empress Augusta, he drank and said: "To our ladies!"

And a series of toasts began, toasts offered with the gallantry of boozers and old troopers, mingling with obscene jokes and made even more brutal by the girls' ignorance of German.

The men rose one after another, trying to be witty, striving to be funny; and, their eyes blank, their lips pasty, the women, so drunk that they were practically tumbling off their chairs, frantically applauded each effort of the soldiers.

The captain, no doubt wanting to give the orgy a gallant appearance, raised his glass yet again and exclaimed: "To our victories over hearts!"

Lieutenant Otto, a bear from the Black Forest, got to his feet, inflamed, saturated with drinking. And, suddenly imbued with alcoholic patriotism, he shouted: "To our victories over France!"

Inebriated as they may have been, the women hushed; and Rachel, shuddering, turned around: "Listen, you wouldn't say that in front of certain Frenchmen that I know!"

But the little marquis, still holding her on his lap, started chortling, very cheerful because of the wine: "Ah, ah, ah! I for one never saw any. The instant we show up, they take French leave!"

The raging girl yelled into his face: "You're a liar, you bastard!"

For a second, he fixed his clear eyes on her just as he always fixed them on the paintings that he riddled; then he resumed laughing: "Ah, yes! Let's talk about it, beautiful! Would we be here if they had any guts!?" And he livened up: "We are their masters! France belongs to us!"

She jumped off his knees and flopped down on her chair. He stood up, held out his glass to the center of the table and repeated: "France and the French belong to us—the woods, the fields, and the houses of France!"

The other officers, totally plastered, suddenly shaken by military enthusiasm, an enthusiasm of brutes, grabbed their glasses and hollered: "Long live Prussia!" And they chugalugged them. The girls, frightened and reduced to silence, didn't protest at all. Rachel likewise held her tongue, powerless to respond.

Then the little marquis placed his refilled flute of champagne on the Jewess's head and cried: "And all the women in France belong to us, too!"

She leaped up so fast that the crystal turned over, emptied the yellow wine on her black hair, as if for a baptism, and shattered on the floor. With quivering lips, she confronted the still guffawing officer, and, choking with anger, she stammered: "That, that, that ain't true, damn it! You ain't gonna have no women in France!"

He sat down to laugh to his heart's content, and, attempting a Parisian accent, he said: "Dat is very goot, very goot—den vot are you doink here, my girl?"

Flabbergasted, she was initially tongue-tied and too upset to catch his drift; but once she had grasped what he was saying, she yelled, indignant and vehement: "Me! Me! I ain't no woman, I ain't, I'm a hooker! And that's all the Prussians can get!"

She had barely finished when he slapped the wind out of her; but as he brandished his hand again, the girl, boiling with frenzy, reached toward the table, grabbed a small, silver-handled dessert knife, and, so swiftly that at first nobody caught on, she stabbed him right in the neck, just above the breastbone.

A word was cut short in his throat; and he sat there, with a gaping mouth and a dreadful stare.

The company roared, and they all jumped up tumultuously; but, after hurling her chair against Lieutenant Otto's legs, sending him crashing down full-length, the girl dashed toward the window, opened it before anyone could seize her, and plunged into the night, through the still-pouring rain.

Within two minutes, Mademoiselle Fifi was dead. Fritz and Otto drew their swords, about to massacre the women, who were kneeling at their feet. The major, not without difficulty, managed to stop that carnage, and he had the four terrified girls locked up in a room guarded by two men. Then, as if preparing his soldiers for combat, he organized the pursuit of the fugitive, quite certain that she'd be captured.

Fifty men, spurred on by his threats, were sent into the park. Two hundred others searched the woods and all the houses in the valley.

Meanwhile, the table, which had been instantly cleared, now served as a bier; and the four officers, rigid, sober, with the stern faces of warriors on duty, stood at the windows, peering into the night.

The deluge remained torrential. A continuous splashing filled the darkness, a drifting murmur of water falling and water flowing, water trickling and water spurting.

Suddenly, they heard a shot, then another very far away; and for the next four hours, they intermittently heard nearby or remote detonations and rallying cries, strange words yelled like guttural appeals.

In the morning, everyone came back. Two soldiers had been killed and three others wounded by friendly fire in the ardent hunt and the confusion of that nocturnal chase.

Rachel was nowhere to be found.

The Prussians terrorized the inhabitants, turning homes upside down, beating, combing, scouring the entire countryside. The Jewess didn't seem to have left a single trace.

The general, upon being notified, gave orders to hush up the whole affair rather than set a bad example for the army; and he then disciplined the commandant severely, who, in turn, punished his inferiors. The general said: "You don't wage war to have a good time and fondle prostitutes." A furious Count von Farlsberg resolved to get even with the entire district. Needing an excuse for his severity, he summoned the priest and ordered him to toll the bell for the Marquis von Eyrik's funeral.

Contrary to expectation, the priest was docile, humble, and highly respectful. And when, carried by soldiers as well as preceded, surrounded, and followed by soldiers all marching with loaded rifles, Mademoiselle Fifi's corpse left the Château d'Uville and headed toward the cemetery, the bell, for the first time during the Prussian occupation, boomed out its death knell in a lively style, as if fondled by a friendly hand.

It tolled again that evening, also the next morning, and every day after that; it clanged as often as anybody could want. On some nights, it even began on its own, gently dispatching two or three peals into the darkness, overcome with singular merriment and awakened who could say why. All the local farmers said the bell was haunted; and no one except the priest and the sacristan got anywhere near the bell tower.

You see, a wretched girl was living up there, in fear and solitude and fed in secret by those two men.

She remained there until the departure of the German troops. Then, one evening, after borrowing the baker's wagon, the priest himself drove his prisoner to the gates of Rouen. Upon their arrival, the priest gave her a hug; she climbed down and briskly strode to the brothel, its proprietress having assumed she was dead.

A short time later, she was taken from the brothel by an unprejudiced patriot who loved her for her wonderful deed, then, eventually cherishing her for herself, married her and turned her into a lady, who was every bit as good as so many other ladies.

THE MASK

That evening there was a costume ball at the Élysée-Montmartre to celebrate Mid-Lent, and, like water gushing through a sluice, the throng surged into the illuminated corridor leading to the dance hall. The formidable uproar of the band, exploding like a musical storm, assaulted the walls and the roof, blasted through the neighborhood, and shook the streets and the interiors of houses, awakening that irresistible yearning to jump around, warm up, have fun—a desire slumbering in the depths of the human animal.

And the denizens of the dance hall were pouring in from the four corners of Paris—people of all classes, who loved gross, rowdy pleasure with a touch of sordid debauchery. These were clerks, pimps, hookers—hookers in all materials, from vulgar cotton to the finest batiste, rich, old, diamond-studded hookers and poor sixteen-year-old hookers raring to carouse, to give themselves to men, to squander money. Elegant black suits, looking for young flesh that had lost its first bloom but was still delectable, prowled through that overheated swarm, peering, apparently sniffing, while the masks seemed inflamed chiefly by a desire to have fun. A dense audience crowded around the famous quadrilles, watching them hopping and leaping. The undulating hedge, the restless drove of men and women encircling the performers, twisted around them like a serpent, now approaching, now receding with the flux of dancers. In each quadrille, the two women, whose thighs seemed attached to their bodies by rubber springs, did astonishing gymnastics with their legs. Their upward kicks were so forceful that those limbs appeared to be soaring toward the clouds, then suddenly flying apart as if splitting down to their bellies, while the centers of their bodies grazed the floor in a big, swift straddling feat that was both hilarious and repugnant.

Their escorts jumped, pranced, shook, wiggling and flapping their arms like stumps of featherless wings, and you could sense that they were panting behind their masks.

One man, who had joined the most renowned quadrille, replacing an absent celebrity, the handsome "Dream About Kid," and straining hard to keep up with the indefatigable "Calf Rib," was doing some bizarre solo maneuvers that aroused the delight and irony of the public.

He was a slender, flashy dresser sporting an attractive varnished mask on his face, a mask with a blond, curly mustache, and a wig full of ringlets.

He resembled a wax figure at the Grévin Museum, a strange and fantastic caricature of the winsome young men in the fashion prints, and he danced with an earnest but clumsy effort and a comical furor. He looked rusty next to the others as he tried to ape their gambados; and he seemed stiff and awkward, like a mongrel frisking about with greyhounds. Derisive bravos goaded him on. And he, heady with excitement, jerked around so frantically that, suddenly swept up in a furious outburst, he charged toward the wall of spectators, which parted to let him pass, then closed together around his inert and prostrate body. Several men heaved him up and lugged him away. Someone yelled: "Is there a doctor in the house?" A gentleman presented him-self, young, very stylish, in a black suit with large pearls on his dance-hall shirt. "I teach at the medical school," he said in a modest voice. They let him through, and, in a small room crammed with file cases as in a business office, he found the still-unconscious dancer being placed across several chairs.

First off, the doctor wanted to remove the mask, and, when doing so, he noticed that it was intricately attached by a legion of tiny wires, which adroitly tied it to the edges of the wig, enclosing his entire head in a solid ligature that only an insider could unravel. The neck itself was imprisoned from the chin down in a false skin, and this glovelike envelope, painted the color of flesh, reached down to his shirt collar.

It took strong scissors to cut through that astonishing contrivance, and when the physician had snipped his way from the shoulder to the temple, he opened that carapace and discovered an old human face, worn, pale, scrawny, and wrinkled. The men who had carried that young, curly-haired dancer were so deeply shocked that nobody laughed, no-body uttered a word.

They gazed at him lying across those straw-bottomed chairs, his eyes shut, his features mournful and smeared with white hair, some of it long, falling over his forehead, some of it short, on his cheeks and his chin, and next to that wretched face, that small, that handsome var-nished mask, that youthful and ever-smiling mask.

After a long stretch of unconsciousness, the man came to; but he looked so feeble, so sickly, that the doctor feared some dangerous com-plication.

"Where do you live?" he asked.

The old dancer seemed to be ransacking his memory, then it hit him, and he named a street that no one had ever heard of. He had to be quizzed for details about his neighborhood. He supplied those de-tails with infinite anguish, with a slowness and indecision that re-vealed his confusion.

The doctor said: "I'll take you there myself."

He felt a sudden curiosity to learn who this peculiar mountebank was, to see where this hopping freak was housed.

And a cab soon whisked both of them off to the other side of the hillocks of Montmartre.

His home was in a tall, squalid building with a sleazy staircase, riddled with windows and flanked by two vacant lots—one of those perpetually incomplete structures, those filthy abodes that shelter a throng of ragged and miserable creatures.

Clinging to the banister, a wooden spiral, to which his hand kept sticking, the physician struggled up to the fourth landing, supporting the dazed old man, who was regaining his strength.

The door they rapped on opened, and a woman appeared, as old as the dancer, neat, in a very white nightcap that framed a bony face with sturdy features, one of those broad, rough, good-natured faces of reliable, hardworking lower-class women.

She cried out: "My God! What happened?"

When the situation was outlined in a few dozen words, she calmed down—and calmed down the doctor himself, explaining that this sort of escapade had occurred quite often.

"Gotta put 'im to bed, Doctor, that's all. He'll sleep it off, and tomorrow he'll be his old self."

The physician objected: "But he can barely speak."

"Oh, that's nothin'. He had too much to drink—that's all. He skipped dinner so he'd be light on his feet, and then he guzzled a few absinthes to stir up his blood. You see, the absinthe revives his legs, but it dulls his mind and his tongue. A guy his age shouldn't dance like that. No, really, I've lost any hope of making him see the light!"

The surprised doctor persisted: "Why does he go dancing like that—at his age?"

She shrugged, reddening under her gradually mounting anger.

"Yeah, why? If you gotta know! So people'll think he's young under his mask, so the girls'll believe he's God's gift to women, and they'll whisper filthy stuff into his ears, so he can rub against their skins, all

their slimy skins with their smells and their powders and their po-
mades.... Oh! It's disgusting! Believe me, I've been through a lot, Doctor! It's been draggin' along for some forty years now! But we'd better
get him to bed so he won't get sick. Could ya gimme a hand? When
he's like this, I can't manage by myself."

The old man was sitting on his bed, apparently drunk, with his lank
white hair dangling over his face.

His companion stared at him with eyes full of pity and fury. She
went on: "Hey, ain't he a looker for his age? And does he have ta dis-
guise himself as a mischievous kid to make people think he's young?
Ain' it a pity though! He *is* a looker, ain't he, Doctor? Wait, I wanna
show you before I put him to bed."

She trudged over to a table with a washbasin, a water jug, soap, and
a comb and brush. She took the brush, returned to the bed, and
pushed up the drunkard's tangled hair. Within a few seconds, she had
given him the face of a painter's model, with large curls falling around
his neck. Finally, stepping back to study him, she said: "Honestly, ain't
he good-lookin' for his age?"

"Very good-looking," the doctor affirmed, starting to enjoy himself.

She added: "And if ya'd known him when he was twenny-five! But
we gotta get him to bed! Otherwise the absinthe'll turn his stomach!
Listen, Doctor, could you pull up his sleeve? ... Higher.... That's
right.... Good.... Now the pants.... Wait, lemme take off his
shoes.... That's fine.... Now hold him up while I turn down the
bed.... That's it.... Roll him in.... If you think he's gonna move later
on to make space for me, you're wrong. I've gotta find my own corner,
I do—no matter where. It don't concern him. Ah, you old skirt-chaser,
there you are!"

Once he felt himself lying between the sheets, the man closed his
eyes, reopened them, closed them again, and his satisfied face was entirely filled with his energetic resolution to sleep.

The doctor, observing him with more and more interest, asked: "So
he plays the young man at costume balls?"

"At all of them, Doctor, and you can't imagine in what state he comes back to me in the morning. You see, it's regret that drives him to wear a cardboard face over his own. Yeah, regret that he ain't what he used ta be, regret that he don't make his conquests no more!"

The man was asleep by now and beginning to snore. She eyed him with pity and then continued: "Ah! He made his conquests, he did! More than you'd believe, more than the handsomest men in society, more than all the tenors and all the generals."

"Really? What kind of work did he do?"

"Oh, you'd be amazed since you didn't know him in his prime. When I first met him, it was at a ball, too, for he frequented all of them. It was love at first sight for me, I was caught like a fish on a hook. He was cute, Doctor, cute enough to make a girl cry, as dark as a raven, with curly hair and black eyes as big as windows. Oh, yeah! He was a handsome guy, all right. He took me home that night, and I've never left him since, never, not even for a day, despite everything! Oh, my, he's put me through some harsh times!"

The physician asked: "Are you married?"

She replied simply: "Yeah, Doctor. Otherwise, he'd've dumped me like he did the others. I've been his wife and his maid, everything, everything he's wanted. . . . And he's made me cry. . . . I've shed tears that I'd never show him! Because he told me about his adventures, told me . . . me . . . Doctor . . . He didn't realize how it hurt me to listen. . . ."

"But just what kind of work did he do?"

"Oh, right! I forgot to tell you. He was the chief assistant at Martel, but an assistant like they'd never had. . . . An artist averaging ten francs an hour. . . ."

"Martel? . . . Who's Martel? . . ."

"The coiffeur, Doctor, the big coiffeur by the Opera—all the actresses were his clients. Yes, all the most elegant actresses had their hair done by Ambroise, and they gave him tips that added up to a fortune. Ah! Doctor! All women are the same, yeah, all of them. If they like a guy, they'll offer themselves to him. It's so easy. . . . And it's so painful to hear about it. You see, he told me everything. . . . He couldn't keep his trap shut. . . . No, he couldn't. Things like that give a man so much pleasure! Maybe even more pleasure to talk about it than to do it.

"When I saw him come home in the evening, a bit pale, content, with shiny eyes, I thought to myself: 'Another one, he must have seduced another one.' And I longed to question him, a longing that ripped me apart and another longing not to know, to stop him from talking if he started. And we looked at each other.

"I knew perfectly well that he wouldn't shut up, that he'd be getting down to brass tacks. I could tell by the way he acted, the way he laughed, just to make me understand. 'I had a great day today, Madeleine.' I'd pretend not to see, not to guess, and I'd set the table, I'd bring in the soup, I'd sit down across from him.

"At moments like that, I felt like my affection for him had been crushed inside me by a rock. It really hurts, awfully. But he didn't get it, he didn't know. He needed to tell somebody, to boast, to show how loved he was. . . . And it was only me he could tell . . . you get it? . . . Only me. . . . And so . . . I had to listen and swallow it like poison.

"He'd start in on his soup and then he'd say: 'Another one, Madeleine.'

"And I'd think to myself, 'Here we go again.' My God, what a man! Why did I ever have to meet him!

"Then he'd go on: 'Another one, and really gorgeous to boot. . . .' It would be a girl from the Vaudeville or else from the Variété, and also big stars, the most famous ladies of the theater. He'd tell me their names, talk about their furniture, and give me a blow-by-blow description, yes, Doctor. . . . Details that would tear out my heart. And he'd start from scratch and recite his story again, from A to Z, and he was so satisfied that I forced myself to laugh so he wouldn't get angry at me.

"Maybe it wasn't all true! He loved to brag so much that he was capable of making it all up. Or maybe it *was* true! On those evenings, he pretended to be tired and he wanted to turn in right after supper. We always ate at eleven P.M., because he had clients at night.

"When he finished his story, he'd smoke cigarettes while he strutted up and down the room, and he was so handsome with his mustache and his curly hair that I thought to myself, 'What he says is true after all. I'm crazy about that man—I am. So why shouldn't other women be nuts about him, too?' Ah! I'd often feel like crying, and shouting, and running away, and jumping out the window, but I'd just clear the table while he kept smoking. He'd yawn with a gapin' mouth to show me how tired he was, and before goin' to bed, he'd say two or three times: 'God, am I gonna sleep well tonight!'

"I don't hold it against him, he didn't realize how deeply it hurt me. No, he couldn't tell! He loved gloating about women, like a peacock spreading its tail. By then, he believed that they all looked at him and desired him.

"It was hard for him to grow old.

"Oh, Doctor! When I saw his first white hair, it knocked me for a loop! But then I felt joy, an ugly joy, a big, big joy. I said to myself: 'It's over. . . . It's over. . . .' I felt like I was about to be released from prison. I was gonna have him all to myself when the others didn't want him anymore.

"It was one morning, in our bed. He was still asleep, and I was bendin' over him, about to wake him up with a kiss, when I noticed something in the curls on his temple—a tiny thread that shone like silver. What a surprise! I wouldn't have thought it was possible! First I figured I'd tear it out so he wouldn't see it! But when I had a closer look, I noticed another thread farther up. White hair! My heart was poundin', and my skin was moist, yet deep down I was really glad!

"It may sound nasty, but that morning, my heart was light when I did the housework, and I didn't wake him up as yet. And when he opened his eyes by himself, I said: 'Do you know what I discovered while you were sleepin'?'

" 'No.'

" 'I discovered that you've got some white hair.'

"He was so shaken and angry that he sat up sharply, as if I'd tickled him, and he snapped: 'It ain't true!'

" 'It's true! Just check your left temple. It's got four white hairs.'

"He jumped out of bed and ran to the mirror.

"He didn't find them. So I showed him the first, the lowest, the small curled one, and I said: 'It ain't astonishin' considerin' the life you lead. Two years from now, you'll be done.'

"Well, Doctor, I was right. Two years later, nobody would've recognized him. How fast a man changes! He was still handsome, but he was losin' his freshness, and women stopped chasin' him. Ah! I had a horrible life during that period! He kept puttin' me through the wringer! Nothing pleased him, absolutely nothing. He switched professions and became a hat maker—and lost a bundle. Then he tried the stage, but it didn't work out. And then he started goin' to public balls. Well, he had the common sense to keep a small nest egg, which we live on. It's enough, but it ain't no gold mine. And to think that at one time he had a fortune.

"Now you know what he does. It's like a frenzy gettin' the best of him. He's gotta be young, he's gotta dance with women who smell of perfume and pomade. Poor old darlin', huh!"

—

Deeply moved, ready to cry, she gazed at her aged husband, who was snoring away. Then softly stepping over, she kissed his hair. The physician had gotten to his feet, and, having nothing further to say in front of that bizarre couple, he was preparing to withdraw.

As he was leaving, she asked him: "Could you give me your address all the same? If he turned any sicker, I'd get hold of you."

THE INN

Like all the small wooden inns planted at the foot of High Alpine glaciers, in those bare and rocky gorges that cut through the white mountain peaks, the inn at Schwarenbach serves as a refuge for travelers going through the Gemmi Pass.

The inn, open for six months of the year, was inhabited by Jean Hauser's family; then, when the snow began drifting, filling up the valley and blocking the descent to Leuk, the women, the father, and the three sons departed, leaving the inn in the hands of the old guide, Gaspard Hari, with the young guide, Ulrich Kunsi, and Sam, the big mountain dog.

The two men and the animal were to remain in this snowy prison until spring, seeing nothing but the immense white slope of the Balmhorn and surrounded by pale and glistening summits, hemmed in, closed off, and buried under the snow, which rose around them, shrouded, gripped, crushed the little cottage, piled up on the roof, reached the windows, and walled up the door.

It was the day on which the Hauser family was to return to Leuk, since winter was approaching and the descent was becoming perilous.

Three mules, loaded with baggage and led by the three sons, trudged out first. Next, the mother, Jeanne Hauser, and the daughter, Louise, mounted a fourth mule and started off in turn.

The father brought up the rear, accompanied by the two guards who were to escort the family to the start of the descent.

First they skirted the small, now frozen lake at the bottom of the large basin formed by the rocky mass that stretches past the inn; then they plodded through the valley, which, as bright as a sheet, is dominated on all sides by the snowy peaks.

A sudden burst of sunshine poured down upon that white, frozen, dazzling desert, illuminating it with a cold and blinding flame; no sign of life appeared in that sea of mountains; no movement stirred in that endless solitude; no sound disturbed the utter silence.

Little by little, the young guide, Ulrich Kunsi, a tall, long-legged Swiss, left Father Hauser and old Gaspard Hari behind in order to catch up with the mule lugging the two women.

The younger woman watched him coming and she seemed to be summoning him with sad eyes. She was a small, blond peasant girl, whose milky cheeks and pallid hair looked as if they'd been discolored by long sojourns amid the ice.

Upon reaching the mule, Kunsi put his hand on its crupper and slowed the animal down. Mother Hauser began speaking to him, enumerating with infinite detail all the things he'd have to take care of that winter. This was the first cold season he'd be living there, whereas old Hari had already spent fourteen winters under the snow, at the inn of Schwarenbach.

Ulrich Kunsi was listening without appearing to understand and he kept gazing at the girl nonstop. From time to time, he'd reply: "Yes, Mrs. Hauser." But his mind seemed far away, and his calm face remained impassive.

They reached Lake Daube, whose long, very flat, frozen surface extended all the way to the end of the valley. On the right, the Daubenhorn exposed its sheer, black rocks by the enormous moraines of the Lœmmern Glacier, which was dominated by the Wildstrubel.

As they neared the Gemmi Col, where the hike to Leuk begins, they suddenly beheld the immense horizon of the Valais Alps, from which they were separated by the deep, broad valley of the Rhône.

In the distance, they saw a throng of white, uneven peaks, flattened or pointed and glowing in the sun: the Mischabel with its twin summits, the powerful massif of the Wissehorn, the corpulent Brunnegghorn, the high and redoubtable pyramid of the Cervin, that killer of men, and the Dent-Blanche, that monstrous coquette.

Then, beneath them, in a tremendous basin, at the bottom of a terrifying abyss, they spotted Leuk, its houses like grains of sand tossed into that enormous crevasse, which, cut off and closed by the Gemmi, opens up to the Rhône down below.

The mule halted at the edge of the fantastic and marvelous trail, which, twisting, coiling, and winding, meanders down the steep mountain, to that tiny, almost invisible hamlet at its foot. The women jumped into the snow. The two old men had joined them.

"Well, friends," said Father Hauser, "good-bye and good luck until next year."

Old Hari repeated: "Until next year."

They embraced. Mrs. Hauser then held out her cheeks; and her daughter did likewise.

When it was Ulrich Kunsi's turn, he whispered into Louise's ear: "Don't forget the people up here."

She responded: "I won't." And her voice was so soft that he guessed her answer without hearing it.

"Well, good-bye," Jean Hauser repeated, "and be well."

And walking ahead of the women, he began to descend.

Soon the three of them vanished around the first bend in the road.

And the two men headed back to the inn at Schwarenbach.

They trudged slowly, side by side, without speaking. That was that, they'd remain alone, one on one, for the next four or five months.

Eventually, Gaspard Hari launched into a description of his life the previous winter. He had remained with Michel Canol, who by now was too old to endure it; for he could have an accident during that long solitude. They hadn't been bored, however; the trick was to accept the situation on the very first day; and ultimately, you create games, amusements, lots of pastimes.

Ulrich Kunsi listened with downcast eyes, his thoughts with the people descending to the village through all the zigzags of the Gemmi.

In a short while, the two guides sighted the so tiny, barely visible inn, a black dot at the foot of a monstrous billow of snow.

When they opened the door, Sam, the big, curly dog, started frolicking around them.

"C'mon, boy," said old Gaspard to Ulrich, "we ain't got no womenfolk anymore, we gotta fix supper, you can peel the potatoes."

And both men, settling on wooden stools, began pouring soup on their bread.

The next forenoon dragged on for Ulrich Kunsi. Old Hari smoked and spit into the hearth, while the young man peered through the window at the dazzling mountain facing the house.

Ulrich went out that afternoon, and, retracing the previous day's route, he looked for hoofprints of the mule that had carried the women. Then, upon reaching the neck of the Gemmi, he lay flat on his belly, at the edge of the abyss, and peered down at Leuk.

In its rocky basin, the hamlet wasn't snowbound as yet, although the snow was very close, sharply cut off by the pine forests protecting the surroundings. From high up, the squat chalets resembled paving stones in a vast field.

The Hauser girl was down there now, in one of those gray homes. Which one? Ulrich Kunsi was too far away to discern the individual chalets. How badly he wanted to hike down while he still could!

However, the sun had vanished behind the huge peak of the Wild-strubel; and the young man doubled back to the inn. Old Hari was smoking. Upon seeing his companion, Hari suggested a round of cards; and they sat down, face to face, at either side of the table.

They played on and on, a simple game called Brisque; then, after supper, they went to bed.

The subsequent days were identical with the first day, bright and cold, without new snow. Old Gaspard devoted his afternoons to watching the eagles and other rare birds that ventured to the icy summits, while Ulrich repeatedly visited the neck of the Gemmi and contemplated the hamlet. Then the two men played cards, dice, dominoes, winning or losing meager stakes to make their games more interesting.

One morning, Hari, the first to rise, called out to his housemate. A deep, airy, drifting cloud of white spray was falling upon them, around them, noiselessly, burying them little by little under a dense and muffling blanket of foam. It wore on for some four days and four nights. They had to clear the doors and the windows, dig a corridor, and cut steps in order to climb above that icy powder, which twelve hours of frost had made harder than the granite of moraines.

Now they lived like prisoners, scarcely venturing outdoors. They had divided up the chores, which they performed regularly. Ulrich Kunsi took charge of the washing, the scrubbing—all the tasks and labors that involved cleaning. He also chopped the wood, while Gaspard Hari did the cooking and tended the fire. Their work, steady and monotonous, was interrupted by long sessions of cards or dice. They never quarreled, both of them being tranquil and placid. They were never even impatient, grouchy, or nasty, for they had made sure to resign themselves in advance to this hibernation among the peaks.

Sometimes, old Gaspard would take his rifle and go hunting for chamois; he'd kill some now and then. That spelled a festive day for the inn of Schwarenbach and a grand banquet of fresh meat.

One morning, old Gaspard went off as usual. The outdoor thermometer registered eighteen degrees below zero (centigrade). Since the sun hadn't yet risen, the hunter hoped to surprise his prey on the outskirts of the Wildstrubel.

Ulrich, left alone, stayed in bed until ten A.M. He was a sleeper by nature; but he never dared yield to this penchant in the presence of the old guide, an inveterate early riser.

The young man had a leisurely breakfast with Sam, who spent his days and nights dozing in front of the fire; but then, Ulrich felt sad, even frightened because of the solitude, and he was overcome by a need to play the daily game of cards—just as a person is seized with a yearning to submit to an invincible habit.

So Ulrich went out in search of his companion, who was supposed to return by four P.M.

The snow had leveled the entire deep valley, filling the crevasses, covering the two lakes, and shrouding the rocks; now there was nothing between the immense summits but a colossal surface, white and even, icy and blinding.

For the past three weeks, Ulrich hadn't gone back to the rim of the abyss, where he had stared down at the village. He wanted to return there before climbing the slopes that led to the Wildstrubel. By now, Leuk was also snowed in, and the chalets, buried under that pale mantel, were indistinguishable.

Next, turning to the right, Ulrich reached the Lœmmern Glacier. He strode along with a mountaineer's long pace, banging his ironclad stick on the rock-hard snow. And with his piercing eyes, he tried to locate the tiny black dot moving far away, across that boundless expanse.

When Ulrich arrived at the edge of the glacier, he paused, wondering if the old man had actually taken this route; then he hiked along the moraines, swiftly and uneasily.

The day was waning; the snow was becoming rosy; dry, icy gusts blasted across its crystal surface. Ulrich yelled out—a long, shrill, vigorous yell. His voice soared through the deathlike hush of the sleeping mountains; it flew far away, over the deep and inert waves of glacial foam like the cry of a bird over ocean waves; then his cries faded, and there was no response.

He began walking again. The sun had dropped behind the peaks, which were still purpled by the reflections of the sky; however, the depths of the valleys were turning gray. And suddenly, the young man felt scared. It was as if the hush, the cold, the loneliness, the wintry death of those mountains were penetrating him, stopping and freezing his blood, stiffening his limbs, transforming him into an inert and frozen being. And he broke into a run, fleeing toward his shelter. He figured that the old man had returned during his absence. He must have taken a different route; he'd be sitting at the fire, with a dead chamois at his feet.

Soon, Ulrich spotted the inn. No smoke was wafting from the chimney. He ran faster, opened the door. Sam dashed over to welcome him; but Gaspard Hari had not returned.

Kunsi was so frightened that he whirled around, as if he expected to discover his companion hiding in a corner. Then he rekindled the fire and made the soup, still hoping to see the old man show up.

From time to time, he stepped outside to watch for his reappearance. Night had fallen, the pallid night of mountains, the wan night, the livid night, illuminated at the edge of the horizon by a dim, yellow crescent that was ready to vanish behind the summits.

The young man reentered the chalet, sat down, and warmed his feet and his hands while picturing all kinds of accidents.

Gaspard could have broken his leg, fallen into a hole, twisted his ankle. And he might be stretched out on the snow, overwhelmed and stiffened by the cold, with an anguished mind, lost, perhaps shouting for help, yelling at the top of his lungs in the stillness of the night.

But where was he? The mountain was so vast, so rugged, its surroundings so hazardous, that it would have taken one or two dozen guides combing in all directions for a week to find a man in that immensity.

Nevertheless, Ulrich Kunsi resolved to head out with Sam if Gaspard Hari hadn't returned between midnight and one A.M.

And he made his preparations.

He put two days' worth of provisions in a sack, took his steel crampons, slung a long, thin, tough rope around his waist, and checked his ironclad stick and his hatchet, which serves to cut steps in ice. Then he waited. The fire was burning in the hearth; the big dog was snoring in the brightness of the flames; the clock, sounding like a heart, was ticking rhythmically in its sonorous wooden case.

He was waiting, straining his ears to catch any distant noises, shivering when the light breeze grazed the roof and the walls.

Midnight struck; he shuddered. Then, trembling and frightened, he placed the kettle over the fire so that he might drink some hot coffee before setting out.

When the clock struck one, he stood up, awakened Sam, opened the door, and tramped out toward the Wildstrubel. For five hours he climbed, scaling rocks with the aid of his crampons, cutting into the ice, steadily advancing and occasionally, from the end of his rope, hallooing the dog, who had remained at the bottom of a sheer escarpment. It was about six o'clock when Ulrich reached one of the summits where old Gaspard often hunted chamois.

And Ulrich waited for the dawn.

The sky was paling overhead; and suddenly an abrupt and bizarre glimmer, goodness knows from where, lit up the immense ocean of wan peaks, which stretched out for a hundred leagues around him. That vague brightness seemed to emerge from the snow itself and extend into space. Little by little, the highest distant summits were all tinged a delicate, fleshlike rosiness, and the red sun appeared behind the heavy giants of the Bernese Alps.

Ulrich Kunsi moved on. He walked like a hunter, bending over, casting about for footprints, telling the dog: "Search, boy, search."

Now the young man was redescending the mountain, his eyes

scouring the gulches, his voice sometimes shouting, letting out a prolonged hollering, which quickly died in the mute immensity. He then
put his ear to the ground, trying to listen; he believed he could discern
a voice, he started running, calling out again, hearing nothing, and sitting down, worn out, desperate. He ate lunch toward noon and he fed
Sam, who was equally drained. Then Ulrich resumed his pursuit.

When evening came, he was still trudging after covering fifty kilo-
meters in the mountains. Finding himself too far away from home and
too weary to endure much longer, he dug a hole in the snow and
curled up inside it with his dog, under a blanket that he had brought
along. And they huddled together, man and beast, warming each other,
yet freezing to their very marrows.

Ulrich scarcely caught a wink of sleep; he was haunted by visions,
and his limbs were shaking.

Day was dawning when he got up. His legs were as rigid as iron
bars, his spirits low enough to make him shout in anguish, his heart
pounding so deeply that it nearly struck him down whenever he
thought he heard the faintest noise.

Suddenly, it hit him that he was also going to freeze to death in this
solitude, and his fear of dying spurred him on, reawakening his vigor.

He now trekked down toward the inn, falling, standing up, followed
by Sam, who was trailing him at a distance, limping on three legs.

They didn't reach Schwarenbach until four in the afternoon. The
chalet was deserted. The young man got a fire going, he ate and went
to sleep, so dazed that his mind was a blank.

He slept a long time, a very long time—an invincible sleep. All at
once, a voice, a cry, a name: "Ulrich," shook his profound torpor and
made him sit up. Had he been dreaming? Was it one of those bizarre
shouts that lunge through the dreams of troubled minds? No, he could
still hear it, that vibrant shout, which had entered his ears, remaining
in his flesh to the very tips of his sinewy fingers. He was certain; someone had shouted; someone had called out, "Ulrich!" Someone was

there, near the house. He couldn't doubt it. He opened the door and hollered: "Is that you, Gaspard?" with all the strength that his lungs could muster.

There was no response; no sound, no murmur, no sigh, nothing. It was night. The snow was pale.

The wind had risen, the icy wind that breaks stones and lets nothing survive on those abandoned heights. Its sudden blasts were more parching and more lethal than the fiery wind of the desert. Ulrich again hollered: "Gaspard! Gaspard! Gaspard!"

Then he waited. Everything remained silent on the mountain! He was shaken with terror to his very bones. He dashed back to the inn, slammed the door, and bolted it; next, he collapsed on a chair, shivering, convinced that his comrade had called out to him while giving up the ghost.

He was sure of it, the way you're sure that you're alive or eating bread. Old Gaspard Hari had agonized for two days and three nights, somewhere, in some hole, in one of those deep and immaculate ravines whose whiteness is more sinister than subterranean darkness. He had agonized for two days and three nights, and now he had just died while thinking about his companion. And his soul, barely liberated, had flown to the inn, where Ulrich had been sleeping, and it had called to him by that mysterious and horrible power with which the souls of the dead haunt the living. Hari's soul had cried out, that voiceless soul, cried out inside the sleeper's worn-out soul; it had cried out its final farewell— its rebuke or its curse on the man who hadn't searched long enough.

And Ulrich felt it there, very close, behind the wall, behind the door that he had just closed. Hari's soul was roaming like a night bird whose plumage brushes an illuminated window; and the terrified young man was ready to scream in fright. He wanted to escape, but he didn't dare leave; he didn't dare and would never dare, for the ghost would linger, day and night, around the inn, until the old guide's corpse was recovered and laid to rest in the consecrated soil of a cemetery.

Daylight came, and Kunsi regained a little confidence with the brilliant return of the sun. He fixed his meal, made soup for his dog, then he settled on a chair, immobile, with a tortured heart, thinking about the old man lying out on the snow.

When the night again shrouded the mountain, Ulrich was assailed by new terrors. He stepped into the dark kitchen, which was barely lit by a candle flame; he strode to and fro, listening, listening, wondering if the terrifying cry of the previous night was going to break the grim silence outdoors. And he felt alone, miserable, like no man who had ever been alone! He was alone in that immense desert of snow, alone at two thousand meters above the inhabited earth, above human homes, above noisy, throbbing, stirring life, alone under the frozen sky! He was racked by a wild yearning to flee no matter where, no matter how, to descend to Leuk by throwing himself into the abyss; but he didn't dare to even open the door—he was certain that the other man, the dead man, would block his path rather than remain alone up here.

Toward midnight, Ulrich, tired of pacing, overwhelmed with fear and anguish, finally dozed off in his chair, for he was scared of his bed the way you are scared of a haunted place.

And suddenly, the shrill cry of the previous evening tore through his ears, and it was so strident that Ulrich stretched out his arms to shove away the ghost and he tumbled back with his chair.

Sam, awoken by the noise, began howling the way frightened dogs howl, and he rushed around, seeking the source of the danger. Reaching the door, he sniffed under it, snorting and snuffling vigorously, growling, his fur bristling, his tail erect.

Kunsi, horrified, had stood up, and, clutching his chair by one leg, he shouted: "Don't come in, don't come in, don't come in or I'll kill you!" And the dog, agitated by that threat, barked furiously at the invisible enemy who was challenged by his master's voice.

Bit by bit, Sam quieted down and stretched out in front of the hearth; but he remained nervous, snarling through his teeth, with his head raised, his eyes shiny.

Ulrich, in turn, regained his presence of mind; but, practically fainting with terror, he removed a bottle of brandy from the cupboard and tossed off several glassfuls in a row. His mind became hazy; his courage revived; a feverish warmth coursed through his veins.

He ate little the next day, sticking to alcohol. And he spent a few days as a drunken brute. Whenever he thought of Gaspard Hari, he resumed drinking until he collapsed on the floor in a drunken stupor. And he stayed there, facedown, dead drunk, snoring, with torpid limbs. But no sooner had he digested the enraging and burning fluid than the same shout "Ulrich!" awoke him like a bullet that had pierced his skull; and he struggled to his feet, extending his arms to keep from falling, and summoning Sam to help him. And the dog, who seemed to be growing as insane as his master, hurled himself against the door, scratching it with his claws, chewing it with his long, white teeth, while the young man, with his neck thrown back, his head in the air, chugalugged the brandy like cool water after a race, and again the liquor quickly darkened his mind, and his memory, and his frenzied terror.

Within three weeks, he gulped down his entire provision of liquor. But all that his constant drunkenness did was to lull his terror, which then awoke more furious because it was impossible to blot out. His obsession, exacerbated by a month of intoxication and increasing endlessly in the absolute solitude, dug into him like a drill. He trod through the chalet like a caged beast, putting his ear to the door, trying to hear if the other man was there, challenging him through the wall.

Then, when vanquished by fatigue and dozing, he heard the voice that made him jump to his feet.

Finally, one night, like a coward pushed to the breaking point, he rushed to the door and yanked it open to see the man who was calling him and to force him to shut up.

He received a blast of cold air in his face; it chilled him to the bones. He instantly closed and bolted the door without noticing that Sam had lunged outdoors. Then, shivering, Ulrich threw some more wood into the fire and sat down in front of it to warm himself; but suddenly, he shuddered, someone was scratching the wall and weeping.

Bewildered, he shouted: "Go away!" The sole response was a long and doleful wail.

Any vestige of his sanity was swept away by his terror. He kept reiterating, "Go away," while whirling around, looking for a corner to hide in. The other person, still weeping, moved along the chalet, rubbing against the wall. Ulrich tore over to the oaken cupboard, which was crammed with tableware and provisions, and, lifting it up with superhuman force, he dragged it to the door, forming a barricade. Then, piling up whatever furniture was left—mattresses, straw pads, chairs—he stopped up the window as one does against an enemy siege.

But the person outside was now moaning loudly and grimly, and the young man was responding with his own moans.

And days and nights wore by, filled with endless mutual howling. One being kept circling the chalet, scratching the walls so powerfully as if trying to demolish them; the person inside followed all those movements, bent over, his ear to the stone, and he answered all those cries with dreadful shouts.

One evening, Ulrich heard nothing; and when he sat down, he was so broken with fatigue that he instantly nodded off.

He awoke with no memory, no thought, as if his entire mind had been drained during his profound sleep. He was hungry, he ate.

———

The winter ended. The Gemmi Pass reopened; and the Hauser family headed back to their inn.

Upon reaching the top of their climb, the women mounted their mule and they talked about the two men they'd soon be finding.

They were astonished that, despite the cleared road, neither man had descended several days earlier to tell them about their long hibernation.

The Hausers finally sighted the snowbound inn. The door and the window were shut; a thread of smoke was curling up from the chimney, which reassured Father Hauser. But upon drawing nearer, he spotted a big skeleton lying on its side at the threshold, the bones picked clean by eagles.

They all examined the skeleton. "That must be Sam," said the mother. And she called out: "Hey! Gaspard!" A cry resounded from the interior, a shrill cry that sounded like an animal's shriek. Father Hauser repeated: "Hey! Gaspard!" They heard a second cry, similar to the first.

Then the four men—the father and his three sons—tried to open the door. It resisted. Going to the deserted stable, they grabbed a long beam as a battering ram and they smashed it full force into the door. The wood groaned, yielded, shattered to pieces; then a loud noise shook the chalet, and, peering inside, behind the overturned cupboard, they saw a man standing, his hair down to his shoulders, a beard down to his chest, his eyes shining, his body covered with rags.

They didn't recognize him, until Louise Hauser exclaimed: "It's Ulrich, Mama!" And the mother saw that it was Ulrich, even though his hair was white.

He let them come over; he let them touch him; but he didn't reply to their questions; they had to bring him to Leuk, where the physicians confirmed that he was insane.

And no one has ever found out what happened to his companion.

That summer, Louise Hauser nearly died of decline, an illness attributed to the cold mountain air.

A Day in the Country

For five months now they had been planning to have lunch beyond the outskirts of Paris in order to celebrate the birthday of Madame Dufour, whose patron saint was Saint Pétronille. And so, having eagerly looked forward to this excursion, they had risen very early in the morning.

Monsieur Dufour, borrowing the milkman's cart, drove it himself. This was a very nice two-wheeler; its hood was supported by four iron poles, and the attached curtains were pulled up so the passengers could see the countryside. Only the back curtain fluttered in the wind like a flag. The wife, at her husband's side, looked splendid in an extraordinary cerise silk gown. Finally, an old grandmother and a young girl sat on two chairs, while all that was visible of the boy was his blond hair, since, for lack of a seat, he stretched out on the bottom of the conveyance.

After heading down Avenue des Champs-Élysées and crossing the fortifications at the Gate of Maillot, the travelers got to see the country.

Upon reaching the Neuilly Bridge, Monsieur Dufour said: "The country at last!" And, at that cue, his wife waxed maudlin about nature.

At the Courbevoie traffic circle, they were overwhelmed with admiration for the vast sweep of the horizons. To the right lay Argenteuil with its towering church spire; above it, they could see the knolls of Sannois and the Orgemont Hill. To the left, the Marly aqueduct stood out against the clear morning sky, and the group could also view the far-off terrace of Saint-Germain; while, facing them, some removals of earth at the end of a chain of hills marked the new fort of Cormeilles. Way, way in the tremendous distance, beyond the plains and the villages, they spotted the somber greenery of forests.

The sun was starting to burn the passengers' faces; the dust kept filling their eyes; and, on both sides of the road, an endlessly naked country unfolded, grimy and smelly. It seemed ravaged by leprosy, which was chewing away at the very houses, for the dilapidated and abandoned skeletons of small cottages, left unfinished by penniless entrepreneurs, each held their four roofless walls gaping aloft.

Here and there, the barren soil emitted tall factory chimneys—the sole vegetation in these putrid fields, where the spring breeze carried the stench of schist and petroleum mingling with an even less agreeable odor.

Eventually, they crossed the Seine a second time, over a bridge with a ravishing view. The river was exploding with light; a mist was rising, dried by the sun; and the travelers felt a sweet tranquillity, a bountiful freshness when they were finally breathing a purer air that had not swept through the black smoke of factories or the miasmas of refuse dumps.

A passerby told them the name of the region: Bezons.

The vehicle halted, and Monsieur Dufour began to read the appealing outside menu of a cheap eatery: "Restaurant Poulin, fish stews, fried fish, private rooms, arbors, and swings."

"Very well, Madame Dufour. How do you like it? Are you gonna make up your mind finally?"

His wife read the sign in turn: "Restaurant Poulin, fish stews, fried fish, private rooms, arbors, and swings." Then she gazed at the house for a long time.

It was a white roadside country inn. The open door revealed the brilliant zinc of the counter, where two workers were lingering in their Sunday best.

Finally, Madame Dufour made up her mind: "Okay, it's nice," she said. "And besides, there's the view."

The cart rolled behind the restaurant, into a vast courtyard filled with big trees and separated from the Seine only by the towpath.

The passengers got out. The husband jumped down first, then he opened his arms to receive his wife. There was quite a gap between the vehicle and the footboard, which was held up by two iron branches, and in order to reach it, Madame Dufour had to expose the bottom of a once slender leg, which was now disappearing under an invasion of fat from the thighs.

Monsieur Dufour, already exhilarated by the country, sharply pinched her calf; then, taking her into his arms, he deposited her heavily on the ground as if she were an enormous bundle.

She dusted off her silk dress and then peered around.

Madame Dufour was a woman in her mid-thirties, corpulent, in full bloom, and a delight to see. It was a struggle for her to breathe, tightly laced as she was in her harsh corset; and the pressure of that device shoved the fluctuant mass of her overabundant bosom up to her double chin.

Next, the girl, placing her hand on her father's shoulder, lightly sprang out by herself. The yellow-haired youth had gotten down by putting one foot on a wheel and he now helped Monsieur Dufour to bring down the grandmother.

Then they unhitched the horse and tied it to a tree; and the cart swooped on its nose, with the two shafts on the ground. Pulling off their frock coats, the men washed their hands in a bucket of water, then rejoined their ladies, who were already on the swings.

Mademoiselle Dufour tried to swing standing up, all alone, but failed to gain enough momentum. She was a beautiful girl of nineteen or twenty, one of those women who, when you pass them on the street, lash you with sudden desire and leave you, until nightfall, in a state of vague disquiet and an upheaval of the senses. Tall, with a small waist and broad hips, she had a very dark complexion, very big eyes, very black hair. Her dress sharply brought out the solid fullness of her flesh, which was further accentuated by the movements of her haunches as she tried to soar aloft. Her tensed arms held the ropes over her head, so that her bosom heaved, without jolting, at every surge of impetus. Her hat, swept away by a gust of wind, had landed behind her; and the swing lunged bit by bit, each return baring her delicate legs up to the knees and fanning the air of her petticoats into the faces of the laughing men—an air more intoxicating than the fumes of wine.

Madame Dufour, who was sitting on the other swing, kept emitting long, continuous whimpers: "Cyprien, come and give me a push, Cyprien!" Eventually, he went over, and, rolling up his shirtsleeves as if to perform some labor, he had an infinitely hard time pushing his wife into motion.

Clinging to the ropes, she kept her legs straight out to avoid touching the ground and she enjoyed the dizziness caused by the to-and-fro of the swing, and her shaken figure quivered nonstop like jelly on a plate. However, as the swooping and zooming grew more and more intense, she felt giddy and frightened. At each plunge, she emitted a piercing shriek that attracted all the guttersnipes in the area; over there, before her, above the garden hedge, she vaguely discerned a row of mischievous faces that were diversely twisted with laughter.

A waitress came over, and the family ordered lunch.

"Fried catch of the day, sautéed rabbit, a salad, and dessert," Madame Dufour articulated with an air of importance.

"Bring us two liters of wine plus a bottle of Bordeaux," said her husband.

"We'll have a picnic," their daughter added.

The grandmother, seized with affection for the house cat, had been following her for ten minutes and uselessly lavishing the sweetest appellations on her. The animal, inwardly flattered no doubt by all that attention, stayed very near the old lady's hand, but without letting herself get caught, and she tranquilly made the round of the trees, rubbing against them, keeping her tail erect and purring with pleasure.

"Hey!" the yellow-haired youth cried suddenly, scouring the terrain. "Those are fabulous boats!" They all went to have a look. In a small wooden boathouse, two superb skiffs, as beautifully finished as deluxe furniture, were hanging side by side like two tall and svelte girls; suspended in their long, narrow, shiny slenderness, they made you want to float downstream in the soft and lovely summer evenings or clear summer mornings, drift close to the flower-covered banks, where the trees dip all their branches into the water, where the reeds rustle eternally, and where the swift kingfishers dart like blue flashes.

The entire family gazed respectfully at the two skiffs.

"Oh, wow! They're fabulous," Monsieur Dufour repeated earnestly, and he assessed them like a connoisseur. In his youth he, too, had rowed, he, too, he said; and when he'd had them in his hands (and he pulled on imaginary oars), he hadn't given a damn about anybody. He had beaten any number of Brits way back when, at the Joinville regattas; he joked about the word "ladies," the term for the two stanchions that hold the oars, and he said that the rowers never went out without their "ladies"—and for good reason. He grew hot and bothered while speechifying and he obstinately offered to bet that in a skiff like this he could cover six leagues an hour without exerting himself.

"Lunch is ready," said the waitress, appearing at the entrance. They hurried over; but two young men were already occupying the best spot, which Madame Dufour had mentally picked out. The two men must have been the owners of the skiffs, for they sported rowing costumes.

They were stretched out on chairs, almost reclining, their faces were sunburned and their chests were covered with only thin, white cotton jerseys, exposing their bare arms, which were as robust as a blacksmith's. These were two strapping young men, showing off their strength, yet all the movements of their limbs revealed the supple grace that is acquired by exercise, a grace so different from the deformation suffered by a worker's strenuously repeated labor.

The two rowers exchanged a quick smile upon seeing the mother and a glance upon spotting the daughter. "Why don't we give them our place?" said one man. "That way we can make their acquaintance." The other man instantly stood up, and, doffing his red-and-black cap, he chivalrously offered to let the ladies have the only area that wasn't struck by the sun. The family accepted with profuse apologies; and to make the lunch more rustic, they settled directly on the grass without a table or chairs.

The two young men carried their settings a few steps away and resumed eating. The girl was slightly troubled by the sight of their bare arms, which they displayed endlessly. She even pretended to turn her head and ignore them, while her bolder mother, whose feminine curiosity—and perhaps desire—was piqued, kept staring at those arms, comparing them, regretfully no doubt, to her husband's concealed ugliness.

She squatted on the grass, crossing her legs like a tailor, and she kept on wriggling, claiming that ants had gotten into her somewhere. Monsieur Dufour, disgruntled by the presence and the friendliness of the strangers, was trying to find a comfortable position, but failed, and the yellow-haired youth silently crammed down his food like a pig.

"Lovely weather we're having, Monsieur," the fat woman said to one of the rowers. She wanted to be amiable because they had given their place to the family. "Yes, Madame," he replied. "Do you visit the country often?"

"Oh, just once or twice a year, for a bit of fresh air. And you, Monsieur?"

"I come and sleep here every night."

"Ah, that must be very pleasant."

"It certainly is, Madame."

And he described his everyday life, poetically, and these city-dwellers, deprived of grass and starved for country outings, felt their hearts quiver with that idiotic love of nature that haunts them all year long, behind their shop counters.

The girl, deeply moved, looked up and peered at the rower. Monsieur Dufour broke his silence. "Now, that's what I call living," he said. Then he added: "Another bite of rabbit, my dear?"

"No thanks, darling."

She turned back to the young men, and, pointing to their arms, she asked: "You never feel cold like that?"

The two men burst out laughing, and they astounded the family with tales of their prodigious spells of fatigue, their bathing though drenched with sweat, their races during misty nights; and they thumped their chests vehemently to show the results.

"Oh, you look very solid," said the husband, who no longer talked about beating the Brits.

The girl now examined them askance; and the yellow-haired youth, who choked on some wine, was coughing desperately, dripping on Madame Dufour's cerise silk frock; furious, she ordered some water to wash out the stains.

Meanwhile, the heat was becoming terrible. The sparkling river looked like a burning hearth, and the wines were going to the diners' heads.

Monsieur Dufour, overwhelmed by violent hiccups, had unbuttoned his vest and the top of his trousers; while his wife, who was suffocating, was gradually undoing her dress. The youth was cheerfully shaking his mop of flaxen hair and pouring himself glass after glass. The grandmother, feeling tipsy, remained very rigid and very dignified. As for the girl, she revealed nothing; only her eyes lit up vaguely, and her dark cheeks took on a rosier tinge.

The coffee finished them off. The diners spoke about singing, and each person sang his ditty, which the others frantically applauded. Then they struggled to their feet; and while the two women, who felt dizzy, took in some fresh air, the two men, dead drunk, tried to perform gymnastics. Heavy, limp, their faces crimson, they dangled awkwardly from the rings, unable to pull themselves up; and their shirts continually threatened to abandon the trousers and flap in the wind like banners.

Meanwhile, the two boatmen had pushed their skiffs into the water, and they now returned and offered the ladies an outing.

"Monsieur Dufour, do you mind? Please!" his wife exclaimed. He gazed at her, drunk, uncomprehending. Then one boatman came over, clutching two fishing rods. The hope of catching a gudgeon, that ideal of shopkeepers, lit up the husband's dismal eyes; he agreed to anything and he settled in the shade under the bridge, his legs dangling over the river, while the yellow-haired youth dozed off next to him.

One of the rowers sacrificed himself: he took the mother. "Let's go to the small woods on the Ile aux Anglais!" he cried as he left.

The other skiff moved more slowly. The rower was staring so intensely at the girl that he could focus on nothing else, and his strength was paralyzed by his overpowering emotions.

Sitting at the helm, the girl yielded to the gentle flow of the water. She lost all interest in thinking, her limbs were thoroughly relaxed, she felt she was fully abandoning herself, as if utterly intoxicated. Her face was deeply flushed, she was panting. The dizziness caused by the wine was aggravated by the torrential heat rustling all around her and making all the trees bow to her as she passed. A vague need for delight, a fermentation of her blood imbued her flesh, which was excited by that steamy day; and she was also troubled by her tête-à-tête on the water, in the middle of this rustic area, which was depopulated because of the blazing sky—her tête-à-tête with this young man, who found her beautiful, whose eyes kissed her skin, and whose desire was as penetrating as the sunshine.

Their inability to speak augmented their feelings, and so they gazed at their surroundings. Finally, pulling himself together, he asked for her name. "Henriette," she said.

"Hey! My name is Henri," he responded.

The sound of their voices had calmed them; they checked out the bank. The other skiff had stopped and appeared to be waiting for them. The rower called out: "We'll hitch up with you in the woods. We're heading for Robinson, because Madame Dufour is thirsty." Then he bent over his oars and rowed away so quickly that they soon lost sight of him.

Meanwhile, a continuous roar, which they had been dimly hearing for some time, was approaching very rapidly. The river itself seemed to thrill as if that dull noise were mounting from its depths.

"What's that racket?" she asked. It was the noise of the weir, which sliced the river in two at the level of the island. The rower was confusedly explaining it, when, across the hubbub of the waterfall, they caught the very distant warbling of a bird. "Listen," he said, "the nightingales are singing in the daytime. The females must be brooding."

A nightingale! She had never heard one, and the thought of listening to one stirred her heart, arousing a vision of poetic tenderness. A nightingale! The invisible witness of trysts, evoked by Juliet on her balcony; that heavenly music attuned to human kisses; that eternal inspirer of all the languorous ballads that divulge an azure ideal to the poor little hearts of emotional girls!

So she wanted to hear a nightingale.

"Don't make any noise," said her companion. "We can slip into the woods and sit down near the bird."

The skiff seemed to be gliding. Trees emerged on the island, where the bank was so low that your eyes could pierce the density of the thickets. The skiff stopped; it was moored. And with Henriette leaning on Henri's arm, they advanced between the branches. "Stoop," he said. She stooped, and they headed through an inextricable tangle of vines, leaves, and rushes, an undiscoverable sanctuary, which you had to know about, and which the young man called his "private office."

Directly overhead, perched in one of the sheltering trees, the bird was still singing its head off. It emitted trills and roulades, then held lengthy, vibrating sounds that filled the air and seemed to merge into the horizon, unrolling along the river and soaring beyond the plains, across the blazing silence that weighed down the entire countryside.

Fearful of startling the bird, they held their tongues. They sat there side by side, and Henri's arm gradually circled her waist, squeezing it softly. She kept taking that audacious hand, but without anger, and pushing it away whenever it approached her. Though she wasn't at all embarrassed by that caress, as if it were something natural that she was opposing just as naturally.

She listened to the bird, lost in ecstasy. She felt infinite desires for happiness, abrupt tenderness that swept through her, revelations of divine poetry, and a melting of her nerves and her heart—a melting so deep that she wept without knowing why. The young man now held her tight; she no longer resisted, it didn't occur to her.

All at once, the nightingale stopped singing. A distant voice shouted: "Henriette!"

"Don't answer," he whispered. "You'll scare away the bird."

She had no intention of answering.

They remained like that for a while. Madame Dufour must have settled somewhere, for every so often they vaguely heard faint cries from the fat lady, who was probably being teased by the other boatman.

The girl was still weeping, imbued as she was with very sweet sensations, her warm skin alive with unfamiliar pricklings. Henri's head was on her shoulder; and suddenly he kissed her on the lips. She furiously rebelled, and, trying to avoid him, she struggled up. But he threw himself upon her, covering her entire body. He kept pursuing that fleeing mouth for a long while, and, finding it, he placed his lips on hers. Terrified by wild desire, she returned his kiss, hugging him on her bosom, and all her resistance collapsed as if crushed by an overpowering weight.

Everything was tranquil around them. The bird resumed its warbling. First it emitted three penetrating notes, which sounded like an appeal for love; next, after a momentary silence, its weakened voice launched into very slow modulations.

A soft breeze wafted, drawing murmurs from the leaves; and two ardent sighs emerged from the depths of the branches, blending with the singing of the nightingale and the soft breathing of the forest. The bird was intoxicated, and its voice, intensifying like a kindled fire or a growing passion, seemed to accompany a rustling of kisses under the tree. Suddenly, the delirium of the nightingale's throat exploded wildly. Now and then, it swooned for long stretches or went through deep, melodious spasms.

At times, it rested a bit, smoothly warbling just two or three light notes, then suddenly ending them on a high-pitched note. Or else it shot forth wildly, with spurts of scales, jolts, tremors, like a furious love song, followed by cries of triumph.

At last, it stopped singing and it listened to a moan down below, a moan so profound that it could have been taken for the farewell of a soul. The noise lasted for a while and then ended in a sob.

They were very pale, both of them, as they left their bed of greenery. The blue sky looked dark to them; the blazing sunshine was snuffed for their eyes; they perceived only silence and solitude. They walked together quickly, not speaking, not touching, for they seemed to have become irreconcilable enemies, as if disgust had risen between their bodies and hatred between their minds.

From time to time, Henriette shouted: "Mama!"

A tumult was heard under some bushes. Henri thought he had spotted a white petticoat quickly pulled down over a thick calf; and the enormous lady appeared, slightly confused and even more flushed, her eyes sparkling and her bosom stormy, too close, perhaps, to her neighbor. The latter must have seen very interesting things, for his face was wrinkled with abrupt laughter that he couldn't choke back.

Madame Dufour tenderly took his arm, and they returned to the boats. Henri, walking in front, still mute at the girl's side, thought he could suddenly discern a deep, stifled kiss.

They were finally back in Bezons.

Monsieur Dufour, having sobered up, was extremely impatient. The yellow-haired youth was eating a snack before leaving the inn. The cart was ready in the courtyard, and the grandmother, who had already gotten in, was desperately afraid of being overtaken by night in the grasslands since the surroundings of Paris were unsafe.

Everyone shook hands, and the Dufour family departed. "Au revoir!" the boatmen shouted. The only response was a sigh and a tear.

———

Two months later, while walking along Rue des Martyrs, Henri read a sign over a door: "Dufour, Ironmonger."

He went in.

The fat lady was growing fatter at the counter. They instantly recognized one another, and after a thousand courtesies, he asked her for any news. "And how is Mademoiselle Henriette?"

"Very well, thank you, she got married."

"Ah! . . ."

He was overwhelmed; then he managed to ask: "Whom did she marry?"

"Why, the young man who accompanied us, you know. He'll be taking over our business."

"Oh, that's perfect."

He left in a very sad mood, not quite knowing why he felt sad.

Madame Dufour called him back.

"What about your friend?" she ventured timidly.

"Why, he's fine."

"Give him our very best, okay? And if he happens to be in the neighborhood, tell him to drop by. . . ."

She reddened, then added: "Tell him I'd be delighted to see him."

"I won't forget. Good-bye."

"No. See you soon!"

———

The following year, on a very hot Sunday, all the details of that adventure, which Henri had never forgotten, came to him suddenly, and they were so sharp and so desirable that he returned all alone to their chamber in the woods.

He was stupefied when he arrived. She was there, sitting on the grass, melancholy; while at her side, in his shirtsleeves, her husband, the yellow-haired youth, was sleeping a crude sleep.

She blanched so intensely upon seeing Henri that he thought she was about to faint. Then they began talking naturally, as if nothing had ever happened between them.

But when he told her that he loved this place and that he often came to relax here on a Sunday, while thinking about the past, she gazed into his eyes for a long time.

"I think about it every evening," she said.

"Hey, darling," her husband yawned, "I think it's time we headed back."

The Hand

The guests had formed a circle around Monsieur Bermutier, the examining magistrate, who was airing his opinion about the mysterious Saint-Cloud affair. For a month now, Paris had been in a state of alarm about that inexplicable crime. It was beyond comprehension.

Monsieur Bermutier, standing with his back to the hearth, was talking, citing evidence, discussing the diverse views, but reaching no conclusion.

Several women had gotten up, coming over and remaining on their feet as they gazed at the magistrate's clean-shaven lips, which emitted earnest words. The women shivered, shuddered, wincing with their curious fear, the avid and insatiable need for horror that haunts a woman's soul, torturing her like hunger pangs.

During a pause, one woman, paler than the rest, murmured: "It's dreadful. It's almost supernatural. We'll never know the truth."

The magistrate addressed her: "No, madame, we'll probably never know anything. As for the word 'supernatural,' that you have just used, it has no place in this matter. We are dealing with a very skillfully planned, very skillfully perpetrated crime so mystifying that we cannot sever it from its impenetrable context. I myself once had to investigate a case that truly seemed to verge on fantasy. Incidentally, I had to shelve it for lack of clear-cut evidence."

A few women joined in so quickly that their voices sounded as one: "Oh! Tell us about it!"

Monsieur Bermutier smiled gravely, as an examining magistrate should smile. He resumed: "Now, don't think for even a moment that I might have inferred there could be anything supernatural about that affair. I believe purely in normal causes. It would be a lot better if, instead of applying the term 'supernatural' to things beyond our ken, we simply employed the word 'inexplicable.' In any case, what so deeply moved me in this matter was, above all, the overall context, the circumstances leading up to it. Well, here are the facts."

—

At that time, I was an examining magistrate in Ajaccio, a small white Corsican town on the shores of a beautiful gulf enclosed by towering mountains.

The cases I investigated were mostly vendettas. And there are superb vendettas, utterly dramatic ones, fierce, heroic. They include the finest vengeances we can dream of, age-old hatreds, appeased for an instant but never snuffed, abominable ruses, murders that become massacres and almost glorious actions. For two years, I had been hearing about nothing but the price of blood, the horrible tradition that compels a Corsican to avenge any wrong inflicted by him, avenge it even on a perpetrator's near and dear and on his descendants. I had seen old men, infants, cousins with their throats cut; my head was teeming with such stories.

One day, I learned that an Englishman had rented a small villa at the far end of the gulf, intending to stay for several years. He was accompanied by a French manservant he had engaged while passing through Marseilles.

Soon the whole populace was abuzz about this bizarre man, who kept to himself and never went out except to hunt and to fish. He spoke to no one, he never came to town, and he spent an hour or two every morning practicing with his pistol and his rifle.

Rumors sprang up about him. Some people claimed that he was a distinguished person fleeing his country for political reasons; others affirmed that he was in hiding after committing a dreadful crime. People even mentioned some particularly awful circumstances.

In my quality as examining magistrate, I wanted to gather information about that man; but I was unable to find anything. He went by the name of Sir John Rowell.

So I contented myself with keeping a close watch over him; but actually, nothing suspicious was reported to me.

Nevertheless, as rumors about this foreigner continued, expanded, and broadened in scope, I resolved to seek him out; and so I began hunting regularly in the area around his property.

It took me a long time to find an opportunity. One presented itself when I shot down a partridge right in front of the Englishman's nose. My hound brought me the bird; but, promptly taking my prey, I went to apologize to Sir John Rowell and ask him to accept the dead partridge.

He was a tall man with red hair and a red beard, very big, very broad—a sort of placid and polished Hercules. He had none of the stiffness attributed to the British, and, in a sharp English accent, he thanked me profusely for my civility. Within a month we had chatted five or six times.

Finally, one evening, as I was passing his door, I found him smoking a pipe while straddling a chair in his garden. I greeted him and he invited me to come and have a glass of beer. I didn't wait to be asked twice.

He welcomed me with all the meticulous courtesy of an Englishman, spoke glowingly about France and Corsica, and declared that he loved this countryside and this coast.

Very gingerly and feigning very keen interest, I asked him about his life and his future plans. He replied without hesitating and told me that he had traveled a lot: in Africa, India, America. He added with a laugh: "I had much adventure! Oh, yes!"

Then I returned to the subject of hunting, and he supplied the most curious details about hunting hippopotamuses, tigers, elephants, and even gorillas.

I said: "All those animals are dangerous."

He smiled: "Oh, no! The most dangerous of all was man!"

He burst out laughing—the laughter of a big and content Englishman. "I've hunted my share of men too!"

Then he talked about weapons and he invited me indoors to show me various rifle systems.

His drawing room was hung with black silk embroidered in gold. Large yellow flowers, blazing like fire, stood out against the dark material.

He announced: "That's a Japanese fabric."

Then, in the center of the largest panel, something weird caught my eye. A black object loomed out against a red velvet square. I went over: it was a hand, a human hand. Not a clean white skeleton's hand but a dried black hand with yellow nails, bared muscles, and traces of old blood, blood like filth, on the bones, which had been chopped straight through, as if by an ax, halfway up the forearm.

Around the wrist, an enormous iron chain, riveted and soldered, affixed this dirty member to the wall by means of a ring that was powerful enough to hold an elephant.

I asked: "What's that?"

The Englishman tranquilly replied: "That was my worst enemy. He came from America. His hand was sliced off by a saber, flayed by a sharp pebble, and dried in the sun for a week. Ah, it was very lucky for me, I tell you."

I touched that human relic, which must have belonged to a colossus. The fingers, exceedingly long, were attached by mammoth tendons, which had bits of skin here and there. That skinned hand was an appalling sight; it automatically recalled some savage vengeance.

I said: "That man must have been very strong."

The Englishman gently murmured: "Oh, yes. But I was stronger. I put that chain on him to hold him down."

I thought he was joking. I said: "The chain is quite useless now. The hand won't escape."

Sir John Rowell gravely continued: "It kept wanting to leave. The chain was necessary."

I quickly scanned his face, wondering to myself: "Is he crazy or making a bad joke?"

But his features remained impenetrable, benevolent, and peaceful. I changed the subject and I told him how greatly I admired his rifles.

However, I noticed that three loaded revolvers were lying out on the furniture as if their owner lived in constant fear of attack.

I revisited him several times. Then I stopped. The town was now accustomed to his presence; people took him for granted.

———

A whole year wore by. One morning in late November, my butler woke me up and announced that Sir John Rowell had been murdered that night.

Half an hour later, I entered the Englishman's villa together with the police superintendent and the gendarmerie captain. The valet, distraught and desperate, was weeping at the door. I suspected him at first, but he was innocent.

The culprit was never found.

Upon stepping into Sir John's drawing room, I promptly spotted the corpse; it was lying on its back in the middle of the room.

The Englishman's vest was ripped, a torn-off sleeve was dangling, everything indicated that a terrible struggle had occurred.

The Englishman had been strangled to death! His black, swollen, horrifying face appeared to express a gruesome dread; his teeth were clenched on something; and his neck, pierced with five holes that looked like stab wounds, was covered with blood.

A physician joined us. He examined the finger traces in the flesh for a long time and then uttered these strange words: "It's as if he'd been strangled by a skeleton."

I shuddered and I glanced at the wall, at the place where I had seen that horrible flayed hand. It was gone. The broken chain was dangling in the air.

Next I knelt down to view the corpse, and, in the petrified mouth, I found one of the fingers of that vanished hand: the teeth had cut it off or rather sawed it off at the second joint.

Then we began a thorough investigation of the premises. We unearthed nothing. No door had been forced, no window, no furniture. The two guard dogs hadn't awoken.

Here is a brief outline of the valet's deposition:

For the past month, his master had seemed agitated. He had received numerous letters, burning each one.

In an anger verging on madness, he had often grabbed a whip and furiously lashed that dried-out hand, which had been chained to the wall and which, at the time of the murder, had been removed—goodness knew how.

Sir John had always retired very late and locked himself in carefully. He had always had firearms within reach. And he had frequently spoken aloud at night as if arguing with someone.

That night, as it happened, he had kept silent. And it was only upon coming to open the windows that the valet had discovered the murder. He didn't suspect anybody.

I passed on whatever I knew about Sir John to the magistrates and the police officials, and they undertook a scrupulous search of the entire island. They discovered nothing.

Now one night, three months after the crime, I had an awful nightmare. It seemed to me that I saw the hand, the ghastly hand, scuttle like a spider or a scorpion across my walls and my curtains. I awoke three times, I fell asleep three times, I saw the hideous relic gallop around my room three times, using its fingers as legs.

The next morning, they brought me the hand: it had been found on the grave of Sir John, who had been buried in the cemetery because they had been unable to locate any family. The forefinger was missing.

That, ladies, is my story. And that is all I know about that matter.

—

The women were shocked, they were pale and trembling. One of them exclaimed: "But that's no way to finish your story, there's no explanation! We won't get a wink of sleep if you don't tell us what you think really happened."

The magistrate smiled grimly.

"Well, ladies, I guess I'll be giving you scary dreams. I quite simply feel that the legitimate owner of the hand wasn't dead and that he had come to reclaim it with his remaining hand. But I can't figure out how he managed to pull it off. It was a sort of vendetta."

One of the women murmured: "No, that can't be it."

And the examining magistrate, still smirking, concluded: "I did tell you that you wouldn't care for my explanation."

The Jewels

Upon meeting the girl at a party given by the assistant head of his office, Monsieur Lantin fell for her hook, line, and sinker.

She was the daughter of a provincial tax collector, who had died several years ago. She had then moved to Paris with her mother, who frequented a few solid homes in the neighborhood, hoping to find a husband for the girl. They were poor and honorable, quiet and unassuming. The girl seemed the very epitome of the virtuous spouse to whom any sensible young man dreams of entrusting his life. Her unpretentious beauty had the charm of angelic purity, and the imperceptible smile that always haunted her lips seemed like a reflection of her heart.

Everybody sang her praises; anyone who knew her kept repeating, "The man who lands her will be a lucky stiff. You won't find a better wife."

And so Monsieur Lantin, chief clerk at the Ministry of the Interior, with an annual salary of three thousand five hundred francs, asked for her hand and then married her.

He was unbelievably happy with her. She ran the household so skillfully and so economically that they appeared to be enjoying a life of luxury. There was no attention, no delicacy, no refinement that she didn't shower her husband with, and she was so seductive that even six years after their first encounter he loved her more than in the beginning.

There were only two things he reproached her for: her love of the theater and her love of false gems.

Her girlfriends (she knew the wives of some petty officials) always managed to get her a box at the latest hit and even at a premiere or two; and she dragged along her husband—willing or not—to such entertainments, which he found horribly exhausting after a day's work. He'd beg her to attend with some lady in her acquaintanceship, who would then bring her back immediately. It took her a long time to give in, since she didn't find this arrangement quite proper. But she finally yielded just to be nice, and he was tremendously grateful.

Now, because of this love for the theater, she soon needed to adorn herself. Her wardrobe remained simple, true enough, and always in good taste, though modest; indeed, her gentle grace—her humble and sunny, her irresistible grace—seemed to acquire a new charm from the simplicity of her gowns. However, she got into the habit of wearing two big rhinestone eardrops—which glittered like diamonds—plus fake-pearl necklaces, pinchbeck bracelets, and combs studded with varied beads that looked like precious stones.

Her husband, a bit shocked by this passion for frippery, kept reiterating: "Darling, if a woman can't afford real jewels, then she appears only in her grace and beauty. Those are the rarest gems."

But she smiled sweetly and repeated: "What can I say. I like jewelry. It's my vice. I know you're right, but a leopard can't change its spots. I would just love to own some real jewels!"

And she ran the pearl necklaces through her fingers, making the facets of cut crystal flash in the light, and saying: "Just look how well crafted they are. You could swear they were genuine."

He would smile, declaring: "You've got a Gypsy's taste."

On some evenings, when they remained alone at the fireplace, she would put the morocco box on the tea table—the box containing what her husband called her tinsel—and she began examining those imitation jewels as passionately as if savoring some profound and secret delight. And she slipped a string around her husband's neck, laughing with all her heart and exclaiming: "How funny you look!" Then she threw her arms around him and kissed him wildly.

One winter night, upon returning from the opera, she was shaking with cold. The next day she was coughing. A week later, she succumbed to pneumonia.

Lantin nearly followed her to the grave. His despair was so dreadful that his hair turned white within a month. He wept from morning to evening, his soul ravaged by an intolerable agony and haunted by her memory, by her smile, by her voice, by all the dead woman's charm.

Nor did time ease his pain. At his office, when his colleagues were chitchatting about mundane things, his cheeks would often abruptly swell up, his nose would wrinkle, his eyes fill with tears; and with a terrible grimace, he would burst into sobs.

He kept his spouse's bedroom intact and he locked himself in there every day in order to think about her; and all the furniture, all her clothing remained in its place, the same as on the last day.

Normal life proved harsh for him. His income, which, in his wife's hands, had covered all their needs, was now insufficient for him alone. And he wondered, stupefied, how she had managed to provide him with excellent wines and delicate foods that he could no longer afford on his modest resources.

He incurred some debts and chased after money like people reduced to frantic expedients. Then, one morning, finding himself totally penniless an entire week before the end of the month, he wondered if he should sell anything; and he instantly thought about unloading his wife's "tinsel," for in his heart of hearts, he had always resented those phony and irritating trinkets. The very sight of them each day marred his memory of his beloved.

He spent a long time combing through the pile of gewgaws left by his wife, for she had kept buying them obstinately until the very end, bringing home a new object almost every evening. Finally, he decided on the large necklace that had apparently been her favorite, and that, he mused, could fetch seven or eight francs, since the workmanship was actually quite intricate for a bogus gem.

He slipped it into his pocket and headed toward his ministry by way of the boulevards, seeking a jewelry shop that could inspire his trust.

Eventually he spotted one and entered it, a bit embarrassed to be displaying his poverty by trying to sell such a worthless item.

"Monsieur," he said to the jeweler, "I'd like to know the value of this piece."

The merchant took hold of the article, examined it, turned it over, weighed it in his hand, picked up a loupe, called his assistant, murmured a few remarks to him, placed the necklace back on the counter, and gazed at it from a distance in order to judge the effect.

Monsieur Lantin, annoyed by all these ceremonies, was about to say, "Oh, I know it's worthless!" when the jeweler cut him off: "Monsieur, it's worth twelve to fifteen thousand francs, but I can't buy it unless you tell me exactly where you acquired it."

The widower gaped and gawked, unable to comprehend. Eventually he stammered: "What's that? Are you sure?"

The jeweler misunderstood Lantin's amazement and he dryly added: "You can try to do better somewhere else. But I feel it's worth fifteen thousand at the most. Come back if you can't get a higher price."

Monsieur Lantin, dumbfounded, grabbed his necklace and left, yielding to a confused desire to be alone and to reflect.

But once he was out on the street, he was overcome with mirth and he thought to himself: "Imbecile! What an imbecile! And what if I'd taken him at his word? Now, there's a jeweler who can't distinguish between paste and the real stuff!"

And he entered another shop at the start of Rue de la Paix. Upon seeing the necklace, this second jeweler exclaimed: "Damn it! I'm well acquainted with this article. I sold it."

Monsieur Lantin, deeply disturbed, asked: "How much is it worth?"

"Monsieur, I sold it for twenty-five thousand. I'm ready to take it back for eighteen thousand once you indicate its provenance according to the law."

This time Monsieur Lantin sat down, stupefied with astonishment. He went on: "But . . . but examine it meticulously, Monsieur. All this time I thought it was . . . a fake."

The jeweler replied: "May I have your name, Monsieur?"

"Certainly. My name is Lantin, I am an official at the Ministry of the Interior, I live at 16 Rue des Martyrs."

The merchant opened his records, peered hard, and announced: "This necklace was indeed delivered to Madame Lantin, at 16 Rue des Martyrs, on July 20, 1876."

And the two men locked eyes, the official desperately surprised, the jeweler smelling a thief.

The jeweler then said: "Can you leave this object here for just twenty-four hours? I'll give you a receipt."

Monsieur Lantin stuttered: "Of course! Certainly!" And he left, folding up the paper and slipping it into his pocket.

He crossed the street, walked along, realized he was heading the wrong way, doubled back toward the Tuileries, crossed the Seine, perceived his new mistake, walked back to the Champs-Élysées, unable to focus his mind on anything. He tried to understand, to reason it out. His wife couldn't possibly have bought an object that valuable. Not at all! So then it must have been a present! A present from whom? Why?

He halted and stood in the middle of the boulevard. A horrible doubt assailed his mind. She? But then all the other jewels were presents, too! He felt as if the earth were quaking beneath him, a tree collapsing in front of him; he flung out his arms and fainted dead away.

He regained consciousness at a pharmacy, to which he'd been carried by passersby. A cab brought him home, and he locked himself in.

He wept dreadfully until nightfall, chewing a handkerchief to keep from crying out. Then, drained by fatigue and grief, he went to bed and fell into a deep slumber.

He was awoken by a sunbeam and he got up slowly to go to his ministry. It was hard for him to work after all those shocks. He then figured he could ask his supervisor to excuse him and he wrote him a note. Next he thought about returning to the jeweler and he reddened with shame. He reflected for a long time. He couldn't leave the necklace with that man; he dressed and went out.

It was a beautiful day, the blue sky spread over the city, which seemed to be smiling. People were strolling with their hands in their pockets.

Watching them amble by, Lantin murmured: "How lucky a man is if he's rich! With money, you can snap out of any grief, you can go wherever you like, you can travel, you can take your mind off your sorrows! Oh, if only I were rich!"

He realized he was hungry since he hadn't eaten in two days. But his pocket was empty, and then he recalled the necklace. Eighteen thousand francs! Eighteen thousand francs! A handsome sum all right!

After reaching the jewelry shop on Rue de la Paix, he started pacing up and down. Eighteen thousand francs! He nearly stepped inside two dozen times; but shame got the better of him.

Yet he was hungry, very hungry, and also penniless. He brusquely made up his mind, dashed across the street to avoid thinking about it, and hurried in.

Upon seeing him, the merchant came over and offered him a chair with a courteous smile. The assistants likewise showed up and peered askance at Lantin with cheery eyes and smirks.

The jeweler declared: "I've made inquiries, Monsieur, and if you still feel the same way, I am ready to pay you the amount that I offered you."

Lantin stammered: "Certainly!"

From a drawer the merchant produced eighteen large bills, counted them, and handed them to Lantin, who signed a short receipt and pocketed the money with a trembling hand.

Then, about to leave, he turned to the still-smiling jeweler, and, lowering his eyes, he muttered: "I've got . . . I've got other jewels . . . which have come to me . . . from the same legacy. Would you be interested in buying them, too?"

The merchant bowed. "Why, of course, Monsieur."

One of the assistants ran out to laugh his head off; another forcefully blew his nose.

Lantin, flushed and grave, impassively announced: "I'll bring them by."

And he took a cab to pick up the jewels.

He returned one hour later without having eaten. The two men examined the objects piece by piece, evaluating each one. Nearly all of them had been purchased here.

Now Lantin discussed the estimates, lost his temper, demanded to see the sales records, and talked louder and louder as the prices rose.

The huge eardrops were worth twenty thousand francs; the bracelets thirty-five; the rings, brooches, and medallions sixteen thousand; an item studded with sapphires and emeralds fourteen thousand; a solitaire on a gold neck chain forty thousand. The entire lot added up to one hundred ninety-six thousand francs.

With malicious bonhomie the merchant declared: "It all comes from somebody who invested everything in jewelry."

Lantin gravely enunciated: "It's as good a way as any to invest." And he left after arranging for a second opinion the next day.

Outside in the street, he gazed at the Vendôme Column, longing to climb it as if it were a greasy pole. He felt light enough to leapfrog over the Emperor's statue perched up there in the sky.

He had lunch at Voisin and drank wine costing twenty francs a bottle.

Then he hailed a cab and went for a spin around the Bois de Boulogne. He eyed the other carriages a bit scornfully, goaded by a desire to shout at the passersby: "I'm rich, too. I've got two hundred thousand francs!"

Suddenly he remembered his ministry. He drove over, strutted into his superior's office, and announced: "I'm here to hand in my resignation, Monsieur. I've just inherited three hundred thousand francs!" He shook hands with his former colleagues, describing his plans for a new life; then he dined at the Café Anglais.

Finding himself next to a distinguished-looking gentleman, he couldn't resist the itch to tell him, somewhat coyly, that he had just inherited four hundred thousand francs.

For the first time in his life, he wasn't bored at the theater and he spent the night with some prostitutes.

Six months later, he remarried. His second wife was extremely virtuous but she had a temper. She caused him a lot of suffering.

THE MODEL

Curving like a crescent moon, the small town of Étretat, with its white cliffs, its white pebbles, and its blue ocean, lay basking in the sun on a radiant day in July. At the horns of the crescent, the small gate on the right, the big gate on the left, each thrust a leg, that of a dwarf or that of a colossus, into the tranquil water; and the needle, nearly as high as the cliff, wide at the bottom and slender at the top, pointed its sharp head at the sky.

All along the beach, a seated throng was watching the bathers. On the Casino terrace, under the luminous sky, another crowd was sitting or strolling, the women displaying a garden of frocks punctuated by bright red and blue parasols embroidered with large silk blossoms.

At the promenade at the end of the terrace, other people, calm, serene, wandered leisurely, far from the elegant mob.

A young man, well known, renowned, a painter named Jean Summer, was gloomily walking next to a young woman, his wife, who sat in a small wheelchair gently pushed by a servant. The crippled woman gazed sadly at the joy of the sky, the joy of the day, and the joy of the crowds.

They didn't speak. They didn't look at one another.

"Let's stop a bit," said the woman.

They stopped, and the painter sat down on a camp stool that the servant handed him.

The strollers ambling behind the mute and immobile couple glanced at them sorrowfully. Their devotion was legendary. He had married her despite her handicap, deeply moved, it was said, by her love.

At a short distance, two young men were chatting on a capstan, their eyes melting in the horizon.

"No, it's not true. I tell you I'm well acquainted with Jean Summer."

"Then how come he married her? She was already crippled, wasn't she?"

"Definitely. He married her . . . he married her . . . the way people marry—out of stupidity, damn it!"

"But then? . . ."

"There's no then, my friend . . . no then. A man is stupid because he's stupid. And besides, you know that painters are specialists in ludicrous marriages. They almost always marry a model, an old mistress—in short, damaged goods in every sense of the term. And why? Who knows? You'd think that after constantly dealing with that sisterhood of dimwits known as models, a painter would be permanently disgusted by that sort of female. But oh no! After having them pose, the artists marry them. Just read Alphonse Daudet's little book *Artists' Wives*—it's so cruel, so fine, so accurate.

"For the couple you see over there, the accident was very unique and awful. The little woman staged a play or rather a terrifying drama. Indeed, for her, it was all or nothing. Was she sincere? Did she love Jean? Who can say? Who can precisely determine what's true and what's false in a woman's actions? They're always sincere, but their feelings are forever ebbing and flowing. They're passionate, criminal, devoted, admirable, and ignoble. They lie nonstop, without meaning to, without realizing it, without grasping it; yet with all that, and despite all that, they are utterly frank in their emotions and sensations—a frankness they demonstrate with violent, unexpected, incomprehensible, and fanatical resolutions that confound our reasoning, baffle our lucid minds, and upset all our egotistical plans. And because their decisions are so brusque and unforeseen, women remain indecipherable enigmas for us. We keep wondering: 'Are they honest? Are they dishonest?'

"But, my friend, they're both honest and dishonest at once, because it's in their nature to be at both extremes and at neither.

"Just look at the thoroughly honest measures they take to obtain their goals. Their methods are intricate and simple. So intricate that we never catch on to them in advance, and so simple that after being victimized we can't help being astonished and saying: 'Huh? She really played me for a fool like that?'

"And they always succeed, my friend, especially when it comes to marriage.

"But let me tell you Summer's story."

———

The woman is a model, of course. She posed for him. She was pretty—above all, elegant, and she apparently had a wonderful figure. He fell head over heels in love with her, the way you fall in love with any slightly seductive woman that you see a lot of. He imagined that he loved her with all his soul. And that's a bizarre phenomenon. The instant you desire a woman, you sincerely believe that you can't live without her for the rest of your life. You know very well that this isn't your first time, that possession has always been followed by disgust, that to spend your entire existence with another person you need, not a raw physical appetite, which is quickly sated, but a rapport of souls, moods, and temperaments. In yielding to seduction, you have to determine whether it's just a physical thing, an intoxication of the senses, or a profound spiritual attraction.

Well, he believed he loved her; he swore and swore that he'd be true to her, and he shacked up with her.

She was really sweet and endowed with the elegant silliness that Parisian girls so readily acquire. She chattered, she babbled, she mouthed stupidities that sounded witty because of the humorous way they were prattled. Her constant graceful gestures were aimed at charming an artist's eyes. When she raised her arm, when she leaned over, when she boarded a vehicle, when she offered you her hand, her motions were precise and perfect.

For three months, Jean failed to recognize that she basically resembled any other model.

They rented a cottage in Andrésy for the summer.

I was there one evening, when the first doubts began assailing my friend's mind.

Since the night was radiant, we felt like taking a stroll along the river. The moon was pouring its light into the shimmering water, its yellow reflections shredding in the flow, in the eddies, in the broad, lazy current.

We were sauntering along the riverbank, a bit intoxicated by the vague exaltation aroused in us by those wondrous evenings. We yearned to perform superhuman deeds, to love inscrutable and deliciously poetic creatures. We felt ecstasies thrilling inside ourselves, desires, mysterious strivings. And we kept silent, imbued by the serene and vivid freshness of the enthralling night, by that freshness of the moon, which seems to pass through our bodies, penetrate them, immerse our minds, fill them with fragrance, dip them in happiness.

All at once, Joséphine (that was her name) cried out: "Hey! Did you get a load of that fat fish that jumped up over there?"

He responded without glancing or thinking: "Yes, dear."

She was up in arms. "No, you couldn't have seen it, you were looking the other way."

He smiled: "Yes, that's true. The night is so beautiful that my mind's a blank."

She held her tongue. But a minute later, she felt obligated to chat and she asked: "Are you going to Paris tomorrow?"

He replied: "I don't know."

She was irked once more: "If you think it's any fun walking but not talking, then think again! People talk unless they're stupid!"

He didn't answer. Then, sharply sensing, thanks to her perverse female intuition, that she was about to exasperate him, she launched into that irritating ditty that had been dinning into our ears and our minds for two years already: "I was looking aloft!"

He murmured: "Please keep quiet."

She furiously snapped: "Why do you want me to keep quiet?"

He replied: "You're spoiling the countryside for us."

Now the inevitable scene erupted, the odious, moronic scene, with unexpected reproaches, tactless recriminations, then tears. She pulled out all her stops. They headed home. He had let her rant and rave, never interrupting her, numbed as he was by that divine evening and crushed by that tempest of stupid rebukes.

Three months later, he was struggling wildly in those invincible and invisible bonds with which the habit of a relationship entangles a life. She held him tight, tyrannized him, martyred him. They quarreled from dawn to dusk, trading insults, trading slaps.

Eventually, he wanted to flee, break off with her at any price. He sold all his paintings, he borrowed money from his friends, he wound up with a total of twenty thousand francs (he was still unknown back then), and one morning he left the cash on the mantelpiece together with a letter of good-bye.

He sought refuge in my home.

Toward three in the afternoon, someone rang the doorbell. I went to open. A woman pounced on me, knocked me aside, stormed in, and dashed over to my studio: it was her.

He had risen upon seeing her.

She pulled out the envelope containing the banknotes and hurled it at his feet in a truly noble gesture, snarling: "Here's your money! I don't want it!"

She was deathly pale, trembling, ready, no doubt, to commit any folly. As for him, I saw him blanch, too, blanch with anger and exasperation, ready, perhaps, to commit any violence.

He asked: "What do you want?"

She retorted: "I don't want to be treated like a hooker! You begged me and you took me. I didn't ask you for anything. Keep me!"

He stamped his foot: "No! You're going too far! If you think you're gonna—"

I grabbed his arm. "Shut up, Jean! Let me handle it!"

I walked toward her and, gently, gradually, reasoned with her; I emptied the whole bag of arguments that are used in such circumstances. She listened, motionless, staring, obstinate, and silent.

Finally, not knowing what else to say, and seeing that the outcome would be bad, I tried a last resort: "He still loves you, my dear. But his family wants him to marry—you do understand, don't you? . . ."

She gave a start. "Aha! Aha! I get it! . . ." And turning to him, she added: "You're gonna . . . you're gonna . . . get married?"

He rejoined bluntly: "Yes."

She took a step: "If you get married, I'll kill myself . . . you hear?"

He shrugged: "Okay. . . . Kill yourself."

Choking with dreadful anguish, she whimpered: "What's that? . . . What's that? . . . What's that? . . . Repeat it!"

He repeated: "Okay! Kill yourself! If that's what you want!"

Still deathly pale, she murmured: "Don't tempt me! I'll throw myself out the window."

He laughed, stepped over to the window, opened it, and, bowing like a man who lets someone else pass before him, he said: "Right this way. After you."

She gaped at him for a moment with wild and horrible eyes. Then, starting to dash as if to jump over a hedge in a field, she hurried past me, past him, crossed the balustrade, and disappeared. . . .

I will never forget the impact made on me by that open window after I saw that body hurtle down. In that second, the window seemed as vast as the sky and as empty as space. And I instinctively recoiled, not daring to look, as if I were about to plunge as well.

Jean stood there, immobile and terror-stricken.

They brought out the poor girl. Both her legs were broken. She will never walk again.

Her lover, insane with remorse and perhaps also grateful, took her back and married her.

And that's the story, my friend.

———

Night was falling. The young woman, feeling cold, wanted to leave; and the servant began rolling the small wheelchair toward the village. The painter walked at his wife's side without their having exchanged a single word for the past hour.

The Entity (The Horla)

May 8. What a wonderful day! I spent the entire morning lounging on my front lawn, under the enormous plane tree that covers the house, providing both shade and shelter. I love this region, and I love living here because this is where my roots are, those profound and delicate roots that attach a man to the soil where his forebears were born and died, that attach him to what people think and what they eat, to both customs and food, to local phrases, to the intonations of farmers, to the smells of the earth, of the hamlets, of the very air.

I love my house, which I grew up in. Through my windows I can see the Seine flowing alongside my garden, almost across from my house, behind the road—the large, broad Seine, which runs from Rouen to Le Havre, crowded with passing boats.

Over there, to the left, lies Rouen, the huge city with blue roofs under a pointed throng of Gothic belfries. These countless belfries, frail or solid, are dominated by the cathedral's cast-iron spire and filled with bells that peal through the blue air of beautiful mornings, reaching me with their sweet and distant metallic booming, their brass chanting carried to me by the breeze, now stronger, now weaker, depending on whether it wakes up or dozes off.

What a magnificent morning it was!

Toward eleven o'clock, a long convoy of ships inched past, towed by a tugboat that was as small as a dispatch boat and that gasped in agony, vomiting a dense smoke as it struggled past my barred entrance gate.

Two British schooners, their red Union Jacks flapping against the sky, were followed by a superb Brazilian three-master, sheer white and admirably clean and shiny. I was so deeply moved by the sight of that vessel—I don't know why—that I saluted it.

———

May 12. I've had a slight fever for several days, I feel sick or rather I feel sad.

What is the source of those mysterious influences that change our happiness into discouragement and our confidence into distress? One might think that the air, the invisible air, is teeming with unfathomable Powers, whose mystifying presence we endure. I wake up cheerfully, my throat bursting to sing. Why? I stroll along the current; and suddenly, after a brief walk, I reenter my house in a desolate mood as if some misery were awaiting me there. Why? Has a cold shiver grazed my skin, shaking my nerves and darkening my soul? Have the shapes of the clouds, the hues of the daylight, the so variable colors of things passed before my eyes and troubled my thoughts? Who knows!? Everything around us, everything we see without looking, everything we brush past without knowing it, everything we touch without feeling it, everything we encounter without distinguishing it—everything exerts rapid, surprising, and inexplicable effects on us, on our organs, and, through them, on our ideas and even on our hearts.

How profound it is—that mystery of the Invisible! We cannot fathom it with our wretched senses, with our eyes, which cannot perceive the smallest thing or the biggest, the closest or the farthest, the dwellers on a star or the dwellers in a drop of water; we cannot fathom that mystery with our ears, which deceive us, for they transmit the vibrations of the air into sonorous notes. They are fairies who work the miracle of changing that movement into noise, a metamorphosis that gives birth to music, that turns the mute agitation of nature into song. Nor can we fathom that mystery with our sense of smell—which is weaker than a dog's—or with our sense of taste, which can barely discern the vintage of a wine!

Ah! If we had other organs that could work other wonders for us, how many more things could we discover around us!

—

May 16. I am sick—decidedly so! I was so healthy last month! I have a fever, an atrocious fever, or rather a feverish state of jangled nerves, that makes my soul as ill as my body! I incessantly feel that awful sensation of ominous danger, that apprehension of imminent misfortune, of impending death, that inkling which is, no doubt, the first sign of a still-unknown illness sprouting in my blood and in my flesh.

—

May 18. I've just consulted my doctor, for I've been unable to sleep. He found that my pulse is too rapid, my eyes are dilated, my nerves on edge; but no alarming symptom whatsoever. I have to take showers and drink potassium bromide.

—

May 25. No change! I'm truly in a bizarre state. When evening sets in, I am invaded by an incomprehensible anxiety as if the night were hiding some terrible threat for me. I wolf down my dinner, then I try to read. But I can't grasp the words; I can barely distinguish the letters. So I pace up and down my parlor, crushed by a confused and irresistible fear, the fear of sleep and the fear of my bed.

Around ten P.M., I go up to my bedroom. Once inside, I turn my key twice and I shoot the bolts; I'm scared . . . of what? . . . I've never been afraid of anything until now. . . . I open my closets, I peer under my bed; I listen. . . . I listen. . . . For what? . . . Is it strange that a simple malaise, a circulatory problem perhaps, an irritation of the nerves, a slight congestion, a very minor disturbance in the so imperfect and so delicate functioning of our human machine, can turn the most joyful of men into a melancholic and the bravest of men into a coward? Then I get into bed and I wait for sleep as you'd wait for an executioner. I fearfully await its arrival, and my heart pounds, and my legs shudder; and my whole body shakes in the warmth of the sheets, until I suddenly doze off as you'd plunge into a chasm and drown in its stagnant water. I do not feel, as I once did, the coming of that perfidious sleep, concealed nearby, watching me, about to grab my head, close my eyes, annihilate me.

I sleep—a long time—two or three hours—then a dream—no—a nightmare clutches me. I truly feel that I'm lying and sleeping. . . . I feel it and I know it. . . . And I also sense that someone is approaching me, looking at me, touching me, climbing into my bed, kneeling on my chest, clutching my neck and squeezing . . . squeezing . . . strangling me with all his might.

As for me, I struggle wildly, bound by the atrocious incapacity that paralyzes us in our dreams. I try to yell—I can't. I try to move—I can't. Panting and desperately floundering, I attempt to turn, to hurl off the creature that is crushing me and suffocating me—I can't!

And suddenly, I wake up in a panic, bathed in sweat. I light a candle. I'm alone.

After that crisis, which recurs every night, I at last sleep peacefully until dawn.

—

June 2. My overall state has gotten worse. What's wrong with me? The bromide doesn't help; the showering doesn't help. A while ago, I went for a stroll in the Roumare Forest to tire my body, which was fatigued anyway. I initially believed that the fresh air, light and sweet, and redolent of grass and foliage, would pour new blood into my veins and new energy into my heart. I walked along a wide avenue, then, turning off toward La Bouille, I followed a narrow path between two hosts of exceedingly high trees that formed a thick, green, almost black roof between the sky and me.

Suddenly I shuddered, not a shiver of cold, but a strange shiver of fear.

I walked faster, nervous about being alone in these woods, stupidly, unreasonably frightened by the profound solitude. All at once, I felt that someone was following me, that someone was hard on my heels, very close behind me, able to touch me.

I whirled around. I was alone. All I could see behind me was the straight, wide path, deserted, flanked by lofty trees—fearfully deserted; and in the other direction, the path stretched as far as the eye could see, the same in every respect, equally terrifying.

I shut my eyes. Why? And I began spinning on one heel, very swiftly, like a top. I nearly collapsed; I opened my eyes; the trees were dancing, the ground was floating; I had to sit down. Then, ah! I didn't know how I had come here! A bizarre idea! Bizarre! A bizarre idea! My mind was a blank. I swerved off to my right and I came back to the avenue that had led me to the middle of the forest.

———

June 3. Last night was horrible. I'm leaving town for a couple of weeks. I'm certain that a brief trip will put me back on my feet.

———

July 2. I'm home again. I'm cured. In fact, I had a splendid time. I visited Mont Saint-Michel, which I had never seen before.

What a vision when you reach Avranches, as I did, with the waning of the day! The town lies on a hilltop; and I was taken to the public garden at the edge of Avranches. I uttered an astonished cry. An endless bay stretched out before me as far as the eye could see, with the two widely flanking coasts fading into the distant mists; and at the center of that immense yellow bay, under a clear and golden sky, a small, strange mountain rose up, dark and pointed, from the sand. The sun had just disappeared, and the still-blazing horizon revealed the silhouette of that fantastic rock, which carries a fantastic monument on its peak.

At dawn I headed there. The tide was out as it had been on the previous evening, and, as I drew closer, I watched the amazing abbey loom higher and higher. After walking for several hours, I reached the enormous heap of rocks that bears the small townlet dominated by the grand church. Upon climbing the narrow and precipitous street, I stepped into the earth's most admirable Gothic dwelling built for God, a construction as vast as a city, full of low rooms crushed under vaults and high galleries supported by frail columns. I entered that gigantic granite jewel, which is as delicate as lace, clustered with turrets and slender belfries that are filled with twisting staircases, and that thrust their bizarre heads into the blue skies of days, into the black skies of nights—heads bristling with gargoyles, devils, fantastic beasts and monstrous flowers, and linked together by subtle and elaborated arches.

When I reached the top, I said to the monk escorting me: "Father, how wonderful you must feel here!"

He replied: "It's very windy, monsieur." And we started chatting while gazing at the rising tide as it washed across the sand, covering it with steel armor.

And the monk told me stories, all the ancient stories of this place, legends, and still more legends.

One tale struck me to the quick. The people of the mountain and the surrounding area claim that they can hear voices on the sand at night, that they can hear two goats bleating, one very loudly, one very softly. Skeptics maintain that those are the cries of seagulls, cries that at times resemble bleating, at times human wailing. But the fishermen returning in the dead of night swear that between tides they have encountered an old shepherd prowling over the dunes, near the tiny far-flung hamlet, swathing his head in his cloak, and leading a billy goat with a man's face and a nanny goat with a woman's face, both of them sporting long, white hair and talking a blue streak, quarreling in an unknown language, then suddenly pausing and bleating with all their strength.

I asked the monk: "Do you believe that?"

He murmured: "I don't know."

I went on: "If other beings besides ourselves exist on the earth, how come we haven't known about them long since, how come you've never seen them, how come I've never seen them?"

He responded: "Do we see even the hundred-thousandth part of existence? Look, here is the wind, which is nature's most powerful force, which knocks over men, flattens buildings, uproots trees, raises the sea into mountains of water, destroys cliffs, and hurls great ships against reefs—the wind that kills, that whistles, that moans, that bellows—have you ever seen the wind and can you see it? Yet it does exist."

I held my tongue against that simple reasoning. This man was a sage or perhaps a fool. I couldn't tell for sure; but I held my tongue. I had often thought about what he was now saying.

—

July 3. I've slept badly; there must be a feverish influence hereabouts, for my driver is as sick as I am. Upon coming home yesterday, I noticed his strange pallor. I asked him: "What's wrong, Jean?"

"I can't doze off at night, Monsieur, my nights gobble up my days. It's been like a bad spell on me ever since you left, Monsieur."

The rest of the staff is well, however, but I'm terrified of having a relapse.

—

July 4. I've definitely suffered a relapse. My old nightmares keep haunting me. Last night, I felt something crouching on top of me, holding its mouth on mine, sucking out my life between my lips. Yes, it was draining my life from my throat as a leech might have done. Then, sated, it got off me, while I woke up, so terribly crushed, broken, exhausted that I was incapable of moving. If this goes on for the next few days, I'll certainly leave again.

—

July 5. Have I lost my mind? What occurred last night, what I saw was so bizarre that my head spins at the mere thought of it.

I locked myself in my bedroom as I now do every evening; then, feeling thirsty, I drank half a glass of water, whereupon I happened to notice that my carafe was brimful, all the way up to the crystal stopper.

Next I went to bed and I fell into one of my dreadful slumbers, until some two hours later, when I was shaken by an even more horrible shock.

Picture a man who is asleep, who has been murdered, who wakes up with a knife in his lung, with a death rattle in his gullet, who is covered with blood, unable to breathe, about to die, and who doesn't know why he's been attacked—that was how I felt.

Regaining my sanity, I was thirsty again; I lit a candle and headed toward the table where my carafe was standing. I took hold of it and tilted it over my glass; nothing came pouring. The carafe was empty! It was completely empty! At first I couldn't grasp it; then all at once, I was so terribly overwhelmed that I had to sit down—or rather, I collapsed on a chair! Then I jumped up and peered all around me! Then, wild with fear and amazement, I sat down again in front of the transparent crystal! I gaped at it, trying to find an explanation. My hands were trembling! So someone had drunk the water? Who? I? I, no doubt? Could it have been anyone else? Well, then I was a sleepwalker; without realizing it, I was living the mysterious double life that makes you listen for two beings inside you or listen for an alien being, unknowable and invisible, listen to it animating your captive body in moments when your soul is torpid and your flesh obeys that other being as it obeys you—indeed, your body obeys that other being more willingly than it obeys you.

Ah! Who can comprehend my abominable anguish? Who can understand the agitation of a sane, alert, rational man, gazing in dismay through a glass carafe, searching for some water that disappeared while he was asleep! And I stayed there until daybreak without daring to return to my bed.

———

July 6. I'm going crazy! Someone drained my carafe again last night. Or rather: I drained it!

But was it me? Was it me? Who was it? Who? Oh, my God! Am I going crazy? Who will save me?

—

July 10. I've been gathering some remarkable evidence!

I'm definitely crazy! And yet . . .

On July 6, before turning in, I placed some items on my table: wine, milk, water, bread, and strawberries.

Someone drank up—I drank up—all the water and a bit of the milk. No one touched the wine, the bread, or the strawberries.

On July 7, I repeated the experiment, and it produced the same results.

On July 8, I omitted the water and the milk. Nothing was touched.

On July 9, finally, I set out only water and milk on the table, first taking care to envelop the carafes in white muslin and tie down the stoppers. Next I rubbed graphite into my lips, my beard, my hands, and I went to bed.

Invincible sleep grabbed hold of me, soon followed by atrocious awakening. I hadn't stirred; my sheets were spotless. I hurried over to my table. The cloths around the carafes were immaculate. Throbbing with terror, I undid the strings. All the water had been drunk! All the milk had been drunk! Ah! My God! . . .

I'm leaving for Paris shortly.

—

July 12. Paris. I guess I've taken leave of my senses during these past few days! I must have been prey to my feverish imagination, unless I truly walk in my sleep or have fallen victim to one of those recorded but still inexplicable phenomena that are called "suggestions." In any case, my panic verged on lunacy, and now twenty-four hours in Paris have sufficed to restore my self-assurance.

Yesterday, after I did some shopping and paid some visits, which breathed fresh and bracing air into my soul, I capped off my evening at the Théâtre-Français. It was performing a play by the younger Alexandre Dumas; and that keen and powerful mind completed my cure. Solitude is certainly dangerous for active intellects. We need to be surrounded by men who think and speak. When we are alone for a long time, we fill the emptiness with phantoms.

Taking the boulevards, I very cheerfully headed back to my hotel. Amid the jostling throng, I mused—not without mockery—about last week's terrors and suppositions. For I had believed—yes, believed—that an invisible being was dwelling under my roof. How weak the mind is, how easily distraught, how swiftly bewildered, when struck by something slight and incomprehensible!

Instead of concluding with these simple words, "I don't get it because the reason eludes me," we instantly picture horrible mysteries and supernatural forces.

———

July 14. Bastille Day. I roamed the streets. I was as entertained as a child by the flags and the firecrackers. Yet it's very silly to be joyful on a date fixed by a government decree. The populace is a moronic flock, alternating between stupid patience and fierce revolt. It is told, "Have fun." It has fun. It is told, "Go and fight your neighbor." It goes and fights. It is told, "Vote for the emperor." It votes for the emperor. Then it is told, "Vote for the Republic." And it votes for the Republic.

The men who rule it are likewise fools; but instead of obeying other men, they obey principles, which can only be asinine, sterile, and bogus, simply because they are principles—that is, ideas accepted as certain and indisputable in a world in which we are sure of nothing, since light is an illusion and noise is an illusion.

———

July 16. Last night I witnessed things that deeply upset me.

I was dining at the home of my cousin, Madame Sablé, whose husband is in command of the 76th Light Infantry in Limoges. There were also two young women, one of whom had married Dr. Parent, a physician focusing on the nervous ailments and the extraordinary phenomena currently manifested by experiments in hypnosis and suggestion.

He talked on and on about the prodigious results obtained by British scientists and by the physicians of the School of Nancy.

The data he cited struck me as so bizarre that I declared my utter incredulity.

"We are," he affirmed, "on the verge of exposing one of Nature's most important secrets—that is, one of her most important secrets on this earth; for she undeniably has far more important secrets up there, among the stars. Ever since man began to think, ever since he learned how to state and set down his thoughts, he has been vaguely haunted by a mystery that is impenetrable to his crude and imperfect senses, and he has deployed his intelligence to make up for his physical inadequacy. When his intelligence was still in a rudimentary stage, that obsession with invisible phenomena took commonplace but terrifying forms. It gave rise to the popular beliefs in the supernatural, the legends of restless spirits, fairies, gnomes, ghosts—I would even say God. For our notions of the creator-and-laborer, from whatever religion they may come, are the most mediocre, most dim-witted, and most unacceptable inventions ever concocted by a frightened brain. Nothing could be truer than Voltaire's maxim: 'God made man in his own image, and man has returned the favor.'

"For over a century, however, we have apparently sensed something new. Mesmer and a few others have taken us along an unexpected road, and, especially for the past four or five years, we have truly achieved some amazing results."

My cousin, likewise very incredulous, was smiling. Dr. Parent said to her: "Would you like me to put you under, Madame?"

"Yes, I would."

She sat down in an easy chair, and he began to stare at her hypnotically. As for me, I suddenly felt a bit queasy, my heart was thumping, my throat tightening. I saw Madame Sablé's eyelids grow heavy, her lips tense, her bosom heave.

Ten minutes later, she was asleep.

"Get behind her," said the physician.

And I settled behind her. He placed a visiting card in her hands, saying: "This is a mirror. What do you see in it?"

She replied: "I see my cousin."

"What is he doing?"

"He's twisting his mustache."

"And now?"

"He's drawing a photograph from his pocket."

"Who is it a photo of?"

"Him."

It was true! And that photograph had just been delivered to me that very evening, at the hotel.

"What is he doing in his portrait?"

"He is standing there, holding his hat."

She was looking at that card, that white cardboard, as if she were looking into a mirror.

The young women, horrified, were saying: "Enough! Enough! Enough!"

But the doctor ordered her: "You will get up tomorrow at eight A.M. Then you will visit your cousin at his hotel and you will beg him to lend you five thousand francs, which your husband is asking you for and which he will demand on his next furlough."

The doctor then woke my cousin up.

Heading back to the hotel, I mused about that curious session, and I was assailed by doubts: not about my cousin's absolute integrity; having known her since childhood, virtually her brother, I consider her above suspicion. I actually thought the doctor capable of a hoax. Could he have concealed a mirror in his palm, showing it to the young woman along with his card? Professional magicians pull off far more singular feats.

So I went up to my room and got into bed.

At around eight-thirty the next morning, I was awakened by my valet: "It's Madame Sablé. She wants to see Monsieur immediately."

I tossed on my clothes and welcomed her.

She sat down, greatly disturbed, lowering her eyes, and, without lifting her veil, she murmured: "My dear cousin, I've got a great favor to ask of you."

"What is it, Cousin?"

"I'm awfully embarrassed to tell you, but I have no choice. I need, absolutely need, five thousand francs."

"Come on! You?"

"Yes, I, or rather my husband, who's told me to get the money."

I was so dumbfounded that I stammered by way of responding. I wondered if she and Dr. Parent were playing a trick on me, if they had designed a practical joke and were putting on a very skillful act.

But as I scrutinized her, all my doubts faded. Her request was so painful to her that she was trembling in anguish, and I realized that her throat was filled with sobs.

I knew that she was very rich and I went on: "Come on! Your husband doesn't have five thousand francs at his disposal? Look, just think about it! Are you sure he told you to ask me?"

She hesitated for several moments as if arduously ransacking her memory; then she answered: "Yes.... Yes.... I'm sure."

"Did he write you?"

She hesitated again, reflecting. I could tell that her mind was in torment. She understood nothing. All she knew was that she had to borrow five thousand francs for her husband. So she ventured to lie.

"Yes, he wrote me."

"When was it? You said nothing to me yesterday."

"I received his letter this morning."

"Can you show it to me?"

"No ... no ... no.... It contains intimate things ... too personal.... I ... I burned it."

"Well, then has your husband incurred debts?"

She hesitated again, then murmured: "I don't know."

I brusquely declared: "Look, I don't have five thousand francs available at this moment, my dear cousin."

She uttered something like an agonizing cry.

"Oh! Oh! I beg you, I beg you! Find the money!"

She was growing more and more agitated, clasping her hands as if praying to me! I heard her tone of voice change; she was weeping and stammering, harried and overpowered by the unrelenting order she'd been given.

"Oh! Oh! I beg you.... If you only knew how horribly I'm suffering.... I need the money today!"

I took pity on her.

"You'll have it shortly, I swear."

She exclaimed: "Oh! Thank you! Thank you! You're so kind!"

I went on: "Do you recall what happened at your home last night?"

"Yes."

"Do you recall that Dr. Parent put you under?"

"Yes."

"Well, he ordered you to come here this morning and borrow five thousand francs, and at this moment you are obeying his suggestion."

She mused for several moments, then replied: "But it's my husband who's asking for the money."

I spent an hour trying to convince her, but got nowhere.

After she left, I hurried to the doctor. He was just on his way out and he smiled as he listened to me. Then he said: "Do you believe me now?"

"Yes, I have no choice."

"Let's go to your cousin."

She was dozing on a chaise longue, thoroughly exhausted. The doctor checked her pulse, then peered at her for a while, holding one hand in front of her eyes, which she gradually closed under that unbearable magnetic force.

When she fell asleep, he said: "Your husband no longer needs the five thousand francs. You are going to forget that you asked your cousin to lend you the money, and if he broaches the topic, you will not understand."

Then he woke her up. I drew a wallet from my pocket.

"Here, my dear cousin, is what you asked me for this morning."

She was so surprised that I didn't dare belabor the point. I did try to rouse her memory, but she forcefully denied everything; she thought I was poking fun at her, and she very nearly lost her temper.

———

There! I returned to the hotel; and I was so upset by my experience that I couldn't eat a bite of lunch.

———

July 19. Many people to whom I've described my adventure have laughed in my face. I'm at my wit's end. The wise man says, "Perhaps?"

———

July 21. I dined in Bougival, then I spent the evening at the rowing-club dance. It's obvious that everything depends on the place and the surroundings. To believe in the supernatural on the Island of La Grenouillère would be the height of madness. . . . But what about on the peak of Mont Saint-Michel? What about in India? We submit terrifyingly to our environment. I'll be going home next week.

———

July 30. I arrived home yesterday. Everything is fine.

———

August 2. Nothing new; the weather is superb. I spend my days watching the Seine flow by.

———

August 4. Quarrels in my staff. My domestics claim that someone is breaking the glasses in the cupboards at night. My valet accuses my cook, who accuses the linen maid, who accuses the other two. Who is the real culprit? It would take a fine mind to solve the mystery.

———

August 6. This time I'm not crazy. I saw. . . . I saw. . . . I saw! . . . I can no longer doubt it. . . . I saw. . . . I'm still icy cold down to my fingertips. . . . I'm still terrified down to the marrow of my bones. . . . I saw it! . . .

At two P.M. I was strolling in broad sunshine among my rosebushes, along the path flanked by the autumn roses, which were budding.

As I paused to study a Giant of Battles, which had three magnificent blossoms, I saw, I distinctly saw, very close to me, a rose stem bend as if twisted by an invisible hand, then snap as if plucked by that hand! Next, the flower moved up the curve that would have been described by a hand bringing it to lips, and the blossom remained suspended in the transparent air, remained alone, immobile, a dreadful red splotch three paces from my eyes.

Desperately I threw myself on the rose, trying to grab it! I found nothing; it had vanished. I was furious at myself; after all, a sane and serious person is incapable of such hallucinations.

But was it a hallucination? I turned to look for the stem, and I promptly found it, freshly broken, on the bush, between the other two roses on the branch.

I stepped indoors, utterly distraught; for now I'm certain, as certain as the alternation of days and nights, that an invisible being exists near me, a being that feeds on milk and water, that can touch things, take hold of them, shift them, that it is consequently endowed with a material nature, though imperceptible to our senses, and that dwells, like me, under my roof. . . .

—

August 7. I slept peacefully. It drank water from my carafe, but did not disturb my sleep.

I wonder if I'm crazy. While strolling along the river just now, in broad daylight, I was assailed by doubts about my sanity: not the vague misgivings I had been experiencing, but precise and concrete doubts. I've known madmen; I've known some who've remained lucid, intelligent, even clear-sighted about all things in life—except for one point. They spoke about everything shrewdly, easily, and profoundly—when all at once, their minds hit the reef of their madness, smashed to pieces, scattered, and sank in that terrifying and infuriated ocean full of mists and squalls and bounding waves that are called "dementia."

I would certainly believe I was crazy, absolutely crazy, if I weren't completely sentient, if I weren't perfectly acquainted with my mental state, if I didn't fathom it by analyzing it with total lucidity. I would then basically be hallucinating with a rational mind. Some unknown turmoil must have afflicted my brain, one of those disturbances that physiologists are currently trying to record and pinpoint; and this disturbance has apparently opened a profound crevice in my mind, in the order and logic of my thoughts. Similar phenomena occur in dreams that lead us through the unlikeliest phantasmagorias without surprising us, for the verifying apparatus, the sense of validation, lies dormant, while the imaginative faculty watches and operates. Could it possibly be that one of the imperceptible keys of my cerebral keyboard is stuck fast inside me? An accident victim may lose his memory of proper nouns or verbs or numbers or merely dates. By now, all sections of the mind have been conclusively localized. So why would it shock me that my faculty for verifying the unreality of certain hallucinations should be dulled at this moment?

I was musing about all these things while ambling along the water. The sunshine covered the river, immersing the earth in sweet delight, filling me with a love of life, a love for the swallows, whose agility is a joy for my eyes, a love for the riverbank plants, whose rustling enchants my ears.

Yet little by little, an enigmatic malaise took hold of me. A force, a mysterious force, seemed to be numbing me, stopping me, keeping me from advancing, calling me back. I experienced that excruciating impulse to go home, a need that oppresses you when you have left a beloved patient at home and you have a sudden inkling that he has taken a turn for the worse.

So I reluctantly headed back, certain that upon reaching my house, I would learn some bad news, find a letter or a telegram. There was nothing; and I was more surprised and apprehensive than if I had suffered another fantastic vision.

———

August 8. Yesterday evening was horrible. It no longer shows itself, but I can sense it near me—spying on me, watching me, penetrating me, dominating me, and more frightful by concealing itself than by relying on supernatural phenomena to hint at its invisible and consistent presence.

Nevertheless, I managed to sleep.

—

August 9. Nothing, but I'm scared.

—

August 10. Nothing; what's in store for me tomorrow?

—

August 11. Still nothing; I can no longer stay here with these fears and these thoughts in my soul; I'm going to leave.

—

August 12, ten P.M. I tried to leave all day long; I couldn't. I wanted to perform this so easy and so simple act of freedom: get out, climb into my carriage, and head for Rouen. I couldn't. Why not?

—

August 13. When you are stricken with certain illnesses, all the springs in your physical being seem broken, all your energy seems drained, all your muscles seem slack, your bones as soft as your flesh and your flesh as liquid as water. I feel this in my spiritual being, feel it in a bizarre and disheartening way. I have no strength left, no courage, no self-dominion, no power even to stir my will. I can no longer will; someone wills for me, and I obey.

—

August 14. I'm doomed! Someone has taken possession of my soul and rules it! Someone controls all my actions, all my movements, all my thoughts. I am nothing on the inside, nothing but an enslaved spectator terrified of all the things I do. I wish to leave. I can't. It doesn't want me to; and, panicky and shuddering, I remain in the easy chair, where it keeps me sitting. All I want to do is rise, stand up, so I can believe that I am still in control of myself. I can't. I'm riveted to my chair; and my chair adheres so tightly to the floor that no power can lift us up.

Then all at once, I must, I must, I must go to the end of my garden, pick some strawberries, and eat them! And I go there! I pick strawberries and I eat them. Oh, God! Oh, God! Oh, God! Is there a God? If there is, deliver me, save me! Help me! Forgive me! Pity me! Have mercy on me! Save me! Oh, what agony! What torture! What horror!

—

August 15. That was precisely how possessed and controlled my poor cousin was when she tried to borrow five thousand francs from me. She was submitting to an alien power that had entered her, a power like another soul, like a parasitical and autocratic soul. Is the world about to end?

And the being that dominates me: what is that invisible, that unknowable entity, that prowler of a supernatural race?

So the Invisible Ones do exist! Then why, since the creation of the world, have they failed to manifest themselves in a precise way as they do for me? I have never read about anything like what has been happening in my home. Oh, if only I could leave my house, if I could go, depart, and never come back. I would be saved then—but I can't.

—

August 16. Today I managed to escape for two hours, like a prisoner who happens to find his cell door open. I felt that I was suddenly free and that it was far away. I ordered my servant to hitch up my horse on the double, and I sped to Rouen. Oh, what joy to command an obedient servant: "Go to Rouen!"

I halted in front of the library and I asked to borrow the great treatise penned by Dr. Hermann Herestauss about the unknown inhabitants of the ancient and modern worlds.

Then as I climbed back into my brougham, I wanted to say, "To the train station!" and I shouted—I didn't speak, I shouted—so loudly that heads turned in my direction: "Take me home!" And, in panicky anguish, I collapsed upon the cushion in my vehicle. It had found me and possessed me again.

—

August 17. Oh! What a night! What a night! And yet it strikes me that I ought to rejoice. I read until one A.M.! Hermann Herestauss, a doctor of philosophy and of theogony, has written down the histories and manifestations of all those invisible beings that prowl around man or have been dreamed up by him. He describes their origins, their domains, their powers. Yet none of them resembles the entity that haunts me. It would seem as if ever since he began to think, man has sensed and feared a new being, stronger than man, his successor in this world, and that, feeling his immediacy but unable to probe the nature of his master, he has, in his terror, created the whole fantastic tribe of hidden beings, vague phantoms born out of fear.

And so, having read until one A.M., I went and sat down at my open window to cool my forehead and refresh my mind in the calm wind of the darkness.

The night was fine, it was warm! How deeply I would have enjoyed that night in the past!

No moon. The stars were glimmering and flickering in the depths of the black sky. Who inhabits those worlds? What life-forms, what creatures, what animals, what plants are out there? The beings that think in those far-off universes—what do they know more than we? What can they do better than we? What things do they see that we are utterly unacquainted with? Will one of them travel across space sooner or later and appear on our planet and conquer it just as the Normans once crossed the seas to subjugate weaker nations?

We are so frail, so defenseless, so ignorant, so tiny, we humans, on this speck of mud that swirls so feebly in a drop of water.

I nodded off while dreaming like that in the cool evening wind.

Now, after sleeping for some forty minutes, I opened my eyes without stirring, awoken by some sort of confused and bizarre emotion. At first, I saw nothing; then, all at once, a page of the open book on my table seemed to have turned on its own. No breath of air had come wafting through my window. I was surprised and I waited. About four minutes later, I saw, I saw, yes, I saw with my own eyes another page rise and drop upon the preceding page as if moved by a finger. My easy chair was empty, seemed empty; but I realized that *it* was there, it, sitting in my seat and reading. In a furious leap, the leap of an enraged beast trying to rip out its tamer's guts, I charged across the room to grab it, strangle it, kill it! . . . but before I could reach it, my chair toppled over as if something were fleeing me, my table wobbled, my lamp crashed down and went out, and my window closed as if a wrongdoer caught red-handed had dashed into the night, slamming the shutters.

So it had taken flight; *it* had been scared, it was scared of me.

Well, then . . . then . . . tomorrow . . . or later on . . . or someday, I will be able to clutch it in my fists and crush it on the floor! Don't dogs sometimes bite their masters and rip out their throats?

—

August 18. I have been mulling all day. Yes, yes, I'm going to obey it, abide by its impulses, carry out all its wishes, act humble, submissive, cowardly. It is stronger than I. But the time will come. . . .

—

August 19. I know . . . I know . . . I know everything! I've just read the following in a scientific journal.

A rather curious bit of news has reached us from Rio de Janeiro. Insanity, an epidemic of insanity, comparable to those contagious dementias that afflicted European nations during the Middle Ages, is raging at this moment in the province of São Paulo. The panicky inhabitants are leaving their homes, deserting their villages, abandoning their fields, claiming that they are being pursued, possessed, controlled like human cattle by invisible yet tangible beings, creatures like vampires, which feed on their vital energy while these victims sleep, and which also drink water and milk without appearing to touch any other kind of aliment.

Professor Don Pedro Henriquez, accompanied by several medical scientists, has departed for the province of São Paulo in order to study in situ the origins and manifestations of this astonishing insanity and to propose to the Emperor of Brazil measures that would strike him as the most appropriate to restore the minds of these frenzied populations.

Ah! Ah! I recall, I recall the glorious Brazilian three-master that sailed past my windows on May 8 as she headed upstream! I found her so lovely, so cheerful, so white! And the Being was aboard, coming from there, where its race was born! And it saw me! It also saw my white home and it jumped ashore. Oh, God!

Now I know, I've fathomed it. Man's reign is over.

It has come, the Being that was feared by the earliest nations, the Being that was exorcised by the anxious priests, that was evoked on dark nights by the sorcerers, who never saw it appear, the Being that the inklings of the world's temporary masters endowed with all the monstrous or graceful shapes of gnomes, sprites, spirits, fairies, or hobgoblins. After the gross conceptions produced by primitive dread, more perspicacious men developed a clearer sense of *it*. Mesmer caught its gist, and ten years ago the physicians exposed its precise character before it could act on it itself. They have played with this weapon of the new Lord, the domination of a mysterious willpower over the enslaved human soul. They have dubbed it magnetism, hypnotism, suggestion—and goodness knows what else. I have seen them delighting in that horrible force like imprudent children! Woe to us! Woe to man! It has come—the ... the ... Just what is its name? ... The ... It seems to be shouting its name at me, and I can't hear it ... the ... yes ... it is shouting its name. ... I listen ... I can't ... Repeat ... the ... Entity ... I heard it ... the Entity ... that's it. ... The Entity ... it has come! ...

Ah! The vulture has eaten the dove; the wolf has eaten the lamb; the lion has devoured the sharp-horned buffalo; man has killed the lion with an arrow, with a sword, with gunpowder. But the Entity will make man into what we have made the horse and the ox: his chattel, his servant, his food, by the sheer power of his will. Woe to us!

However, the animal sometimes revolts and kills the man who tamed it. . . . I, too, want . . . I will be able to . . . But we have to know it, touch it, see it! Scientists tell us that the beast's eyes, being different from our eyes, cannot see as we see. . . . And my eyes cannot distinguish this newcomer who is oppressing me.

Why not? Oh! Now I remember what the monk said to me at Mont Saint-Michel: "Do we see even the hundred-thousandth part of existence? Look, here is the wind, which is nature's most powerful force, which knocks over men, flattens buildings, uproots trees, raises the sea into mountains of water, destroys cliffs, and hurls great ships against reefs—the wind that kills, that whistles, that moans, that bellows—have you ever seen the wind and can you see it? Yet it does exist!"

And I also mused: my eyes are so feeble, so imperfect, that they can't distinguish even hard objects that are as transparent as glass! . . . If a sheet of plate glass bars my path, my eyes throw me against it the way a bird trapped in a room smashes its head against the windows. And a thousand other things hoodwink my eyes and lead them astray. So is it any wonder that my eyes can't perceive a new object that light can pass through?

A new being! Why not? It was bound to come! Why should we be the last? And why can't we distinguish it as we can distinguish all other beings that were created before us? The reason is that its formation is more perfect, its body finer and more refined than our bodies, which are so weak, so awkwardly conceived, encumbered with organs that are always weary, always strained like overly intricate springs, our bodies, which live like plants and like beasts, arduously nourished on air, grass, and meat, live machines prey to diseases, deformations, putrefactions, wheezing, poorly regulated, naïve and bizarre, ingeniously misconstructed, a fragile, makeshift work, a rough sketch of something that could be intelligent and marvelous.

Varied creatures have been scarce in this world, from oyster to man. Why not one more being once we have completed the intervals that separate the successive emergences of all the diverse species?

Why not one more? Why not more trees with immense and daz-zling flowers that imbue entire regions with their fragrances? Why not more elements in addition to fire, earth, air, and water? There are only four, nothing but four—of those nourishers of all beings! What a pity! Why aren't there forty, four hundred, four thousand? How poor everything is, how wretched, how miserable! Grudgingly given, badly designed, ineptly executed! Ah! The elephant, the hippopotamus—how graceful! The camel—how elegant.

But, you will say, how about the butterfly? A flying blossom! I picture one the size of a hundred universes, with wings whose shape, beauty, color, and motion I cannot express. But I can see the butterfly. . . . It flits from star to star, refreshing them, perfuming them in the soft and harmonious breath of its passage! . . . And the nations up there are ravished and ecstatic as they watch it flutter by! . . .

—

What's wrong with me? It, it, the Entity, keeps haunting me, keeps making me visualize these follies! It is inside me, it is becoming my soul; I will kill it!

—

August 19. I will kill it. I've seen it! Last night, I sat down at my table and I pretended to be absorbed in what I was writing. I knew that it would come and prowl around me, very close to me—so close that I might perhaps touch it, grab it? And then! . . . Then I would have the strength of a desperate man; I would have my hands, my knees, my chest, my forehead, my teeth, to strangle it, crush it, bite it, tear it to shreds.

And I watched for it, with all my body parts seething with excite-ment.

I had lit my two lamps and the eight candles on my mantelpiece as if I could have distinguished my visitor in all that light.

In front of me, my bed, an old oak four-poster; to my right, my fire-place; to my left, my door, which I had carefully locked after leaving it open for a long time in order to lure my visitor; behind me, a very high mirrored armoire, which I used daily when shaving and dressing, and in which I viewed my reflection from head to foot each time I passed by.

So I pretended to be writing in order to fool it, for it was observing me, too; and all at once, I sensed, I was certain, that it was reading over my shoulder, that it was grazing my ear.

I leaped up, stretching my arms and whirling around so fast that I nearly fell. Well? . . . The room was as bright as day, but I couldn't see my mirror image! . . . The mirror was empty and deeply clear and radiant! My reflection was gone, yet I was standing right in front of the mirror! I scrutinized the vast limpid glass from top to bottom. And I gazed with panicky eyes; I didn't dare come closer, I didn't dare move, sensing, as I did, that *it* was there, but that it would escape me after its imperceptible body had devoured my reflection.

How frightened I was! Then suddenly, I began seeing myself in a mist, in the depth of the mirror, like a mist across a watery surface; and the water seemed to be gliding from left to right, shifting slowly, making my image more precise from second to second. It was like the end of an eclipse. Whatever was hiding me didn't seem to have a sharp outline, instead it had a sort of translucent opaqueness that was gradually clearing.

I could finally view myself completely as I do every day when peering into the mirror.

I had spotted it! My dread still haunts me, making me shudder.

———

August 20. Kill it—but how? After all, I can't touch it? Poison? But it would see me mix the poison into water; and besides: would our poisons have any effect on its imperceptible body? No . . . no. . . . Absolutely not. . . . Well, then how? . . . How? . . .

———

August 21. I summoned a locksmith from Rouen and ordered him to install iron shutters in my bedroom, the kind used on ground floors in certain Parisian townhouses to keep out intruders. He will also craft me a door to match. I may look like a coward, but who cares! . . .

—

September 10. Rouen, Hôtel Continental. It's done. . . . It's done. . . . But is it dead? My soul is still overwhelmed by what I saw.

Yesterday evening, after the locksmith finished installing my new door and shutter, I left them open until midnight even though it was starting to get cold out.

All at once, I sensed that it was there, and I was filled with joy, a wild joy. I slowly got up and I ambled to the right, to the left, on and on, to keep it from suspecting anything. Then I took off my boots and casually put on my slippers; next, I closed my iron shutter, and, tranquilly heading to the door, I double-locked it. Returning to the window, I padlocked it and pocketed the key.

All at once, I realized that it was moving around me, that it was now scared in its turn, that it was ordering me to open the door and allow it to escape. I nearly gave in; but I didn't give in. Backing against the door, I barely opened it, just enough to let me squeeze through; and since I'm very tall, my head touched the lintel. I was sure it hadn't managed to flee, and I locked it in all alone, all alone. What joy! I had it! I dashed downstairs; rushing into my parlor, which lies right under my bedroom, I grabbed my two lamps and I poured out their oil on the carpet, the furniture—everything; then I set the oil on fire and hurried away after double-locking the huge front door.

I hid in a clump of laurels deep in the garden. How long it took! How long! Everything was black, hushed, immobile; not a puff of air, not a star, mountains of clouds, barely visible yet weighing so heavy, so heavy on my soul.

I watched my house and I waited. How long it took! I was starting to believe that the fire had gone out on its own or that *it* had snuffed it— when a ground-floor window caved in under the might of the fire, and a flame, a big red and yellow flame, long, tender, and caressing, rose up the white wall, licking its way to the roof. A light flashed through the trees, the branches, the leaves, as did a shudder, a shudder of fear. The birds awoke; a dog began to howl; the day seemed to be dawning! Two more windows burst, and I saw that the entire main floor of my house was nothing but a dreadful conflagration. Then a shriek, a shrill, horrible, wrenching shriek, a woman's shriek, tore through the night, and two garret windows flew open! I had forgotten all about my servants! I saw their panicky faces and their flailing arms! . . .

Wild with dread, I raced toward the village, yelling: "Help! Help! Fire! Fire!" I ran into some people who were already responding, and I doubled back with them to see what was happening!

By now, the house was no more than a horrible and magnificent funeral pile, a monstrous pyre illuminating the entire earth, a pyre where men were burning, and where *it* was burning, too. It, It, my prisoner, the new Being, the new master, the Entity!

Suddenly, the whole roof collapsed between the walls, and a flaming volcano spurted toward the sky. Through all the windows revealing the furnace, I saw the blazing cauldron and I thought to myself that It was there, in that oven, dead. . . .

Dead? Perhaps? . . . Its body—through which daylight passed? Wasn't its body invincible against the weapons that kill our bodies?

What if it wasn't dead? . . . Perhaps time alone holds sway over that Visible and Redoubtable Being. Why that transparent body, that unknowable body, that spiritual body, if that Being likewise had to fear ills, wounds, infirmities, premature destruction?

Premature destruction? That is the wellspring of all human dread! After man, the Entity.

Man, who can die on any day, at any hour, at any minute, through any accident, is followed by the Being who must die only on Its day, at Its hour, at Its minute because it has reached the limit of Its existence!

No . . . no. . . . There is no doubt, there is no doubt. . . . It isn't dead. . . . And so . . . And so . . . I will have to kill myself, myself! . . .

JOACHIM NEUGROSCHEL's translations include definitive renderings of Kafka, Mann, Racine, Molière, Bataille, and almost two hundred others. His translations of de Sade's *Philosophy in the Boudoir* and Dumas's *The Man in the Iron Mask* are forthcoming from Penguin. Awards received include the French-American Foundation Translation Prize, the Goethe House/PEN Translation Prize (three times), and Guggenheim and NEA grants. He lives in Belle Harbor, New York.

A Note on the Type

The principal text of this Modern Library edition
was set in a digitized version of Janson, a typeface that
dates from about 1690 and was cut by Nicholas Kis,
a Hungarian working in Amsterdam. The original matrices have
survived and are held by the Stempel foundry in Germany.
Hermann Zapf redesigned some of the weights and sizes for
Stempel, basing his revisions on the original design.

MODERN LIBRARY IS ONLINE AT
WWW.MODERNLIBRARY.COM

MODERN LIBRARY ONLINE IS YOUR GUIDE
TO CLASSIC LITERATURE ON THE WEB

THE MODERN LIBRARY E-NEWSLETTER

Our free e-mail newsletter is sent to subscribers, and features sample chapters, interviews with and essays by our authors, upcoming books, special promotions, announcements, and news.

To subscribe to the Modern Library e-newsletter, send a blank e-mail to: **sub_modernlibrary@info.randomhouse.com** or visit **www.modernlibrary.com**

THE MODERN LIBRARY WEBSITE

Check out the Modern Library website at
www.modernlibrary.com for:

- The Modern Library e-newsletter
- A list of our current and upcoming titles and series
- Reading Group Guides and exclusive author spotlights
- Special features with information on the classics and other paperback series
- Excerpts from new releases and other titles
- A list of our e-books and information on where to buy them
- The Modern Library Editorial Board's 100 Best Novels and 100 Best Nonfiction Books of the Twentieth Century written in the English language
- News and announcements

Questions? E-mail us at **modernlibrary@randomhouse.com**
For questions about examination or desk copies, please visit
the Random House Academic Resources site at
www.randomhouse.com/academic